THE MAN WHO LOVED TOO MUCH

Jay Trott

Copyright © 2024 Jay Trott

All rights reserved.

ISBN: 979-8-3302-8416-0

The story and characters depicted in this book are fictitious. Any resemblance to real persons, living or dead, is purely coincidental.

LEAVE YOUR PLOW

IT WAS WHEN JANET DIED of ovarian cancer, eaten from the inside out, that Mike decided to go into the ministry. He was forty-nine at the time, the kids were through college and (pretty much) out on their own, and he was tired of going to a meaningless job and sitting in a cube.

The corporation was all about appearances and everyone was a salesman—of himself. Mike did not relate to any of that. He was tired of it, the big talkers and little-doers, the endless tedious meetings with fancy PowerPoint presentations and posturing and jockeying for the floor, the competition. It all seemed so empty to him now, so pointless after his wife died, after he watched her die in agony and he himself died a little watching her.

His heart was for his family, and when Janet died his heart was broken, too broken to see any reason to go to work anymore just to pay for the house where he no longer felt at home. *She* had been the reason, he realized it now; he saw it clearly for the first time. She and the kids were the reason he crawled out bed on frozen January days and scraped the hard frost off the windshield and dragged himself in for "another day in paradise."

There was one thing he had always wanted to do, though, or thought he wanted to do, and that was some kind of ministry. Their life was structured around their community church, his and Janet's. Faith was like bread to them, like water. He loved God and the words of life and the love of the cross was strong in him. It was his inspiration, his though:-being.

But ministry? Really? Actually the idea had been suggested by many people over the years, including pastors, but he was always too self-effacing to take it seriously. True, when he did readings in church something strange happened to him. He went into the grip of something—he did not know what. People commented on it, on how much his reading meant to them, how it made the words meaningful. Then there was the Bible study they asked him to lead. It turned out he was a bit of a natural. Everyone told him so.

In any case he had been thinking about the ministry for some time, somewhere in the back of his mind, more and more as the years went by and his job went round and round in circles. He and Janet used to talk about it. Was he being called? Was it possible even to have a call at his rapidly advancing age? Why not? It had happened to others, people they knew. He felt alive when he was at church and doing things, thinking about how to spread the "good news." This was exciting stuff for him.

His actual job? Meh. Not that he wasn't grateful to have an actual job. But there wasn't any joy in it for him anymore. He was not an "agent for change" or "serving the customer" or whatever the company blather de jour happened to be. He was a fixer for Management. He analyzed markets and helped them shape their forecasts and then correct course with year-end adjustments when things went awry, as they often did. One percent over budget in sales and plus-territory for profitability—amazing the things you can do with price increases and inventory adjustments.

You know what it was all about in the end? It dawned on him one day. It was about Management getting their annual bonuses and not looking like idiots at the next shareholders' meeting. His entire job was about that and only that. And this began to grind on him over the years. He saw CEOs come and he saw CEOs go, good men, bad men, indifferent men. Some deserved bonuses and some deserved a kick in the pants. But it didn't seem to matter. They all got their bonuses in the end because they had Mike and Mike knew how to make it happen.

Then Janet died and he was shaken. He went into a gray zone and stayed there for a long time. Getting up in the morning became harder and harder and smiling at people who didn't smile back became positively painful—until he decided he'd had enough. Yes, he made that momentous decision they tell you never to make while you are still grieving. He would give up being one of the corporate dead in order to see if it was possible to live.

He told the kids what he was thinking. They were a little hurt when they realized it would entail selling the house they had grown up in but did not protest very much. To tell the truth they were still so much in shock over the loss of their mother that they lacked the strength or will to resist him. Besides, it wasn't a complete surprise. They knew he had been thinking about it for some time. They'd heard him talk about it when he thought they weren't listening.

Once the decision was made, doors just seemed to open. He put the house on the market and it sold almost immediately. He was glad to be rid of it and all the painful memories of his beloved wife coming home to die. She was there and she wasn't there. A flickering light, a glimmer at the top of the stairs; not a ghost exactly—at least he didn't think so—his own mind playing tricks on him—bringing her home—why couldn't she come home?

Of course she couldn't come home. That was one of the main reasons he had to get out of there. He gave the kids everything they wanted from the house, and this seemed to mollify them—and him, his conscience—giving away everything their mother loved, which had to be done if he was going to move on, if he was going to pursue his new plan.

He knew it was hard for them. Janet had been their best friend, their confidante, their cheerleader, their strength and their support in good times and bad, always there for them no matter what, unconditional love and so much more. They loved her for it and it grieved them to come home to the place where she no longer was, where all they could think about was her cheerful greetings and how much they missed her, where their father was moping around sad and solitary and a little unkempt and trying to pretend he was happy—for their sake.

This hurt Mike too because he realized he couldn't fill that hole for them. She had her place in their lives, she was Mom, and he could not fill the aching void she left behind, and this made him sad and made him feel inadequate and small.

Anyway, the house sold for a good price. Mike found temporary quarters in an in-law apartment in a local farmhouse and started sending out applications to seminaries. Somewhat to his surprise the first one was accepted, at Gordon-Conwell. It seemed like another sign that he was on the right path. So he quit the precious job he didn't really want and said goodbye to his friends at work without fanfare and prepared himself for the next great adventure in his life: serving God and man.

It was at Gordon that he first discovered he had something of a knack for preaching. He did not have to downplay this gift because he was *supposed* to be preaching; and in this sanctioning he found a new freedom and voice. It wasn't necessary to labor for hours over a blank Word document like his younger peers. He could figure out what he wanted to say, jot down a few notes, and then stand up and open his mouth and a sermon would just come out of him.

He learned the secret of the One Grand Idea—find something big to talk about, something people were hungry for—and hang the whole sermon on that one thing. His message: "God is love." The cross and the commandment to "Love one another" was what inspired him. Love for God and for each other—the church living in humility and gentleness—this was the plain meaning of the text, in his view; this was paradise restored, the core of his preaching.

In his internship he discovered something strange. It seemed he was able to sense the mood of the congregation while he was talking and adapt to it on the fly. He was not committed to any set course because he wasn't reading his sermons. He could wait for the wind to blow and follow where it led him. The more he opened himself up to this feedback mechanism, this strange intuition, the more the congregation seemed to respond. They leaned in close, they were together.

Oh sure, there were some outliers, the perennially unimpressed, the yawners, the snickerers. What was someone his age doing going into the ministry? What was this nonsense about talking without notes and looking right at them and even into their eyes while he spoke? Pastor Bob never did that. And did they really have to love their neighbor?

Pastor Bob told him to ignore the cavilers. Those were literally his words. "Get used to it," he told Mike after he had been at the church about four months. "There are some in every congregation and more in some congregations than others. I call them the 'joy killers.' No, not the kill-joys. That seems too mild."

And what did Pastor Bob think about Mike and his gift? He was impressed. He was not a great preacher himself and had the good sense to know it, but he was not jealous of Mike. After all, he could afford to be generous; Mike would be gone at the end of the year. Bob supported him and praised him lavishly, and Mike was grateful because he still wasn't sure, changing course so late in life, following the call he thought he felt—did he really feel it?

Mike noticed an ad for an opening at a large church in southern New Hampshire when he was finishing up his internship. Almost on a whim he applied. Of course they don't call it "applying," but he knew what it was all about. He worked hard on his Ministerial Profile, a résumé with a nicer name. It felt a little funny to be so careful. Jesus called the disciples and they just came, didn't they? Seems they didn't need a Ministerial Profile back then.

He did the things he knew he would have to do in order to win over a call committee, having been on a couple himself. Not that he concealed anything; he was open about his beliefs. But he gave in enough to the process to say things he knew they would want him to say and avoid the little traps into which he had seen many other candidates fall.

Whatever he did, it must have worked, because the search committee came to hear him. They weren't conspicuous, twelve strangers sitting together in the third pew from the back in a half-empty church—not at all. Mike gave a particularly good sermon. Before he stood up, he prayed silently, "Lord, humble me so that you can be glorified," and then the Spirit descended on him in the stillness of a New England summer morning. The committee was all smiles afterwards and Mike and Bob both had a good feeling about what had just happened.

Twelve? Yes, twelve. The church they represented was large and growing and had a dynamic senior pastor. And a youth pastor. And a small group and Christian ed pastor. And a calling pastor. The opening was for "assistant pastor"—someone to help out with extra services and anything else the senior pastor did not have time to do. The number twelve did not make Mike think of the tribes of Israel or the disciples, however. It made him think of a jury.

Still, he felt confident enough to make a good impression. He shook hands firmly and looked each person in the eye. A few weeks later he heard from them again. They wanted him to come up to "meet" them. This was the way they couched the job interview. He prepared for it just as he would for any job interview. He researched Pine Cove Community Church and talked to all the pastors he could think of and made sure he was fully prepared to make a good impression.

The committee was impressed. He could tell. He gave straight-arrow answers to tough questions about doctrine and current controversies. He did not try to be coy about his beliefs, but they happened to be the same beliefs Pine Cove was looking for in a candidate. It seemed they were well-matched in orthodoxy. Mike went home in high spirits, fairly confident of success.

They called and asked him to come speak at their church. It was a little out of the ordinary, like an audition, but Bob told him it was not unheard of. Mike was nervous about talking before such a large crowd—stumbled around in the beginning while he tried to get his bearings—but before long he was back in his groove and did pretty well. Anyway, they seemed to think so. They thought he would make a very acceptable assistant pastor.

Mike was amazed, even a little dazed. It had all gone so smoothly—selling the house, getting through divinity school without too much of a struggle, in spite of Greek and Hebrew, and then obtaining his first call. It was confirmation of his momentous decision to change paths mid-life.

PEACE AND GRACE TO YOU

IT WASN'T HARD for Mike to uproot and move, since he had pretty much divested himself of all his earthly belongings, letting the kids take what they wanted and the dump take the rest. He arrived in his new home town with clean hands and a clean heart and was eager to get started and do some good, if he could.

The welcome was warm. Pine Cove was a thriving church, and everywhere he looked he saw a sea of smiling faces, there were so many people, happiness everywhere. His first impressions were confirmed, from his interview and later when he came to preach. It was a friendly church with sound teaching and committed Christians full of love and zeal.

How many times was he invited out to dinner in those first dizzying months! A wave of sympathy swept over the church as the news spread that he was a widower. He was glad for all the invitations and felt he was ramping up nicely on getting to know people and the crucial exercise of putting names to faces—crucial for a pastor, anyway.

He was very impressed with the people who were running the church, both their commitment and their competence. It was remarkable that so many high-powered people were willing to take time from their demanding work schedules to serve the church and the Lord. He was impressed with them as people. They were down to earth. They were loving and generous.

He was glad to see that his new church had taken up the banner of love and was actively living it. There was kindness everywhere he went in those happy days when they were all getting to know each other, gracious greetings and gracious words. He pinched himself. How had he wound up in such a church, so alive, so genuine and warm? How had he been so blessed?

Not everything went perfectly smoothly, of course, there at the beginning of his ministry and the new life he had chosen for himself. Mike had been on board for six months or so before he became aware of the Cantors. No, not worship leaders; a couple by the name of Cantor, who sang in a very different way, or so it seemed to him.

Fred Cantor was on the board of deacons and was a striking character with a strong-brewed personality. Apparently he was a potentate in finance in Boston; Mike found out later it was insurance. He knew the type well from his long sojourn in the corporation. They're the tall ones who stand out in meetings even when they don't talk, the ones with the Mysterious Influence over others, like Saul.

Mike became much more aware of the Cantors, however, after he found himself invited to a Bible study at their house. Acutely aware, we might say. By that time he had visited many studies and was impressed with the level of Bible literacy in the church, which was by no means the case in other churches. Here was a church where small groups of parishioners were able to read the Bible together and discuss what they'd read with insight and sophistication.

But nothing prepared him for what he heard that night. It seems he stumbled into a discussion of Revelation, and specifically a certain notorious chapter that he, until that moment, did not realize was notorious. Somehow he had managed to glide through divinity school without having his clothes snagged by this small chapter in the midst of a strange and indecipherable book.

Mike had set Revelation aside in his mind because it was imposing and he did not really understand it. Coming dead last among the sixty-six books of the Bible, it seemed like a caboose, optional and interesting but obscure, more difficult than rewarding. He was the kind of guy who went straight to the Beatitudes when he thought of the Bible. The esoteric visions of Daniel and John were harder to warm up to.

We gravitate naturally to the things we like and understand; but now Mike was wearing the weeds of a teacher. Not that he saw himself that way, necessarily. In his mind he was still just a guy in jeans going to a Bible study at someone's home and feeling kind of awkward, a guy who not long ago had been sitting in a corporation cube and whiling away the hours with coffee. But *they* did. He was the ordained pastor and presumably the expert in exegesis.

He could sense this deference in them, this two-edged sword, as he sat there in the comfortable leather chair in the Cantors' rec room with the fire glowing in the hearth. It was with some discomfort that he realized he did not have anything to offer them when it came to the passage under consideration. Someone read the words and he sat there listening like everyone else—and he *was* just like everyone else because the words were strange to him, exotic and strange. No grand insights came to mind.

He knew there were many opinions about Revelation. There were some who thought its dire prophecies had been fulfilled with the destruction of Jerusalem and unhappy events occurring within the timeframe in which it was written. There were others who saw it as a prophecy of the end times. Mike knew their interpretations could be colorful, although he had not expended the time or energy to find out exactly what they were and how he felt about them.

The traditional view made sense to him. He was content with it. This strange beast coming up out of the sea represented the different empires that had crushed the Jews, the most mighty and terrible of all being the Roman Empire, which prevailed at the very time John was writing in exile on his hard rock. It made sense that the beast was Rome and its self-worshipping emperors, who had become increasingly vicious since the time of Augustus.

Mike used this soothing logic to put the controversy to bed in his own mind. It was about to be rudely awakened, however. Fred Cantor was leading the study, and it dawned on Mike, as his new friend unfolded his interpretation, that they were heading into murky waters. Somehow Fred had gotten the idea into his handsome head that the second beast, the one with the feigning horns of the lamb, was the Roman Catholic Church. This was the interpretation he now proceeded to unfold for his rapt listeners.

The presentation of this interpretation was not clumsy. Would that it were! But no, the same sophistication and thoroughness Mike had observed in other Bible studies at Pine Cove were on display here as well. Obviously Fred had spent some quality time with the commentaries, parsing out the apparent meaning of the colorful symbolic descriptors and finding ways to ascribe them to Catholicism. It was all very convincing. No one protested.

Not until Brenda Carlson spoke up, that is. "I'm a little confused. Are you saying Catholics aren't Christian?"

"I'm talking about the church, the institution," Fred replied, his tone changing from plainspoken friendliness to the one you hear when something is in play. "I'm sure there are many sincere Catholics, but unfortunately they are deceived. It's counterfeit Christianity."

"I don't think that can be right," Brenda's husband chimed in. "I don't see how they can be counterfeit. I mean, look at all the Catholic churches out there."

"Of course you don't. Nobody does. That's the whole point of the prophecy, to help us see things we can't see. This beast has the horns of a lamb. It looks like Christ, but it isn't Christ. It isn't Christian. It's fake, and in the end times it will be repudiated."

There was complete silence in the room as the eleven participants—five couples and Mike—mulled over this startling claim. Mike looked at them and wondered what they were thinking. Could they actually be buying this?

"What do you say, Pastor?" he heard Brenda saying. "Do you really think this is about the Roman Catholic Church?"

"I believe it's generally interpreted as being about the Roman *Empire*," Mike replied cautiously. "The counterfeit could be the emperors who had themselves declared god."

"That's not what the commentaries say," Fred said boring in. "I did a lot of research on this, and it's pretty clear that the Protestant view is that this represents the pope."

"Well, there are a lot of different opinions about it, because it's so obscure. But I doubt there are too many serious commentaries saying it's the pope. Especially since he didn't exist yet."

"How about Matthew Henry? Is he 'serious' enough for you?"

Mike blinked. "He's very serious. But I doubt he said that."

"He certainly did. Here it is. You can see for yourself."

He handed him a thick gray book, open to the appropriate page. Mike looked down at it and saw the passages that Fred or someone had highlighted in yellow: "Those who would think the first beast signifies Rome pagan by the second beast would understand Rome papal, which promotes idolatry and tyranny, but in a more soft and lamb-like manner."

His first reaction was shock in comprehending that the second beast was indeed being linked to "Rome papal." Was it possible? Did Matthew Henry believe the second beast was Catholicism? Then he latched onto "Those who would think" like a life raft.

Henry was not equating the beast with the Roman church; he was saying there were some unspecified people who did. He was putting distance between himself and them.

For a moment Mike felt better. But then he began to wonder if this was just a rhetorical trick. Henry was insulating himself by putting all this speculation into the mouth of "those," but it also seemed to be his own view. Or at least he was not offering any alternative views. Everything he had to say about the passage indicated that the beast and the pope were one.

Mike sat there blinking at the page while the room grew very quiet. "I wasn't aware of this commentary," he said at last. "To tell you the truth, I'm not really an expert on Revelation. I'll just say it's a very hard book, and we might want to be careful about drawing conclusions from things that aren't really clear."

"Not an expert. I see. But they seem clear to Matthew Henry," Fred persisted. "It makes sense, what he's saying. All of the things he talks about there make sense, it seems to me."

"Well, not to contradict him, but I very much doubt that's the case. I have read commentators who say this is about the Roman Empire and their blasphemies, or what he calls 'Rome pagan.'"

Fred seemed perturbed at being contradicted. "So you don't believe there's a problem with the Catholic Church. You're one of these relativists. Anything goes."

"I wouldn't call myself a relativist. I consider Catholics my Christian brothers and I respect them and their sincerity."

"What about Luther? He called Rome the 'whore of Babylon.'"

"He also wanted us to leave Revelation out of the Bible," Mike said with a genial laugh. In Mike's mind, Luther was a complex man who sometimes said provocative things that were not supposed to be taken too literally, as in his *Table Talk*. This was a sophisticated perspective, however, as he surmised from the looks of dismay on the faces of his two hosts.

He did not know it yet, but he had made powerful enemies. Fred was not happy about being corrected in his own Bible study. He felt Mike was wrong, but even if he wasn't wrong there were other ways to handle things. It was not necessary to humiliate a man in his own home, in front of his friends, laugh at him.

The one who really turned, though, was Susan. Mike had gone after her man. Her husband was a god to her, not only a wonderful provider but a man of faith and wisdom who studied the Bible and read commentaries and was no lightweight. She adored him for his integrity and the position of eminence he enjoyed in the church, in her view so well-deserved.

Mike, the new pastor, the guy who came to their home in jeans, had disrespected him. That was how she felt about the unfortunate incident. He did not give her husband his due. He made him look small and ordinary, and for this she could not forgive him.

A couple of weeks later Mike was summoned by Charles Ridley, the senior pastor.

"So tell me about what happened at the Cantors'?" Charles said with a friendly but concerned smile.

Mike was surprised—he wasn't expecting this. "Oh—I guess you mean the Bible study."

"I heard there was a bit of a row."

"'Row'? Well, no, not really. They had an interpretation of Revelation that was—well, less than edifying. I simply tried to add some perspective, that's all."

"I understand there was some sort of disparaging comment about Luther."

"Disparaging? No. Luther can't always be taken at face value. Sometimes you have to be careful when you cite him as an authority because he doesn't always mean what he seems to say."

"I don't know if he does or he doesn't, but a word of advice. You might want to consider treading a little more lightly with Fred Cantor in his own home. He's not someone to trifle with. Besides, they were raised Lutheran. So they tend to be a little touchy on the subject, what with a Postmodernist lurking around every corner."

"I'm hardly a Postmodernist—whatever that is," Mike said. "I was just trying to diffuse the situation with a little humor. They were saying the whore of Babylon is the Pope. I really don't think we want to have that sort of thing going on in our Bible studies."

"Well, as you may have guessed by now, I have my own differences with 'Rome.' But be that as it may, I'm counseling you as a friend. Fred Cantor is a remarkable man in many ways. He does a lot for this church. But I can tell you one thing—you don't want to get on his bad side. You will regret it."

"Should I go to him—apologize?"

"Do you have something to apologize for?" Charles said, giving him a searching look.

"I guess maybe I was a little too flip. I laughed when probably I shouldn't have—defensively. But this is something I feel strongly about. We can't go around talking about the love of God and the unity of the Spirit and then call the entire Catholic Church the whore of Babylon. That just doesn't seem very loving to me."

"Well, you know, you can overdo that love thing. It isn't the be-all and end-all of the Bible, like some people make it out to be."

Mike was shocked by the tone of this comment. "But the Bible says 'God is love.'"

"That was what the old Thomists believed, too, and I suppose you know it was a major bone of contention with the Protestant theologians. Yes, 'God is love,' but God is a lot of things. God is 'holy, holy, holy.' You don't want to get too cozy with God, as the Israelites found out at Mt. Sinai. That's a blind alley, too."

"But I thought God's holiness *was* his perfect love. Isn't that what Jesus was talking about when he said all the law and all the prophets were summed up in two commandments?"

"I'm not going to get into a theological debate with you. I'm just trying to help you. This is a big church with a lot of people who have diverse backgrounds and diverse opinions. You don't want people like the Cantors against you. Fred's the chairman of the board of deacons, basically your boss. They're good people, they have the best interests of the church at heart, and we just need to remember that not everyone has the kind of training we have and knows things the way we do. Believe me, you're going to hear a lot of weird things in the course of your ministry. This is not the hill to make your stand on."

"So should I go apologize? I would be perfectly happy to do so. I can see how my laughing might be taken the wrong way."

Charles looked at him. "No, I think I would let sleeping dogs lie at this point. If you really don't feel you did anything wrong it could just make things worse. Let's let the dust settle and see where we are. He really is a good man, once you get to know him."

THE HOUSE BUILT UPON A ROCK

BUT WHAT WAS that hill, if not love? The meaning of the Bible verses seemed clear to Mike—"Love one another"; "No man has ever seen God; if we love one another, God abides in us and his love is perfected in us"; "I pray that you, being rooted and grounded in love, may have power, together with all the saints, to grasp how wide, how long, how tall, how deep is the love of Christ"; "The greatest of these is love"; "Beloved, let us love one another, for love is of God, and he who loves is born of God and knows God"—and so forth.

Mike was aware of the controversy to which Charles alluded. He remembered it being discussed briefly at Gordon. His professor did not seem inclined to dwell on it, and Mike was not inclined to dwell on it either—because it was painful. It was personal for him. If love was not the center and essence of the gospel and church life, which is what he believed and felt with all his heart, then what was he doing in the ministry?

A dark cloud entered into his soul through this discussion with Charles. Even as they sat there smiling at each other he could feel a spirit of opposition rising between them. Mike had been in difficult situations before. He'd had a couple of bosses who simply did not like him very much. It did not matter how hard he worked or how good his work was or how pleasant or cooperative he tried to be—they had taken it into their heads to oppose him. One of them succeeded in making him miserable for about a year until she finally stepped on a landmine and was fired.

One of the great implacable truths of human existence is that some people simply do not like us. And now Mike had a dark foreboding about his relationship with Charles. He did not want to have this foreboding—more than anything he wanted to be friends with Charles—but he could not pretend to be unaware of the negative signals coming from the senior pastor, something in his tone, something vaguely threatening beneath the show of warmth and ostensible Christian meekness. Was he headed into stormy waters in the very first church he served?

Because come on, Fred Cantor was wrong. Not only was there no Scriptural warrant for his attack on Catholics, but it was hateful and perverse. Fred was using Luther to equate the Catholic Church with the whore of Babylon. Should Mike have let it stand? No, he could not. It went against everything he believed in, everything he stood for. It made him physically ill just to think about it.

But did Charles agree with Fred? He couldn't—but he was being cagey. He would not condemn him, and this restraint put him in de facto alliance with Fred, whether he agreed with him or not. Mike had heard Charles make occasional comments about Catholicism in worship services that struck him as being unfair or unnecessary, like the swipe he took at transubstantiation a couple of weeks earlier. At the time he had smiled along with everyone else at the prophetic utterance of the senior pastor—but now it came back to him and rubbed him the wrong way.

Was Charles a closet bigot? Was it possible that his new mentor, the spiritual leader of a large and prominent church, was a hater of Rome? It had been hundreds of years since the Puritans cut off the ears of Catholics who persisted in polluting the Massachusetts Bay Colony with their unwanted presence; but the prejudice itself, it seems, had not died. This came as a rude surprise to Mike, who had little exposure in his life to this particular prejudice. His parents never breathed a word of it. Janet would not have let them attend a church that even hinted at it. Her lifelong best friend and godmother of their first daughter was a devout Catholic.

The same intuitive power that helped Mike with his sermons now turned against him with a vengeance and started telling him things he did not want to hear. In short, he had a premonition that difficult times were coming his way. He thought about the irrationality of human existence. He thought about the best and kindest person he had ever known being attacked and destroyed by a relentless biological killer. If someone like Janet could be taken off in such a horrible way, then why should he be spared suffering? There was no reason why he should, none he could think of.

Suffering was headed his way and there was nothing he could do about it. This unpleasant thought took hold of him and would not let go. Not that he saw himself as being above suffering. "No servant is greater than his master." Nor was he the sort of person who spent a lot of time wondering why "bad things happen to good people." His view of human nature was much closer to Romans: "No one is righteous; no not one." And from that point of view, why should he not suffer? Why should his life be any more pain-free than the Savior he worshipped?

Suffering is the way of purification. The Bible was clear on this. Men are sinners and suffering is to be welcomed as the means by which their dross can be turned into gold. Mike was not proud of his exchange with Fred Cantor. He had been far too glib. He had a Yankee's congenital sharp tongue—and he knew very well what Proverbs had to say about men with sharp tongues. He regretted that he was not as good as the man who wrote Proverbs. Then again, if he was so good why did he write? Books like Proverbs are written to scold ourselves as much as others. Solomon most of all was in need of his own instruction.

Life is a course of correction for the wise, and Mike knew he needed plenty of correcting. Still, he did not relish the prospect of suffering in his new calling. He could see it coming—ever so clearly, based on past experience—for the church was no different from the corporation in the matter of sinfulness. It wasn't holiness that made the church different but repentance and the love of God and mercy. Mike understood all this on an intellectual level, and on that same level he was willing to suffer. He could see suffering coming and he was willing to endure it.

But he did not want to suffer. He wanted everything to go well in his new calling. He went to Charles again in an attempt to heal the rift that he sensed opening up between them—but Charles would not understand him. He went right back to the Luther thing and his cagey position. Mike could not get around the roadblock that had been thrown in his way, could not maneuver himself out of the unpleasant situation his mentor was creating—not without saying something he did not believe—not without acknowledging Fred might just be right and dropping his principled opposition.

This was something he simply could not do in good conscience. He felt in the strongest terms that Fred's coldhearted judgment was both wrong and contrary to the spirit of Christ. More than anything he wanted the church to be one. He hated the religious jingoism that caused members of the denominations to malign each other just as a Manchester partisan might condemn the footballers from Merrimac. It was not possible for him to go to Charles and pretend these were not his real feelings.

Unfortunately it was also impossible to go to Charles and reason with him about his position. He just seemed to get himself into more trouble. Charles had hardened against him, like Pharaoh hardening his heart. Since he could not win Charles over with honest persuasion, and since it was not in his nature to dissemble, his only option seemed to be to keep a low profile and hope that the Cantors would forget about the perceived slight in time. He kept his head down and applied himself diligently to his duties, working long hours, staying humble, and making no demands.

But there was one way in which he could not avoid giving offense. This was his natural aptitude for preaching, the gift that is so coveted in churches. He had been given the Saturday night service. Charles dismissed it as the "orphan service," but Mike liked the low visibility. He eased right into his role. His sermons started out strong and only got stronger as he became acquainted with his congregation. He was a little surprised to see the numbers gradually increasing. The 60 or so souls with which he had been entrusted grew to 75 and then shot up to 100 and beyond.

People rushed up to him after the services to say how much they enjoyed his sermons and how meaningful they were. He overheard the whispers—"Such a good preacher! As good as Charles!" Mike was embarrassed by these comments. He did not want to be as good as Charles. It was not his intention or desire to challenge the senior pastor in any way. "Do nothing out of selfish ambition" were words that he tried to live by. But Charles did not seem to feel the same way. The more the congregation grew, the more evident his coolness became.

But why? Charles was the star. Church was packed on Sunday mornings. People drove thirty miles just to hear him. No, there had to be some other reason for the coolness. For that matter, was it even coolness at all? Mike watched him with the other pastors. He seemed to treat them in much the same way—friendly but always keeping his distance. Besides, Charles did not actively *mistreat* him. There had been no more unhappy confrontations after the conversations about the Cantors. To tell the truth, there was hardly any contact between them at all.

But this is just what troubled him. He'd had such a good relationship with Bob Diamond during his internship. They would go out for breakfast in the little one-stoplight town and just chat. Bob took mentoring seriously, and Mike was grateful for the support. Of course Charles was a lot busier than Bob. Charles had a flock of about two thousand souls and a seemingly endless barrage of activities to oversee; Bob was lucky to see 70 in church on a Sunday and had an abundance of free time to lavish on receptive protégés—or his woodworking.

Charles was always in a meeting of one kind or another, if not at the church itself then in town or in Boston or some exotic venue, connecting with various dynamic ministries and coming back with glowing reports that he shared during his sermons. He knew everyone at the top of the loose-ranged Evangelical hierarchy and seemed to consider himself one of them. This effort alone—to keep himself in the top echelon where he felt he belonged and where he said the church needed him to be—took up a huge amount of his time.

Mike got it. They had a busy church. That was why there were so many pastors and why he was there. They were a church on the move, a church with a mission. There were a lot of things to do and everybody was doing them—and at the top of this pyramid was Charles himself, a veritable whirlwind of activity and creative ideas, every day shaking things up and putting people on their toes and making them go "out of their comfort zones."

Charles did not have time to be like Bob and take the other pastors under his wing. They had to fly on their own. In fact they were expected to lift *him* up. That was why they were there—to help his ministry soar. This was never openly stated, of course, but Mike saw it. And he did not object. He was willing to have such a role. After all, Charles had unique gifts, as he often reminded them. There are some gifts we have and some gifts we don't have, and the way to make yourself and others unhappy was to try to be gifted in areas where you were not.

There were a lot of areas where Charles was not gifted. He was not gifted at working with young people, which was why they had a youth pastor. He was not gifted at visiting parishioners, which is why they had a visiting pastor. It seemed a lot of the things he wasn't "gifted" at were the grubby things, the hard things, like bringing communion to the old woman in the nursing home who was no longer one of the church's bright lights—that sort of thing.

Mike found himself becoming a little skeptical about this use of the concept of spiritual gifts. It was originally intended to draw the church together, not to single out individuals for special privileges. There are all kinds of gifts, according to St. Paul, and all of those gifts are vital to the body; thus no one has the right to lord it over others. It was human nature to boast and glorify ourselves, but the "more excellent" way was to love one another. This was not what Charles had in mind, however, when he talked about his gift for preaching and teaching. Instead he seemed to be excusing himself from ministerial duties that he found distasteful or boring.

Be that as it may, Mike did not mind the system at Pine Cove, on the whole. After all, it was true that Charles was highly gifted in the pulpit. He was highly gifted at standing up in front of a large crowd and providing them with an intense spiritual experience—there was no other way to put it. The church was packed on Sunday mornings, and it was definitely because of Charles. It had never been packed before; in fact it had almost closed its doors. People came to hear him preach and find out what incredible, moving, challenging thing he would say and do next. Without him and his extraordinary gift, they would not be there.

The other pastors were expected to complement Charles and fill in the gaps left by his various self-identified deficits. They were not there to be nurtured by him. And yet Mike could not help wishing for a little nurturing from the senior pastor. He longed to have a good relationship with him; he longed for them to be Christian brothers, to feel a sense of kinship and camaraderie and not just shared aspiration. None of this was forthcoming. There was no open breach in their relationship, there were no more arguments and no hostility on the surface, but Mike felt a certain tension between them. He felt a coldness from Charles, and it hurt him.

He was still trying to suppress these apprehensions as he blew past his first anniversary date. Outwardly everything was fine. After all, he was a bit of a rising star, with the growing popularity of the Saturday night service. Then Bill Atkinson dropped by his office one summer evening. Bill was one of Mike's favorite people at Pine

Cove. He had been there when Charles first arrived, when it was just another floundering New England Protestant church, and had supported Charles from the start, unlike those who fought his changes every step of the way and were eventually appeased with their own traditional service (albeit at eight in the morning).

Actually Bill was supportive of all the pastors; Mike was no different. But there was a connection between them. They were the same age and had been through the same corporation mill, which made it easy for them to talk. They also had a similar small-town Yankee background and the ironic affect that comes along with it. They understood each other implicitly, but not everybody else understood *them*.

Bill stuck his head in the door to Mike's office. "Mind if I come in for a moment?"

"Be my guest," Mike replied, although there was something about the way he said this that put him on his guard.

Bill closed the door behind him, and Mike noticed. "So listen, I just wanted to tell you what a great job you're doing. I don't get to Saturday night very often, but I went a couple of weeks ago and it was amazing. Truly. Great stuff."

"Oh, thanks. And right back at you. You are very supportive, and it means a lot."

"Have you always had that—the preaching thing?"

"No," Mike said self-consciously. "I had no idea I had any ability of that kind until I actually tried it. I was as surprised as anybody else."

"Well, you definitely do. In fact I'm starting to think you may mount a challenge to Charles himself," he said, looking at Mike with an inquisitive expression.

Mike just laughed. "I'm not interested in challenging anybody. Charles is amazing. I'm just trying to do the best I can and stay out of trouble."

"'Trouble'? What do you mean? Is everything okay between you and Charles?"

"Of course. Why wouldn't it be?"

"I don't know. You tell me. We had a meeting with some of the deacons last week and he said something sort of strange, so I didn't know if something was going on between you two. I hope not."

Mike was now forced to choose whether he wanted hear this strange something. "You mean about me?"

"Yes, I guess. Or at least I thought it was strange. Maybe I'm missing something. Anyway, someone complimented you on your preaching and the way the Saturday service keeps growing by leaps and bounds. Charles looked at her and said, 'Let's just hope he can keep it going'—just like that. We were kind of shocked. Someone asked him what he meant and he said all you ever talk about is love. 'People could get the wrong idea.' Which surprised me, because I thought that's what it was all about."

Mike was tongue-tied. He knew what he wanted to say on the subject of love, had been working on it in his head ever since his conversation with Charles, preparing himself and layering his defense with increasingly elaborate arguments, but for this very reason it now seemed like there was no purpose in replying. It was too complicated to explain. For one thing, he felt he was being caricatured. He did *not* just preach about love. He was the only pastor on the staff who followed the traditional lectionary and disciplined himself to talk about the topics it raised each week, instead of simply defaulting to whatever was top of mind.

For another, he was far from being some sort of cultural accommodationist. Charles seemed to be implying that his message of love made him soft on sin. But Mike did not portray love as a soft force. On the contrary, love was the hard edge between sin and righteousness. "The commandments, 'You shall not commit adultery, You shall not kill, You shall not steal, You shall not covet,' and any other commandment, are summed up in this sentence, 'You shall love your neighbor as yourself.' Love does no wrong to a neighbor; therefore love is the fulfilling of the law."

He did not put love in opposition to the law and accountability, as Charles intimated; he was not a smiling simpleton spooning out pabulum and pretending that anything goes and God cannot be provoked. But how could he explain all this to Bill when it was Charles who was sitting on the other side? The caricature Charles was using was effective for the very reason that it was a caricature. It demolished the complexity of his views. Most of all it was effective because it came from Charles and carried the full weight of his authority.

"I didn't realize he had reservations about what I was preaching," Mike relied carefully. "He hasn't said anything to me about it. I would be happy to discuss it with him."

"Oh, I know. I'm sure he just wants you to do well. And I may be reading too much into it. I wasn't going to say anything, but I happened to see you sitting here…"

"No, I'm glad you did. If I'm being talked about in deacon meetings, then I definitely want to know about it. I'm not a seasoned veteran, despite my age. I'm well-aware I have a lot to learn and a lot of room for improvement."

"Well, I don't know about that. As I said, I think you're fantastic. I love your sermons, and a lot of other people do too. I guess I was just worried that there was some kind of rift between you two guys, which I would certainly hate to see."

Mike sat there in shock after his friend left. Why was Charles making disparaging comments about him? Why didn't he come directly to him if he had a problem with his preaching? Why choose a public venue where Mike wasn't even present to benefit from the correction? Was he sending a message? If so, it had been received. Mike was flanked and he knew it. If it came down to him against Charles, he knew he would lose.

Him against Charles! The very words were acid. He did not want to be against Charles. It was the last thing he wanted. He had done everything he could to fit in and be a good soldier, had not presumed to challenge Charles in any way, although there were things he felt that should have been challenged. And his reward for this meekness and humility was a public slap in the face. Clearly that was the way Bill saw it. That was why he closed the door.

His intuition was right. Something had gone seriously awry in their relationship. Was it because of his doctrine? No, he was right down the middle when it came to that. In fact in some ways he was more orthodox than Charles. Was it because he preached about love? It seemed unlikely. All Christian preachers preach about love. They can hardly avoid it when the New Testament has so much to say on the subject.

No, something else had caused this outburst in front of the deacons. It came in response to someone commenting on the growth of the Saturday night service. Was this what was bothering Charles? Was he—*jealous* of him? Was he trying to dismiss the growth because he felt it diminished his own success? If so, this would put them in natural opposition to each other in a way that could not be circumvented.

Mike fought this debilitating idea. It was ridiculous to think the senior pastor had any reason to be jealous of a junior associate and his "orphan service" when his own services were packed every week and he was the celebrated author of three well-known books on revival and church growth. What he had done to soften hearts in the granite state was legendary.

So he couldn't be jealous of poor Mike. Could he? Because if he was, then Mike now found himself in an impossible and bizarre situation. The better he preached, the more he put himself in jeopardy. He could not help getting better. Not only did he love preaching, but every week he learned something new about how to reach people and how to strip down his message to pure essence and carve out all unnecessary gestures.

He was getting better; he couldn't help it. Anyone who does something over and over again gets better, whether he wants to or not—and Mike wanted to. But did this mean his relationship with Charles would continue to get worse? It was a terrible thought, and he was not completely successful in his efforts to pray it away.

THE SINFUL WOMAN

As attendance on Saturday night continued to grow, Mike noticed someone new—an attractive blonde who started coming in the summer of his second year. Not that he was on the lookout for attractive blondes just then. He was still very much in mourning for Janet. Besides he was too busy for a relationship of that type, with all the meetings and events and the counseling he was doing for people who were coming to him on a chronic basis.

Anyway, he noticed her because she always came early and sat in the front row. She introduced herself—her name was Clarissa. Her attendance became more regular as summer turned into fall. Then one day she waited until the room was pretty much empty before approaching him. She seemed a little embarrassed.

"Hi! Just wanted to tell you how much I love this service," she said, looking at him but not really looking at him. "I've been to a few churches—in a professional capacity—but this is the first one where I really felt at home."

"Thank you so much! It's great to have you here."

"Someone told me about this church, a friend, so I thought I would just check it out. But it's really great. The services are so meaningful, your sermons, everything. I didn't know church could be like this. Am I babbling?" she said laughing.

"Not at all! It's very kind of you to say so. We try."

"I just wanted to tell you, every time I come there's something I can relate directly to my life. Like today's sermon—looking for the good in people—breaking our own bondage—that was just what I needed to hear right now. And the music! It was great, best ever."

"Yes, we are fortunate with the music. This church happens to have a lot of accomplished musicians who are willing to step forward and help out. And now that they're all back from their summer vacations you can really hear how they sound together."

"Must get kind of expensive though, having a whole band up there like that."

"It doesn't cost us a dime. They're all volunteers."

"Really? Wow. They're good."

"Thanks! Three of them are former music majors, I believe."

"Interesting. I happen to be a former music major myself."

"Are you? What do you play?"

"I'm a violinist. I know—stuffy."

"Not at all. Tough instrument to learn, from what I hear. Strictly a percussion man myself. Wolfeboro High School band."

"Well, you need percussion, too." She paused and looked thoughtful. "Say—do you think they'd be interested in having a little help?"

"You mean—you want to play with them?"

"I know, it's crazy—right? I would love to help, if they wanted it. I think I could make myself useful. I'm pretty good at following directions."

"I don't know. I'm going to see Greg on Tuesday. I'll ask him."

"You must think I'm nuts, inviting myself into the band."

"Not at all. First you have to learn the lingo, though. We call it a 'worship team,'" Mike said with a smile.

"Worship team, got it."

"It's an extremely important part of the service, since worship is what the service is all about. Or at least it should be. Not always true—but that's a different story. Don't get me started on that story. Where was I? Oh, yes. The second thing is we have this crazy concept of the call. The idea is that the Holy Spirit calls us to minister in various ways."

"Is there a cell phone for that?" she said with a laugh.

"It might be why we're standing here having this conversation. The Spirit is this sort of mysterious force in our lives, like the wind—you can feel it, but you don't know exactly where it's going. It's a guiding power. And I can tell you from experience that I believe it's very real. It blew me here when I wasn't even sure I was cut out for the ministry."

"Really? You haven't just always done this?"

"Not at all. I'm a second-career guy. Didn't even manage to get started until last year."

"Wow. I never would have known. So there's hope for me yet."

"Believe me, if there's hope for me there's hope for anybody."

As it turned out, Greg was very open to the idea. She played for him after the service on the following Saturday—she had brought along her violin—and he realized right away that she was a good musician. She didn't need notes in front of her, which was the case with so many classically-trained violinists and his major reservation. He could play a progression and she knew just what to do with it. She was welcomed onto the team with open arms.

About a month later she asked Mike if she could come see him. "Of course!" he said—but not, to tell the truth, with his whole heart. He was beginning to be worn out by all the people who were coming to see him. They thought he could help them but he wasn't so sure. He wanted to help them, but he was beginning to realize that many of them were in complex situations or had intractable problems. They weren't coming to him to be healed per se; they were coming to bend his ear and sometimes to win him over to their misery.

He believed in carrying each other's burdens, but as the congregation grew so did the burdens he was being asked to bear. The problem wasn't a lack of willingness on his part; it was his inability to say no. Some were in unhappy marriages. One was chronically unemployed, and the more Mike talked to her the more he understood why. Another had a possible personality disorder. He attached himself to Mike and scared him a little. There were times when he seemed to Mike like he could be dangerous, if he made up his mind to be.

Everyone who came to him wanted something, and Mike was beginning to wonder how much he had to give. He was pleasantly surprised to find that this was not the case with Clarissa, however. She came to thank him, like the one leper that returned. Not that she didn't have problems; but she felt she had found the answer at Pine Cove Community Church.

Clarissa had lived an—interesting—life. We are tempted to say a modern life, but of course there were many such lives in the past. What made things different today was modern medicine. Women did not have to be afraid of getting pregnant anymore, and drugs took away the threat of disease. Clarissa's life had not been as clear and pure as her name suggested. She had grown up in an agnostic family and never really gone to church, not even on Easter and Christmas. Faith and religion were never discussed in her house—or were dismissed as hypocrisy.

Her parents were "moral people," as she put it, but their influence stopped when she went to college. There, in the music department, she found herself mixed up with a group that had very liberated attitudes toward sex. There were parties and there were bashes and sometimes they went all weekend long and she couldn't even remember half of the nonsense that went on because she was high or drunk.

After college she led what she described as "the musician's life," bouncing around from gig to gig and boyfriend to boyfriend for several years before landing her present position as the strings instructor at a prestigious prep school near Boston, which she supplemented with freelance work and private students. She was a hard-working person and was doing fairly well for herself.

What was not going so well was her love life. There was a series of relationships and they always went farther than she wanted them to and they always ended badly because she was not happy; because her rootless wandering life was not really what she wanted; because the men she was attracted to were bad boys—or maybe they were the ones who were attracted to her—anyway it never worked out for them. They never told her the truth.

She related all this in a perfectly matter-of-fact, almost clinical manner. And no, she was not trying to pull him into her web. It was not Mike himself that drew her to Pine Cove but the message he was preaching of freedom and the possibility of a new life. He had shown her a different path, and it looked beautiful to her. She had a vision of herself leading a very different existence, free from the various addictions and dependencies to which she was prone.

She admitted to being terribly lonely, almost to the point of fraying. She could not find the friendship and sincere love she craved in her work environment, where everyone seemed so phony and too many men wanted to take advantage of her and her singleness. The world was like a war zone to her, psychologically speaking; but the church and the spirit of Christ filled the void she was feeling. She could not wait for Saturday night so she could come to church and be with people who were kind to her and gentle and sincere. She loved being involved in the service and thanked Mike over and over again for his support.

Mike was deeply moved. He believed in the possibility of redemption. "There will be more joy in heaven over one person who repents than over ninety-nine righteous persons who need no repentance." Clarissa insisted that she hated the life she had been living. In order for him to understand why, she had to tell him a little bit about it; but there was nothing boastful or salacious in any of this. No, he realized it was a confession.

He was completely involved in her story from the beginning. For one thing, it was new to him. He had no experience of the lifestyle she was describing, which made it fascinating in the anthropological sense. He realized he had led a sheltered life. Somehow he had gone through his fifty-three years without being exposed to the depravity and aimlessness that were apparently not uncommon in the same community in which he lived. He saw her as a victim who had been drawn into a lifestyle that was a trap and had not known how to get out of it.

But he was also involved because she was so brave. She said things about herself that he could not imagine saying about himself, even if they were true. He mentioned this to her. "Oh, I don't know how brave I am," she said with a laugh. "You get to a point where you just can't go on anymore doing what you're doing. I reached that point long ago. And then again I kind of like telling you. I remember that accountability sermon you gave a while back. I feel almost like if I tell you, then I have to change. Does that make any sense?"

"Of course. Because you feel you owe me something. You feel like you have to change in order to keep the implied promise you've made. But that doesn't make it any less brave. There are a lot of people who could benefit from an arrangement like that—myself included—but that doesn't mean they're going to have the courage to do something about it."

"Funny, I don't think of it as courage. I think of it as need. I have to change or give up the hope of ever being happy. I didn't even know *how* I could change until I came here. I hope you understand what I'm saying. You have been an incredibly important person in my life. Just to feel I can trust men again—"

"Well, there's only one man you should trust. Believe me, I'm just like any other man."

"No, you're not. You have no idea."

Mike tried to deflect this flattery by praising her musicianship—which wasn't difficult. She was a very talented violinist with a pure, sweet tone and great expressiveness. Most of all she projected a beautiful, humble spirit when she was up in front of the congregation. You could see the joy and gratitude on her face. She did let him know, without ostentation, that she was making a bit of a sacrifice to play with the team. Saturday night was a major freelance night, and she had given up many paying jobs over the weeks and months because she did not want to miss church.

Clarissa had come to thank him, but Mike was the one who was astonished and thankful by the end of their hour together. She went out alone into the fetid October night and Mike had an image of her being enveloped by the fog and the orange harvest moon. He prayed for her protection, not just from the evil spirits of this world, but from the invisible dominions and powers that did not have her best interests in mind.

She said he had encouraged her, but she did not know how much she encouraged him. At this strange interlude in his life, when he found himself at odds with his senior pastor and some of the leadership of the church, someone had come to him with no agenda and nothing to gain and given him sincere praise. He did not pretend to be different from other men, but neither was he indifferent to the distinction she seemed to see. He took comfort in it, in the thought that it was possible for him to be salt and light in the world to someone, at least.

Most of all, he felt fortunate to be in a position where he could bring a little joy and comfort to others. His conversation with Clarissa made him feel awkward and strange but it also made him feel renewed. Yes, there was opposition in the church; yes, things were a little difficult for him just then. But to be able to touch people! To preach the Gospel and possibly have a positive impact on their lives! To send them out of church feeling the presence of God and with renewed strength to go back out into the dreary work-a-day world! It was a great privilege for him.

A GREAT MULTITUDE

MEANWHILE MIKE'S PREACHING continued to improve and attendance on Saturday nights continued to grow. They were at 150 or more every week by the end of the summer and beginning to burst out of the small hall where the service was held, constructed as a sound stage for concerts and plays and the other special events that distinguish large Evangelical churches from their sleepy local sisters.

The growth came at a price, however, as Mike continued to have the impression that Charles resented it. There was the habitual smile, the one Charles always wore, the one Mike was beginning to wonder about; there was always that smile and always a hearty handshake, almost like a politician's handshake, when he and Mike met, especially in public venues, smooth and soft; but this show of warmth and affection felt like an empty shell to him. There was nothing behind it. They had no relationship. Not really.

Mike tried. On many occasions he tried to strike up a conversation with Charles and nothing happened. He struck the match, and the match smoldered but would not burst into flame. Charles was all deflection, one hundred percent, at least with him. It reminded him of one of the CEOs he'd known in his former life who was like a senator. No, not a congressman—that was too low on the totem pole—but a senator, truly gifted at deflection, the same relentless cheerfulness, the same apparent energy and enthusiasm at all times and in all situations. Could it be real?

Mike got it. The happy outward appearance was supposed to reflect the Spirit and its abundance. But he could not shake the feeling that it was just a show, or at least partly so. God desires a contrite and broken heart, but this was not what people saw in Charles. No, they saw someone who was on fire for the Lord, who never doubted, never did anything really wrong; whose "confessions" from the pulpit were not of sins but of lovable foibles, and therefore were not confessions at all but something else; who had the perfect marriage and perfect kids—although kids will be kids, as lighthearted stories from the pulpit often illustrated.

Mike was not able to get beyond this outward show of strength and perfect assurance. Over time it began to seem more and more strange. He could never be friends with Charles because he could not get him to drop the façade. He could not have a serious conversation with him of any kind. It was too bad. They were generally of the same mind when it came to things cultural and political, but even on those topics he did not seem to be able to have a decent conversation with the senior pastor. He did not so much talk with you as declaim—and in Mike's experience you were generally intimidated by his commanding tone and reluctant to try to declaim back.

This was how Mike experienced it, anyway. He wondered if anyone else felt the same way. He would look around at people on Sunday mornings and watch as they interacted with Charles. As far as he could tell, he was the only one with these reservations. A smiling old woman, a nobody in the greater scheme of things, although not in the eyes of God, would come up to Charles while everyone was milling about during coffee hour, and he was all hers. He locked onto her like a laser, and then you saw warmth and kindness written all over his face.

But was it really written; and if so, who wrote it? That was the thing Mike could not figure out. Was it just a show for the benefit of anyone who might be looking, this generous outpouring of self to the old woman who was too old to serve on boards and too old to help with church suppers and whose service to the church was long ago forgotten except by a few old-timers like herself? Was it just a show that Charles gave of giving himself to her in this loving way? Mike couldn't quite chase away the doubting angel that whispered such debilitating things in his ear.

He made a point of going to the big service on Sunday morning—at 9:30. There was one at 8:00 and another at 11:15, but the 9:30 service was the one that was always packed, always had a sense of something happening, of drama and excitement. Mike hated to be in any sense political, but he felt he needed to be there, even though he had his own service on Saturday night. He needed to be seen. But this command performance began to get him down and add to his doubts over time. The problem was unanticipated. It seemed the more he knew Charles, the less he liked his sermons.

They were full with all kinds of warmth and depth and lavishing of spirit on his listeners. When Mike first heard them, he was almost overcome. He could not believe the intimate power they had. He could not believe the reaction from the congregation, which was palpable. This is great preaching, he said to himself. He had never seen it before, not like this, not up close, and it was remarkable. Charles would just stand up there and Something Happened. Just in the way he stood there. It was like they were all elevated at once into a zone; it was like they were finding their way to a place of deep profundity and purity of spirit and purpose.

But then Mike began to wonder if there was a little bit of the virtuoso creeping into at least some of these dramatic, inspiring moments. There was laughter, and there was pathos, and there were tears—every single time! In every sermon! All three! No matter what the topic was or what was going on in the world! It began to strike him as being a little too formulaic. The sermons were put together for Maximum Impact. But who was this warm, loving, kind, generous person that the congregation saw on display at the podium? Who exactly was he? Mike didn't see much of this warmth or generosity on a personal level. Were others seeing it?

Speaking of nobodies and shattered lives, an interesting fellow by the name of Frank Crane joined the church that fall. Most of the time he came to the Sunday morning service, but sometimes he came to Mike's service as well. Afterwards he was always in a glow. It was a subdued glow, the glow of someone who has had all of the stuffing knocked out of him, a glow that could only come from the Spirit, Mike felt, since Frank had no spiritedness of his own.

Frank was a recovering alcoholic. He had the broken-down face of a recovering alcoholic and the muted presence. He went to AA every week, never missed, and hung on by his fingernails the rest of the time. He reminded Mike of one the most powerful services he had ever attended. It was a reunion service for people who had gone on a Tres Dias retreat. Instead of a sermon, former retreaters were invited to come and talk about their faith and what it meant to them.

One was a middle-aged woman, thin and unassuming. She began to talk, quietly and in the most absolutely plain terms, about the necessity of her faith in Christ. Turned out she had been an alcoholic. She didn't even try to hide it in front of these largely upper-crust power-Christians. She did not try to hide her weakness, and neither did she flaunt it. She was weak and that was just the way it was. But she loved one of those great verses from St. Paul: it was in her weakness that Christ was made strong. It was through his strength that she had given up her life-long love affair with the bottle. It was through his strength that she had begun to put her marriage and her family and her life back together, bit by bit. To be honest, she didn't know where she was going. She didn't always know if she could make it through another day without a drink. But she was drinking in Him, her living water. She was putting one foot in front of the other. And that was all.

It was the most beautiful testimony Mike had ever heard in his life, completely unpretending and honest. It dawned on him that "faith" wasn't just a word to her. It was her sustenance. It was literally her holding-on, the thing keeping her alive. There was a light in the darkness of her life, and it was this simple faith, and he felt privileged to have seen it in her and have had the opportunity to stop and try to reflect on his own existence and his own faith, which seemed kind of small and pale in comparison.

This same repentant spirit, this sad joy, was what Mike saw in Frank. He would never be one of the movers and shakers of Pine Cove Community Church. The church leaders were almost all professionals, most with six-figure incomes and a few top executives, while Frank was this broken-down guy who was a plumber and didn't live in the right part of town and drove a broken-down old Ford truck to church every Sunday. But that Ford was clean, waxed and clean.

And Frank was clean, his hands were clean, his clothes were not the best but they were clean. He was trying to clean up his life after thirty years of dissolution and darkness and horror and false epiphanies. Actually he was kind of an interesting guy. He would stop and chat with Mike after the services and always had some insight into the day's text, some unique angle that Mike hadn't thought of. Quite profound, in spite of his outward appearance.

There were other things about him that were interesting. He was a poet. He shared some of his poetry with Mike one day when he was at his house and it was beautiful. Homespun, not always elegant in imagery or execution, but beautiful in other ways, most of all in sincerity and depth of feeling. This guy would write poetry;

he would sit out on his porch and write it. He loved nature and he would get inspired and he would grab a pad and pen and start to write. Mike was impressed by that, perhaps even amazed.

He was impressed with his house, too. It was plain, but it was clean, it was neat. Frank had done all of the renovation and wiring and everything else himself. Clearly he had some talent. He showed Mike the ceiling moldings he had made, and they were beautiful. They were unique and beautiful in their own way, in a masculine way, and the coping was perfect, which Mike noticed because he had tried coping himself, with limited success.

As Christmas approached the sexton for the church resigned and moved to Maine ("sexton" was a fancy word for custodian and all-around handyman). Charles mentioned it during the service, and Frank came up to Mike afterwards and asked him if he thought that was something he could do. He was honest about it. He really could use the extra cash. He had lost many of his plumbing customers through his drinking and was having a little difficulty making ends meet.

Mike's heart went out to him. Of course he thought he could do it. He was perfect for it. He was a plumber, and churches always seem to have a need for them, especially in New England in the winter, but he was also handy in all the construction trades, a jack of all trades. He was an honest guy, he was someone who knew how lucky he was just to be alive, and Mike was sure he would make the most of the opportunity.

So he encouraged him to apply. He also put in a good word for him with the trustees, who were in charge of looking for a new sexton. No one else stepped forward to apply for the job, so Frank became the prime candidate by default. Mike told them about his sterling qualities and his versatility, desire to serve, his joy in the Lord. He did not tell them about his former alcoholism. It did not seem necessary or appropriate. Frank wasn't making any attempt to keep it secret, and Mike did not want to prejudice the board against him in any way.

Frank was hired at the beginning of the year and everybody was delighted. He was faithful and always had a smile on his face. He was there to keep the pipes from freezing when it went down to ten below; he seemed to know everything about the physical plant and how to keep it in good shape; he was able to save the church a good deal of money when the furnace died by replacing the burner himself and putting in a more reliable model, better scaled to the need. People who knew his personal history were delighted, Mike among them. There's nothing Americans love more than redemption stories, being an entire nation of recycled lives.

But not everyone was pleased with Frank. In particular Susan Cantor seemed to take it upon herself to keep watch over him and make sure his work met expectations. Trouble began when there was a snowstorm and Frank did not make it to church to shovel the walkways in quite as timely a manner as she desired. He tried to explain that his road had not been plowed, but it did not seem to matter. She had wanted to get into the church with the flowers for the weekend services and had not been able to do so. And she was not happy about this. Why didn't he have a four-wheel drive, like everyone else in New Hampshire?

Then there was a melt and a freeze and there was a lot of black ice. Frank sanded the walkways but did not salt them. This did not go over well with Susan either. Poor Mrs. Braxton had almost slipped on the walkway to the fellowship hall on her way to the sewing circle. Frank's explanation was that the ice did not seem bad enough to necessitate a salt application, especially since a warming trend was forecast for the next day. Besides, he was reluctant to use too much salt, on account of its deleterious effects on grass and plants.

Susan was having none of it. First of all, it wasn't up to him to decide what was or wasn't needed when it came to winter walkways maintenance. The walks were slippery, there was salt—use the salt! Second, what did the sexton have to do with grass and plants? That was the trustees' business. They didn't need some kind of wacko green agenda in the church. They needed safe walkways so people like Mrs. Braxton could come and go with no fear of ice.

Two strikes against poor Frank. Mike heard about it and was mortified. In both instances he was inclined to see things from Frank's point of view and to feel Susan was being unreasonable. But that was part of the problem. He suspected his interest in Frank was playing an unseen role in her eagerness to criticize. He was the one who recommended him, and she still had not forgiven him for what had happened at the Bible study. It seemed likely that Frank was being punished for Mike's sins.

Things went directly downhill from there. To tell the truth, Frank did not do himself any favors. He was a little bit stubborn.

He was a bright guy who knew a lot about things, and he was not altogether eager to back down when he thought he was in the right. In both of these instances he felt he was in the right. He did not apologize to Susan or the board for the way he had handled things. As far as he was concerned, he had acted appropriately.

But Susan was not backing down either. Now that Frank had found his way into her cross-hairs, she became relentless. She was determined to see that he did the job the "right way" or she was determined that he would not be the sexton—one or the other. Mike did not see this contest of wills first-hand, but he heard about it from Bill and others and was heartbroken. Then one day Frank dropped in to see him.

"Mind if I talk to you for a moment?" Frank said, using the opening Mike had come to dread in his brief sojourn in the ministry.

"Not at all, come on in!"

"I got to tell ya, she's driving me crazy. Absolutely crazy."

"Who is?"

"Your friend. You know, what's her name from the trustees, who seems to have taken it into her head that she's my supervisor or something."

"I'm guessing you mean Susan."

"That's the one. I can't do anything right by her. It's like having another wife. I mean, at first it was just a couple of things. But now I get a call from her every other day. I dread it when the phone rings. I'm not kidding."

"What are these calls about?"

"What a bad sexton I am. I didn't do this, I didn't do that. If I did do it, I didn't do it right. I mean, where did this woman get all of this amazing knowledge? She's an expert on everything."

The thought occurred to Mike that Frank had a little of the same affliction. "I know she's just very particular about things. Is it really that hard to get along with her? Maybe it's better to bend a little here and there, if you can."

"I've been doing that. I'm trying to do that. She just won't let it go. It's like I'm her personal project or something. I don't want to be her personal project. I know what I'm doing."

"Well, try not to get frustrated. I think it will blow over. Just hang in there and let her see what a good job you're doing."

"But you think I'm doing a good job?"

"I think you're doing a great job. It's just that different people have different ideas about things. She's not that crazy about me, either, by the way."

"Really?"

"Really. Anyway, don't let it get you down. I'm sure she has better things to do than to follow you around."

"Doesn't seem like it," was Frank's mordant reply.

About a month went by and Mike didn't hear any more about the titanic struggle, but then he happened to go to the March trustees meeting to talk about some improvements that needed to be made to the Saturday night worship space, and much to his dismay it came up.

"Pastor, while you're here we probably need to talk about something that's got a few people in the congregation riled up," said Trent Witzky, who was the chairman of the board and someone Mike liked. Trent was normally a very reasonable guy, a very spiritual guy, but in this case he was being egged on by his close friend Susan, whom he was reluctant to disappoint.

"Okay," Mike said, although it wasn't really.

"It's this situation with Frank Crane. Are you aware of that?"

"I wasn't aware there was a situation."

"Well, unfortunately there is. Personally I like Frank and I think he's doing a good job, on the whole, but some people aren't exactly happy with his work."

"That's one way of putting it," Susan chimed in. "He's a paid employee of the church. He's not a volunteer like the rest of us. He's not just doing this out of the goodness of his heart. We need to have standards. We need to have minimum expectations for people who work for the church."

"Are you saying Frank isn't meeting those expectations?" Mike said with raised eyebrows.

"I'm saying he could be doing a lot better. And it doesn't seem to matter how many times you talk to him about it, the results are always the same. You get a lot of excuses and a lot of promises and double-talk, but nothing happens. Nothing changes."

"Can you be specific? What are we talking about here?"

"Oh, I don't think we need to go into that right now," Trent interjected. "The details aren't that important. The thing is it just seems to be a general feeling with a lot of people. They were looking for something a little different from what they got."

"Did you know he was an alcoholic?" Susan said directly to Mike, sounding a little angry.

"Recovering alcoholic," Mike corrected her.

"I don't care what you call it, he's an alcoholic. Did you know this when you told us to hire him?"

"I didn't tell you to hire him. I just told you I thought he would do a good job."

"Don't change the subject. Did you know about it or not?"

"Yes, I knew. I thought everybody did."

"No, 'everybody' didn't. I certainly didn't know. I think we have to be careful about the people we hire for the church. If someone comes here and volunteers and he's an alcoholic, that's one thing. That's someone volunteering and we're not going to have any specific expectations for someone like that. But if we're actually hiring people, we need to think about what we're doing. We need to make sure they're reliable."

"Are you saying Frank's not reliable?" Mike said, not quite able to hide his incredulity.

"Wow, have you been paying attention? That's exactly what I'm saying. You knew he was an alcoholic, but for some reason you decided to withhold this information. And now it's created an unfortunate situation."

Mike would not back down. "I think Frank's doing a great job. I've gotten to know him a little, and I know he's a very knowledgeable guy, a talented guy, especially when it comes to mechanical things. I know he's a man of faith. As far as the alcoholism goes, he hasn't had a drink in five years. I think we should be willing to give him the benefit of the doubt."

"We did that. We gave him the benefit of the doubt, and look what happened. And who are you to say he's doing a great job? You're not the one who has to supervise him and make sure he does what he's supposed to do. Maybe you should just listen to the people who do have this responsibility instead of trying to brush off all our concerns with your uniformed opinions."

"But there's a Biblical principle at play here. 'Put no stumbling block in your brother's way.' We really should go out of our way to be accommodating, especially to those who may be weak in the faith."

Susan gave him a withering stare. "This is the board of trustees, not the deacons. We're not here to debate doctrine; were here to make sure the church properties are taken care of."

Mike knew it was time to shut up. He didn't trust himself to say anything more. He was burning with anger at this little maneuver. It was the half-truths and the parsed truths and the insinuations that infuriated him. For whatever reason, Susan had hardened her opposition to Frank, and there was no way of changing her mind. He could see it clearly. She was a person of influence; she was strong-willed and had no compunction about using her willpower and persuasiveness when she felt she was in the right, as seemed to be the case in this instance.

The thing that galled him the most, however, was dragging *him* into it. She effectively disarmed him by making him seem like a partisan. It was as if any comment he might make on the quality or timeliness of Frank's work was out of bounds because of his support for Frank, which, in her view, was compromised by dishonesty and concealment. Her determined assault on Frank was also an assault on him. Apparently the old wounds had not healed. Thus he could not be sure whether he was helping or hurting Frank by continuing to try to defend him.

Mike held his tongue, but it galled him to hold it. What she was doing was wrong. She was blowing things way out of proportion to make Frank look like some sort of dismal failure, which was not the case at all. He did things his own way and not the way she wanted them done. That's what it came down to. Even his heroic work on the furnace was now turned against him. Why didn't he go out and get bids? Why didn't he consult with the trustees and make sure everyone was on board with the course of action he had chosen? What if the burner broke down again? There was no warranty now because Frank was the one who had installed it. What then?

Susan had many gifts and admirable qualities, but the sacred gift of magnanimity was not among them. From her point of view, Frank had an indelible stain because of his alcoholism, and this stain could not be washed away, not by a change in heart and behavior exhibited by Frank himself, not even by the blood of Christ. This stain stained everything he did. It was all broken down, it was all wreckage, every bit of his work, in her mind, because that was the way she framed him in her mind: he was a drunk.

Not that she was a teetotaler herself. Far from it. She liked to have her gin and tonic on Friday night before dinner and sometimes on Saturday night, too. She liked a good glass of wine; she and Fred were self-styled connoisseurs and had a sizable collection in their basement. But she was not weak, oh no. She was not like Frank, who could not control himself and let the liquor control him. So he had stopped. Big deal! Did that mean he was strong now, had gained control over his life? Not at all. In her mind the change in him and his faithful attendance at AA showed that he was still weak—too weak to control his desire to get drunk without avoiding alcohol altogether. And if there was one thing she could not tolerate it was weakness.

Mike saw all this and it made him sick. Literally sick in his heart to the point of angina. He was rooting for Frank. He wanted him to conquer his addiction and lead a better life. He wanted him to have the sexton job, first because he needed the money, and second because Mike thought he would be good at it. And he *was* good at it. From the male point of view, which admittedly is not quite as exacting as the female's, Frank was doing a fine job, an admirable job. The way he did things was ingenious. Other people couldn't see it because they couldn't understand it. They had no frame of reference for appreciating him.

Mike did, and it infuriated him to see his protégé beaten down as if he were worthless. Protégé? He hadn't thought of Frank that way before, but now he did, after this devastating conversation with Susan in front of the trustees. He was tied to Frank and Frank to him because he had taken up Frank's cause and recommended him for the job. And ironically, this was the very thing that made it hard for him to defend him. Anything he said was considered to be compromised.

Most of all, though, it was about the sheep and the shepherd. Mike had a very tender concern for this particular sheep. Frank was fragile. It was clearly written in his past and the sagging lines on his face. He was relatively new to the faith, and was this the hard surface that the church was going to show him? Relentless criticism? Personal criticism? Rejection?

Susan was right and wrong. There were two ways of looking at the complaints she had made about Frank. If you looked at them as his shepherd, they seemed baseless. It was not wrong, for instance, for Frank to be concerned about over-salting the walkways. He had sanded generously. No one had fallen. To say that he had no right to be concerned because the trustees were in charge of the grounds was just silly. Christian churches are not about power-plays.

The same was true of her other objections. It was easy for Mike to step into Frank's shoes and see there were two sides to the story. Who was she to judge the poor man for his former alcoholism? And did she actually say "this is the trustees, not the deacons"? What in the world was she implying? How were the trustees in a Christian church supposed to conduct their business if not according to Christian principles?

Mike left the meeting feeling crushed and outraged at the same time. He loved Frank. He wanted to extend the open arms of the church and its Christ to Frank. It seemed to him that Susan and her witch hunt were putting an angry, controlling, unwelcoming face on the church. She was hectoring Frank, and he was becoming more and more upset. The main thing Mike feared was that she would wind up driving the poor man away through her unrelenting legalism.

But somehow she had managed to frame the conversation differently. Somehow she had turned it on him so that she looked like the one who cared about the church and its well-being and he was merely careless. Hiring an alcoholic as a custodian! Hiding the fact from the church leaders! She could drive this one home relentlessly and there was nothing he could do about it.

Her genius was in making him misunderstood. He was trying to be Frank's shepherd, not a radical advocate of alcoholics. But she knew how to win an argument, and he had long ago lost his enthusiasm for winning.

WHATEVER IS CONCEALED

THERE WAS A SPECIAL little ritual for prospective new members at Pine Cove, not something all churches did, called "Testimony Night." Basically it was a forum for them to stand up in front of the congregation and share a little about themselves and why they wanted to join.

Mike had now been through four Testimony Nights at Pine Cove, some of them quite moving, but nothing quite prepared him for what happened when Clarissa stood up in front of a moderate-sized crowd and began to talk in her inimitable way.

Ostensibly Testimony Night was for the whole congregation, a time for new members to say whatever was on their hearts and minds without overextending the already lengthy main service on Sunday morning, where they were actually accepted as members. But in general it was mostly attended by church leadership, who may have felt they had to be there, and any friends and relations of the candidates who wanted to support them.

Mike enjoyed Testimony Night, on the whole. He was excited to see people joining the church and coming to the joy of faith; it was what he was all about. True, the statements of the candidates tended to be a little repetitive, but with fifteen or twenty testimonies in a row this was to be expected. What could the average person say? They were not steeped in theology, nor were they likely to expose their deepest inner feelings in front of a crowd. They were New Englanders, after all. Most depended upon written statements and talked in general terms about their faith and how they felt they had found a home at Pine Cove, etc. Often they used a Scripture passage that seemed appropriate. And there you have it—the Pine Cove testimony formula.

Then there was Clarissa. She had no idea how to use the formula because she had not been raised in a church and knew nothing about church conventions or language. She had never been to a Testimony Night or even imagined such things existed. At the same time she was not cowed by an audience, like the typical new member. She was a performing artist, after all, used to baring her soul on stage and being up in front of people.

You could tell she was different as soon as they handed her the mic. She was used to having one in her hand and used to the sound of her own voice coming back to her over the loudspeakers. She was different in another way, too. You could see her vulnerability written all over her, as if she had a fever and was flushed, the opposite of the polite reserve seen in most of the other candidates. It was in the way she stood and the way she smiled and the way she leaned a little in the direction of her audience as she spoke. No stiffness, no awkwardness, no wall.

Mike was charmed by all this. He might have wished she had been a little more conservative with what she wore—the short skirt and white silk blouse with top buttons unfastened was perhaps a bit much for the Pine Cove crowd—but he could not fault her. He knew she didn't mean anything by it. That was just how she dressed. Besides, she had no idea of the impact she might have on her listeners, no idea of the kinds of thoughts that might be going through their minds as they sat there looking at her. She was being herself, which is what Mike wanted her to be.

"Well—hello!" she said, a little bashfully, and he smiled because he knew what she meant. She was saying, in effect, "I can't quite believe I'm here—can you?" He knew this because of his conversation with her, because he knew her background, knew she had never been in church voluntarily or even thought about being in church until she somehow found her way to the Saturday night service at Pine Cove. He knew about the emotion packed into those few words, hidden in them, and his eyes welled up with tears.

"For those of you who don't know me—which I guess is just about everyone—my name is Clarissa Neumann, and I'm a recovering just-about-everything. I'm not going to say 'alcoholic' because that doesn't seem colorful enough. I've had more addictions than most of you probably even heard of. I'm not proud of it, I'm just trying to tell you where I'm coming from and where I've been. I was a girl looking for love in all the wrong places, but I feel like I've come home now—thanks to Pastor Mike. I've got to say it, thanks to Pastor Mike and the wonderful welcoming people of this church."

Mike tried to merge into his seat. This was not about him and he didn't want it to be about him. It was about Clarissa and most of all it was about the Savior she had found and the new life that had changed her and taken away her pain and her restlessness. The thing about all her addictions?—he assumed it was for comic effect, self-effacing humor. She was being humble and honest and not trying to pull the wool over anyone's eyes, actually overstating the deficiencies of her past.

His heart went out to her as she stood up there in the spotlight on the stage. The room suddenly grew very quiet—she certainly had their attention—and his heart went out to her. He said a little instant prayer: "Lord, please protect her. Send your Spirit to help her right now. Give her strength."

"It's probably pretty hard for you to imagine someone like me," Clarissa continued. "I never went anywhere near a church my whole life—except when I was playing my violin. My parents were atheists and they never even talked about church. To me it was just these curious buildings that people came in and out of on Sundays and I didn't know why. I guess I still sort of feel that way, it's all so new to me. On top of that, I'm a musician—you know how they are. Let's just say I've met some interesting people and been in some interesting places in my life.

"But I said I was looking for love in all the wrong places. Well, I finally found it here. The right kind of love, I mean. The kind of love I never found anywhere else, never in my life. I came here not knowing quite what to expect. I didn't have anything against church. I just didn't know if it was for me. None of my friends went to church. I've heard people talk about 'church shopping,' only I wasn't really coming to buy anything. I was coming to look. More out of curiosity than anything else, or so I told myself.

"Anyway, I drive by this church every day on my way to the school where I teach and on that little board you keep out front there were the words 'We are family.' That was all. I don't know why, but it moved me. I saw the words and I felt like they were for me. I guess the truth is I've been lonely for a long time. I was an only child, so I guess you could say I've been lonely my whole life. Without really knowing it. We have ways of hiding these things. For me it was a party every night or a trip to the bar.

"So those words spoke to me for some reason. I don't know whether it was the mood I was in or the weather or the fact that it was Monday and I had a terrible weekend or what, but they just spoke to me. I made up my mind to come and see what this 'family' thing was all about. Now I've got to be honest with you, I didn't come with any great expectations. It was a Saturday night, I didn't have a gig, I couldn't face the bar scene, so I just decided to come, more out of curiosity than anything.

"But boy, was I in for a surprise! I just sat there looking at how happy everybody seemed and I wanted to be happy, too. And then the music started and everybody stood up and started to praise God and I thought—whoa! What's going on? People raising their hands and everything. At that point I was checking out the exits. But I didn't run away. Actually I wanted to stay. And then the sermon came and Pastor Mike started talking in his warm, loving way, and it just hit me. I am home. I guess that's what I was looking for all this time and didn't realize it. I am home."

She started to sob. She held onto the microphone as if there was more she wanted to say, but then she couldn't say anything so she handed it to the next person.

Mike sat there stunned. It was the most incredible thing he'd ever heard on Testimony Night. It reminded him of *The Seven Story Mountain*, coming in from complete cold, but even better because it was so real and because he knew her personally. He knew there was no pretense in what she said. Her honesty was an act of love. Mike basked in the warmth of these feelings. Hot tears trickled down his face, which he tried to flick away without being conspicuous.

He glanced around the room self-consciously and happened to see Susan Cantor, sitting a few rows away. She was glaring at him.

LEAD US NOT INTO TEMPTATION

CLARISSA'S TESTIMONY was a bright light in the middle of an otherwise heavy winter for Mike. Many more people were coming to him now, as attendance at the Saturday night service grew, looking for solace or inspiration or whatever they thought he could give them. Yes, he was very much in demand, and it was exhausting, but he would never turn anyone away.

One needy person in particular was destined to cause a certain amount of planetary dislocation in Mike's life. His name was Arnie Lascowicz, and he'd been coming to the Saturday night service for some time with his attractive wife and daughters. Arnie made quite an impression. He did not seem to have gotten the Baby Boomer memo about casual dress; in any case he was always immaculately attired. He literally looked like a thousand bucks with his carefully groomed jet-black hair and his expensive freshly-pressed suits.

He was very enthusiastic. He had a bright smile and cheerful greeting for everyone. He sang the praise songs lustily, if not quite on key, and praised Mike up and down for his sermons. His family joined the church at the first opportunity. Mike was pleased. Arnie seemed like an ideal member and an important addition to the community. He was always asking what he could do to help. Finally Mike suggested putting his name in for trustees; it seemed like a good fit. He went on the board in the new year.

So it seemed a little unfair one gloomy day in March when Arnie came to him with a "little problem." Mike was kind of counting on Arnie *not* to be one of the problem-bringers. In Arnie's case, the problem was disappointment—with himself. Apparently he had a weakness for online pornography. He wanted to be able to resist it. He knew it was mind pollution and degrading and ungodly. He was highly ashamed of his weakness.

Mike had just preached a sermon on "confess your sins to each other and pray for each other, that you may be healed." Arnie very much wanted to be healed. He opened up to Mike. It wasn't just his addiction—as he called it—it was everything. He was down on himself, short-tempered at work and at home, depressed and listless, and wondered if the "addiction thing" had something to do with it, befouling his mind and discoloring his world. He needed a fresh start. He needed to get his mojo back, his sense of purpose, his strength, which the electronic Delilah had taken away.

Mike's heart went out to him as he spoke. He wanted to cry for him and for all of them, the American men who found themselves in a strange new world not of their own making and who did not know what to make of this world, who were allowing their minds and imaginations to be polluted—basically because it was too easy; because the Internet was right there in their homes and it was free and it was abundant; because they did not understand themselves; because let's face it, their actual lives were not terribly exciting.

Mike looked at Arnie in wonder. Who would have known, just from his outward appearance, that he had a shameful habit he was unable to control? He seemed so fastidious about himself, so fresh and clean, so enthusiastic about church and religion, so engaged in worship and the sharing time afterwards; who could have seen this demon lurking inside him, as he seemed to see it?

His heart went out to Arnie and he sighed because he felt he did not have a good answer for him. He had a lot of religious answers that he was taught in seminary, where they were well-aware of the problem, and he shared these with Arnie. But as he shared them he wondered if they were good enough. They were high-minded but not very practical. It seemed to him, based on Arnie's own words, that the attraction was just too strong for bromides.

The practical solution, Mike suggested, would be for Arnie to turn off the Internet to avoid temptation. Not heroic, but effective. Mike knew because he had used it on himself. He did not have Internet at the in-law apartment he rented, partly for this very reason. He did not want it in the house because he did not want to be tempted. He did not know if he could resist temptation. He had not always been able to resist it in the past. He was not perfect or a stranger to the perplexing problem Arnie was now facing.

But this solution would not work for Arnie. He could not shut off the Internet. His wife and two daughters were heavy users, especially the girls. What excuse could he possibly come up with to justify such retrograde behavior? It wasn't like he could tell them the real reason. His beautiful wife Donna—he couldn't see himself telling her. It was out of the question. So no, the Internet was not going away. The easiest and most practical solution was out of bounds for poor Arnie—and this meant the temptation would still be there. He wanted to fight it. Would Mike help him fight it?

Mike very much wanted to help him but did not know how. He did not have enough faith in human nature to believe any intervention other than the most obvious one was likely to be very effective. What to do, then? How to talk to poor Arnie about his perplexing problem? There were so many possibilities. For a moment he pictured himself as Charles. He thought he knew what Charles would do. He would keep that warm smile on his face—if it really was warm—and he would be kind but firm and he would scold Arnie, tell him he had to take charge of his life, and then he would reach into the Bible and pull out the breastplate of righteousness and a few other passages that seemed apropos and tell Arnie to "resist the Devil and he will flee from you"— *etc.*

It was Standard Pastoring by the book. And frankly there was a lot to recommend it. First, it might possibly be effective. There was always the chance that such a remedy would work with someone like Arnie. Second, it was completely unassailable. No nosey inquisitor could come in after the fact and identify a clinical misstep of any kind. It was not harsh. It was encouraging. It was Scriptural. The sufferer had been treated with Christian kindness and given good advice straight from the Bible and sent on his merry way.

The only problem with this approach, from Mike's point of view, was it was not likely to work. It was based on a false assumption: the strength of men and perfectibility of human will. Arnie had come to him with a frank admission. He was powerless against temptation. He did not want to do what he was doing. He was embarrassed and hated himself for being weak—but he also did not seem to be able to change. And he so much wanted to change. He so much wanted Mike to help him change.

Mike reminded him of the many passages in the Bible about resisting evil. He advised him to read a bit of Proverbs every day and let it fill his heart and soul, let it become his guiding light and mode of thinking. He also told him to begin the day with prayer, including the all-important words "thy will be done"; to pray for strength every time he felt temptation coming on; and to make a conscious effort to stay away from any potentially compromising situations.

Still, the modern age with all of its incredible conveniences created a difficult situation for men like Arnie. It turned out that he was very much like Frank, although outwardly he did not resemble him at all. With Frank, you frankly knew he did not have his act together. You could see it on his face and in his posture. Things were very different with Arnie. On the outside, he seemed like the most confident guy in the world—and yet he had an addiction, an Achilles' heel, just like Frank; a weakness he could not overcome.

He wanted to pray, he wanted to follow God and seek his will, because he wanted abundant life, because he wanted to be happy and not filled with gloom and self-recrimination and shame. He wanted to follow the Way because he knew it was the right way, the way of life, good for him and good for the soul—but he couldn't. He tried to but he could not overcome. He could not make himself perfect. The ubiquitous temptation was too strong.

Mike felt terribly uncomfortable as he listened to Arnie and his confession. For a moment he wished he had never put himself in this foolish position, never pretended he was qualified to be a teacher and spiritual advisor, a pastor. Arnie came to him begging for relief from his burdens, but Mike felt very unequal to the task. He sympathized deeply with him, but that was the problem. He knew the weakness and he knew how difficult it could be.

It made him think of the well-known passage from Romans. St. Paul had talked about this very problem—the inability to perfect human will. His own sin made him miserable. He could not do the good he wanted to do, but the very evil he did not want to do—"that is what I do." No one knew what his "thorn in the flesh" was, but Mike knew that such thorns do exist. They are real and they are caught in "the flesh," the sum total of a man. Therefore they are not likely to be removed by any mortal surgeon.

Unfortunately this pessimistic way of thinking ran directly contrary to the expectations of the larger culture. It is universally believed and taught in the West that man is in charge of his own destiny. That is the whole meaning of philosophy and its therapeutic stepchild, psychology. Human vanity requires us to conquer our demons and show ourselves to be strong; but St. Paul very plainly taught that we are weak. We have no reason to boast of our self-control. We are no better than the worst of sinners—not on the inside; not in the heart, where it really counts, since God does not look on appearances.

We can look like Arnie on the outside and still feel like garbage on the inside because we know we fall short of the glory of God. We can fool others but cannot fool ourselves. We love spiritual things in our innermost being—but when we actually *try* to be spiritual, we find that we cannot hit the mark. And yet, "Thanks be to God!" God's goodness and love are greater than our own depravity. That is Paul's message. God loves us and has already paid the price for our transgressions. The way to be happy, then, is to put our trust in him and not in our own strength.

But would Mike be able to explain all this to Arnie? That was the question. He knew it would be hard because he had tried to explain this passage in the past. He vividly remembered preaching a sermon about it when he first started out and seeing the blank expressions on the faces of his listeners. The passage is hard for people to absorb because it runs directly against the current of human pride, which is ashamed of our weaknesses. We do not want to be hopeless and wholly dependent on God and his purifying love. We want to save a little honor for ourselves.

Romans 7 was wildly comforting in a strange counterintuitive way; and it was this strangeness that made Mike wary of going into it with Arnie, although he felt it was the only medicine that could relieve his pain. He was careful. He started by talking about the rich young ruler who came to Jesus seeking the kingdom of life and how he was asked to give up just one thing—and how deeply it grieved him. His riches were his wall against nothingness, his identity; he did not want to give them up by any means. He did not want to give up the very thing that was standing between him and true happiness, which comes from depending wholly on God, since only God can give life.

Then Mike took a deep breath and dove into Romans with its dark view of human nature. He used the passage that had been so reassuring to Luther in an attempt to reassure Arnie and let him know he was not alone. He reminded him about St. Paul's thorn in the flesh. Paul prayed to have it taken away but God saw fit to leave it. Why? Perhaps as a way of reminding him of his mortality; perhaps as a way of driving him to the cross instead of trying to save himself. Mike did not know why, exactly. All he knew was God had not removed the thorn.

Arnie brightened. He had never heard Romans talked about like this before. It made God's grace seem more real to him and not just a concept, which Mike thought was a very insightful comment. But then he became curious. How did Mike know this was what St. Paul had in mind? How did he know the thorn could not be removed? Maybe in his case it *could* be removed. Maybe he was just not a good enough Christian. Maybe he didn't have enough faith.

Mike had a difficult counseling decision to make. Would he be like Paul or like Charles? In Romans, Paul let down his defenses. He let us see him as he really was in order to offer us grace and comfort. This was something Charles would never do, not in a million years. He would never let down his guard, the mask of the Perfect Christian. He could sympathize with someone like Arnie but not empathize. He would never go into the dangerous places where Paul went and make himself vulnerable. His riches were his honorable appearance.

Mike decided to follow Paul's lead and be honest and open about his own shortcomings. He would become vulnerable, show his wounds, so Arnie could take comfort in his vulnerability and hopefully be relieved of some of his suffering.

"To tell you the truth, I am not completely immune to the temptation myself," he confessed.

"Really?" Arnie replied, looking surprised.

"No, I'm far from perfect. I am not unlike Paul. Believe me, Romans 7 is very important for me as well. I live on it every day."

"Wow, I never would have guessed that. The way you preach and everything…"

"We all have our masks that we wear," Mike said with a tight smile. "If I've given the impression of being holier than I actually am, I apologize. I guess I have to work on that in the future. But let me assure you, I am no less human than you are."

"So—I mean—where are you at now?"

"Where I'm at now is an apartment where there is no Internet. I'm in kind of a unique position because I can actively remove myself from temptation. I get any email I need here at church, so I don't really need it at home. But that doesn't mean I'm not tempted. That doesn't mean I'm any better than you are or have any reason to boast of my holiness."

Arnie sat there looking at him for a moment. "So you don't really have an answer for me, then."

"I don't have a magic wand to make the problem go away, no. I do know what you're dealing with because I've been there. When my wife was alive and the kids were still at home we had the Internet, and I know how hard it is to resist temptation. All I can tell you is what I've already told you. First of all, do what Paul says. Arm yourself with God's word and with faith. Read the Bible every day. Pray, pray, pray. But if you fall, remember Paul's own struggles and the grace of God. I'm afraid that's the best I can do."

Arnie clearly was not happy with this outcome. Mike could understand why. He had come to him thinking he could cure him, thinking Mike would have the answer he needed in order to get past the predicament he found himself in. That was why he was so open. But Mike could not in good conscience do this. He knew the temptation too well. He did not think it was fair to expect more from Arnie than he knew he could expect from himself. He did not think there was anything to be gained by hiding his own weakness.

He prayed with Arnie before he left. Oh, how he prayed. There was not one conventional phrase in the entire prayer, not one homogenized religious sentiment, no boilerplate, just pure heartfelt emotion and love born in starts and fits and still struggling on. The farther Mike got from himself and his formulas the more present the Spirit felt to him—but there was no discernable change in Arnie. He still seemed dissatisfied. Maybe even a little peeved.

This conversation weighed on Mike terribly in the days and weeks to follow. He was not satisfied with himself and the answer he had given. Arnie had come to him for healing and he could not heal him. He was not even sure a healing was possible, at least not in the sense that a broken bone can be healed. It seemed to him from what he observed of contemporary culture and what he knew about men that dealing, not healing, was the best that could be expected.

Had he helped Arnie at all? He wondered. He *wanted* to help him. He felt badly for him, knew what he was going through. But maybe the Charles strategy, as he imagined it, was the best one after all. Maybe it was better in the end to keep everything on the surface and put on a mask. He could not hold himself responsible for saving Arnie, who would have to put his faith in a higher doctor if he wanted to be healed.

A thought occurred to him—what was it like to be a psychiatrist? Someone who is suicidal comes to you for help. You want to help, you are duty-bound to help. You follow all the best practices for treatment, make yourself completely available to him, but he commits suicide anyway. Is it your fault? Did you fail? So hard to say when in a way you were doomed to fail. You were dealing with forces greater than yourself and your imagination.

This was how Mike felt after his conversation with Arnie. He could not give him the help he needed because he was not the Good Teacher. He was just a guy who believed in God and needed God to live. But had this feeling compromised him and his ability to help? Had he been too skeptical at the outset about Arnie's prospects for breaking the addiction that plagued him? He did not know. He certainly hoped he hadn't. More than anything he wanted to help.

The thing is Arnie would never have gone to Charles with his dilemma. Arnie had come to Mike because Mike deliberately cultivated a persona of openness, humility and acceptance, both from the pulpit and in his interactions with others. He had come to Mike because Mike seemed successful in doing what he was trying to do. But Mike did not feel he could heal him. It was his very commitment to openness that made it impossible, not to mention his own shortcomings.

Had his comments about Romans been misunderstood? He did not want Arnie to think he was giving him permission to give up trying to resist the troubling addiction. "Should we go on sinning? By no means!" He did not want him thinking that holiness was unimportant or it was impossible to become more spiritual than we currently are, by God's grace, even while Paul also said that we are unspiritual by nature. Mike did not have an antinomian bone in his body and worried now that he might have seemed too cavalier.

This encounter with Arnie was not the only thing weighing on his mind. Charles asked him to stop by for a chat. He had not received such an invitation from Charles in quite some time and did not know what to think. Then he had one of his famous intuitions. Charles had heard about Frank and the dust-up between Mike and Susan. He was right. That was exactly what the senior pastor wanted to talk about.

"I understand you and Susan tangled horns again," Charles said with the usual smile and calm composure.

"I guess you mean with the trustees. Yes, that was unfortunate."

"Why don't you tell me about it?"

"What would you like to know? It's poor Frank Crane. This guy has enough on his plate as it is, and now it seems he has to deal with the supervisor mentality from his own church."

"But they do have a responsibility to supervise him. I mean, he does work for them."

"I suppose so, but it's not exactly like a boss-employee relationship. It's not that cut and dried, or that cold. He's a member of the church and a guy with a lot of struggles of his own, and I just think we should take these things into account."

"Okay, but the bottom line is the job has to be done right. Don't you agree?"

"In my view, it is being done right. I think he's doing a great job, and I know there are a lot of people who agree with me, including some on the Trustees."

"Well, apparently there are also people who do *not* agree. Starting with Susan. What I'm saying is I think you need to step back and take into account the possibility that you may be wrong or you may be a little prejudiced in the way you're looking at this."

"Prejudiced! She's the one who's prejudiced. In her mind, he's an alcoholic. Doesn't matter that he hasn't had a drop to drink in five years. Once an alcoholic, always an alcoholic."

"But how do you know that's true? How do you know he hasn't had a drop to drink, I mean—isn't drinking now? These people can be very persuasive."

"I understand all that, I understand the self-delusion thing. *I* believe him, but I guess I can't expect you to believe him too. In any case, the bottom line is he's doing the job. She's wrong; he is not a screw-up. He's a hard-working guy, a dedicated guy, he loves the church and I would hate to see him get hurt."

"Maybe you should have thought of that before you recommended him for the job. Because now we have a bit of a problem. As far as Susan is concerned, and apparently as far as a lot of people are concerned, he's not doing the job. He is not earning what we're paying him. Other people are having to take up the slack, and they're not too happy about it."

"If a lot of people are thinking that way, then that's because that's what she told them. She's on some kind of crusade against the poor guy."

"I give up. I don't know what to say to you. This is Susan Cantor we're talking about. She's one of the most respected and prominent leaders in the church and the Cantors are probably our biggest donors, thirty thousand a year, at least. Or weren't you aware of that?"

"I thought we weren't supposed to show favoritism to the rich."

"'Favoritism'! This isn't favoritism. This is just common sense. You're pitting yourself and your friend against two of the pillars of the church. And I'm telling you, be careful. You don't know where this could lead."

"I don't think this should be about 'pitting' anybody against anything. I am concerned about Frank as a person, pure and simple. And frankly I think her opposition to him has something to do with her attitude toward me. Be that as it may, the guy needs this church. At this point we are about all he has in his life. He's divorced. His kids don't want to see him because of past hurts. We are like a lifeline to him, and I hate to think there's even a possibility of that lifeline being broken over trivial things."

"According to Susan, they aren't trivial. That's the problem. Look, I understand your passion. You want to help the guy. But sometimes people have to help themselves. It seems like he's not helping himself right now, and I'm just trying to tell you—you are putting yourself right in the middle of it. If I were you, I would let it go. Let Frank take care of himself. He's a big boy."

Mike didn't see any point of going on. Charles was not judging fairly or with clear eyes. It seemed he was favoring the Cantors because they were rich and because of what they could do for him and his ministry. And if a guy like Frank had to suffer because of it—well, so be it. As Charles said, he can take care of himself.

But this was just what Mike feared—that Frank could *not* take care of himself. He had seen the joy when Frank first started coming to church and he realized now he had banked on that joy psychologically. He had put Frank in the "saved" bracket and wanted to keep him there.

What if Frank was not destined for the saved bracket? What if he was like the poor soul that receives the seed with joy but then the snares and weeds of life creep in and take it away along with his new-found faith? What if the course of benign neglect being recommended by Charles was actually the wise one? After all, Mike could not save everyone who came to him. Mike could not save the world, as much as he might want to.

Was he being unfair to Charles? He wrestled with this thought through the long dark winter night like Jacob with the angel but was unable to come up with an answer. He was tempted to accuse Charles of favoritism, but was that really what it was? Or was he just being realistic? It was true that people had complaints about Frank's work. And Frank's reaction was a little troubling. He was an employee, after all. Employees have a financial obligation not to fight with their masters.

In the end Mike did not know quite what to think about the whole mess—but this did not relieve him of the burden he felt for Frank. He loved Frank, for all his faults, and wanted him to succeed on the path to sobriety. He hated to think the church might in any way contribute to his failure. He hated to think the church might chase this lost sheep away.

GREET ONE ANOTHER WITH A HOLY KISS

WOW! THAT was quite a conversatION with Charles. Coming on top of the Arnie thing, it left Mike feeling bruised and battered just at Easter, when the gloom of winter was supposed to be lifting and taking the human spirit along with it.

Actually there was some similarity between the two situations. He felt a burden for someone or something that seemed impossible—in Arnie's case, healing him of his addiction; in Frank's case, shielding him from the wolves. In both cases the person he cared about needed to take matters into his own hands at some point in order for there to be a satisfactory conclusion. And this seemed unlikely. Mike was left with the ache and the burn and sense of impending doom.

Then there was Susan Cantor. She had never forgiven him, he was sure, and was therefore determined to make him look foolish and misinterpret everything he said and did. He thought about her attitude towards Frank. Is it true that people can never change? An alcoholic can never get his life back in order? He remembered the look she gave him after Clarissa's testimony. Was he due for some unhappiness there as well?

And what about Charles? He felt oppressed in spirit whenever he thought of him and their most recent conversation. Could he follow Charles's lead when it came to the painful conflict between Susan and Frank? What about the nagging suspicion he had that Charles was favoring Susan because of her money? He wished this suspicion would go away—which is like trying to forget your own name. It would not go away because it was his.

It was the strangest Easter he'd ever had, and the loneliest. He got up in front of the congregation on Saturday night and put on a smile he did not really feel and delivered a barn-burner of an Easter sermon he did not really feel—and it was all very strange. He was preaching and trying to break down the wall, just as he always did, but he was also thinking about his conversation with Charles and about Susan and Frank and Arnie and the ambiguities. Both at the same time.

So many people came up to him after the service eager to shake his hand or hug him and thank him for the beautiful, uplifting sermon he had just delivered, some with tears in their eyes, real tears! He did not know how to respond. Eventually the hall emptied out and he felt relieved. He turned off the lights and was on his way out the door when he remembered his umbrella—it was a drizzly spring night. Where did he leave it? He remembered. It was in the equipment room behind the stage.

He dragged himself up the stairs, exhausted by his conflicting emotions and the effort he had just put in at seeming fine when he was reeling, and was startled to hear noises as he crossed the proscenium—it sounded like people laughing. Then he turned the corner and saw Clarissa and Greg giving each other a hug. They pulled apart when they saw him and exchanged awkward greetings (or at least they seemed awkward to him).

Mike put on a fake smile and picked up his umbrella and walked out as if nothing had happened, but it was too late. The image of the hug was burned into his mind. Greg was married with a lovely wife and two daughters. He was the worship leader not just at the Saturday night service but also the main service on Sunday morning. He was a bit of a star in the church, more featured than anyone else in those inspirational three-minute videos they showed on Sunday mornings. He was the one leading worship week after week, with a look of poignancy or ecstasy on his face, depending on the song and context.

Mike tried to chase away the terrible thought that darkened his mind. After all, it could be perfectly innocent. There was no reason why they could not give each other an Easter hug. The worship team was close. It had been a wonderful service, for all of Mike's own ambivalence, and Greg and Clarissa had played beautifully. Plus he knew Greg, knew him well. They had worked together for almost two years now, meeting weekly at the worship planning sessions, doing prayer groups and men's breakfasts together. He had been to Greg's house and spent time with him and Audrey on many occasions. A wholesome Christian home and family. A good man.

Still, it was a hug, and they were alone, and for some reason he could not stop thinking about it. He tried to analyze it away. After all, what had he really seen? He came around a corner and saw a hug; that was all. Nothing more than a friendly hug. Musicians were like that. They had a special kinship, like athletes. Not being one himself he didn't fully understand it, but he had observed it over the years. It was especially true at Pine Cove. They were a vibrant fellowship group all unto themselves, the worship team.

Yes, it was just a hug. There had not been anything really untoward. But for some reason he could not get this hug—innocent as it might be—and he was sure it must have been innocent—out of his mind. He did not want it in his mind but he also could not get it out. He kept telling himself it was nothing, but apparently some part of him was not in full communication with himself because he still wondered if it was something.

It was more because of Clarissa than Greg, to be blunt. He knew more about her than he wanted to know. Was he just an old prude? The thought crossed his mind. But Clarissa rattled him. As pleased as he was to have her in church, as much as he enjoyed her playing and enthusiasm, as grateful as he was for her new-found faith and the changes she said were taking place in her life—in spite of all of these good things he also remembered some of the things she told him about her past, things he now wished he did not know, things he had no desire to know. This was what made him wonder just how innocent the hug really was, at least on her side.

He now realized he'd had certain misgivings about her all along. There was a little too much make-up and a little too little length in her skirts and a whole air of Me that just did not fit in very well at Pine Cove. He did not know how to talk to her about it without offending her. He did not want to turn her off or take away any of her glow or new-found enthusiasm. He wanted to give her the freedom to be who she was and not be too eager to judge her on outward appearances.

And yet this was just what he found himself doing. Was she really changed? He wanted to believe she was, with all his heart he wanted to believe it; but then there were the outfits, and there was the vaguely flirtatious behavior—and now there was the hug. Oh how he wished he had not seen that hug! How much happier he would be and how much tidier his little world would be if he had not seen it! His whole state of being was thrown into chaos. After all, he was the one who had brought Clarissa into the church.

Should he do something? Then again, what *could* he do? Somehow he could not picture himself sitting down with her to talk about his misgivings and seek assurance that she was not interested in getting her claws into Greg. As far as he knew, the hug might have been nothing. He did not want her to think he didn't trust her, she who had been so open, so giving of her time and talents. The very thought of such a conversation made him feel judgmental and small-minded.

But what about Greg? Could he talk to him? The problem was he did not see how he could explain himself or why he felt the need to have such a conversation. What he actually wanted to do was to warn Greg about Clarissa. Not that Clarissa was necessarily someone Greg needed to be warned about, but she might be. Mike knew things about her that Greg did not know, and this worried him. She was likely to seem less attractive to him if he knew those things as well. But was this really what he was going to do? Tell Greg things that were said to him in confidence in order to warn him about something that he may or may not have any need to be warned about?

No, he wasn't. As unnerving as the hug had been, Mike decided to watch and wait. He kept a close eye on them over the next few weeks, kept his antennae up, with the determination of saying something to one or both of them if he saw anything else that seemed suspicious, but there was nothing. There was friendly attachment and sincere affection, but no more so than with the other members of the worship team. In the end he told himself it was just his imagination. It was his pastoral involvement with Clarissa, through which lens he may or may not have been seeing her clearly. He should trust her. It was ungallant to do otherwise.

Anyway he had other things on his mind just then. A new small-group pastor had come to the church by the name of David Taylor. Yes, "David," not Dave—a very serious young man, dark and slender, with a serious plan in mind, as Mike later discovered.

At first, everything was fine. David was welcomed into the church with open arms, fresh out of Princeton Seminary, full of the right words and affect. The staff went out for lunch together to welcome him and he seemed like a nice young man. He talked about his enthusiasm for the gospel and all the things he had already done in college and seminary and his successes in working with youth. He talked about the people he had brought to Christ even at as tough a place as Princeton. He talked about his own conversion experience, naming the day and the hour.

It was only later that this soft self-portrait came into focus for Mike. It seemed David was a doctrinaire Calvinist who felt a need to purify the Protestant religion of its various accumulated heresies and flaccidities. He was a righteous crusader against the works-righteousness of the Catholic Church, as he saw it, and of any leaning in that direction amongst Protestants, who after all got their name from resisting the "bank of holy merits" and indulgences and pilgrimages and other excesses of the Middle Ages that came from gorging too much on Aristotle and his immanent God.

Mike found out about David's reform mission in a roundabout way. It did not come up at the monthly gathering of the pastors over coffee. No, the news reached him, as it often did, through his friend Bill, who dropped in on him one day seeming rather puzzled or upset—or both.

"Did you hear about this?" he said waving a piece of paper in the air.

"What is it?"

"Our new 'faith statement.' They brought it up at deacons last night. Apparently we're all going to be required to sign it if we want to lead Bible studies."

"What!" Mike said, his hair standing up on the back of his neck. "Who is 'they'?"

"Pastor David and friends. Seems there are 'concerns' about the doctrine being taught in the church. Which is interesting, because I never heard anything about it until now."

"Me either. May I see it?

"Be my guest. Can't wait to hear what you think," Bill said slyly. Mike began to read:

1. There is only one God, the Maker of heaven and earth, Who is "holy, holy, holy," and Who exists in three persons, Father, Son and Holy Spirit.
2. There are four main attributes of God: loving kindness, righteousness, holiness, and judgment. None of these is more important than the others; all must be taken into account in knowing God and worshipping him in spirit and in truth.
3. From the time of Adam and Eve, man is a fallen, sinful being. There is nothing good in him in his natural state and nothing he can do, apart

from God's grace and election, that is good or pleasing in the sight of a holy and righteous God.
4. Jesus Christ saved man from damnation and washed his sins away on the cross. In Him only is our merit. There is none in ourselves or in our works.
5. God is sovereign in all things. By divine election, he chooses those whom he would save and give eternal life and condemns those whom He hates. No one can resist His election, and any good that man might do comes from divine election and no other source. Those who are elected cannot fall away from God.
6. Since man is a lump of damnation, pure and genuine religion consists of confidence in God coupled with serious and clean fear.

Mike felt a premonition come over him as he read the prickly document. "They're actually going to ask people to sign this?"

"That's what they said. Supposedly these faith statements are a big thing in Evangelical churches now. But I can't sign this thing. It's way too negative for me."

"To tell you the truth, I can't either."

"It's different for you. You're a pastor. You don't have anything to worry about."

"I wouldn't be so sure about that. I don't see how the clergy can expect the Bible study leaders to sign it without setting an example and signing it themselves."

"Tell me if I'm wrong, but basically what this seems to be saying is if you don't agree with this stuff you're not a Christian."

"Sounds like somebody wants to draw a line in the sand," Mike agreed. "But is Charles on board with this?"

"Now that's a very good question. He didn't say anything at the meeting. I assume he would have spoken up if he had a problem with it."

"He didn't say anything—he didn't have any input at all?"

"No, none. He just sat there. Which surprised me. That's not like him. Usually he has plenty to say—about everything."

Mike forced himself to maintain a pleasant smile throughout this conversation, for Bill's sake, to reassure him and to keep the peace; but inside he was exploding. As soon as his friend left he began to study the document more closely, reading it over and over again as if he could make the words say something other than what they seemed to say. Alas, the meaning was only too plain.

He kept coming back to the second article. "Love is an attribute of God." What did it mean? It sounded like an attempt to put love in its place, as it were; to suggest love was not the most important thing about God. Was it a rebuke to people who teach that God is love? It felt personal to Mike. After all, he was the one who had been called out by Charles for being "all about love"—and not in a positive way. Was it an attack on him and what he was teaching?

He Googled "faith statement" and found several that were similar to David's, even containing some of the same language. The term "neo-Calvinism" kept popping up in connection with these. Unfortunately the commentators seemed to have different ideas about what this actually was, so Mike went directly to the source. It did not take long to see that the *Institutes of Religion* was indeed the basis of David's faith statement. Most of the articles had been taken directly from the first two books—including article two, almost verbatim.

Mike had read excerpts from Calvin's famous book in seminary but had not studied it in depth. He found the prose sweet and easy to read, unlike many theologians, but one thing that did not seem so sweet, at least to his mind, was the emphasis on God's wrath. Not that Mike doubted the wrath of God; the Old Testament was full of it. His dark view of human nature caused him to agree that we are all objects of wrath apart from grace. But Calvin seemed to be a good deal more interested in this wrath than Mike himself was; interested in it for its own sake.

There had been Calvinists at Gordon-Conwell, and Mike realized at the time that they had a somewhat different spirit from himself. But it was quite possible to go through seminary without having any deep engagement with the "pure doctrine"—which is just what he had done. He tended to gravitate to professors who were like him and shared his views; thus he had never seriously considered what could happen if the wrath of the pure doctrine came into contact with what he believed.

There was diversity at Gordon. The Calvinists were there, and the people who didn't consider themselves Calvinists were there; but since the former did not attempt to compel the latter to join them or adopt their views, there was, at least to Mike's uninquiring eyes, peace on campus. It seemed possible in that environment to go beyond the old wounds that divided the Protestant church. People with different ideas were living and working together. They seemed to get along. Why not the church?

He was beginning to see why. David's faith statement felt like a vigorous, forthright attack on him and what he believed. Were they really going to try to make people sign it? Was *he* going to be asked to sign it? There was no way he could.

After several days of increasing agitation he went to see the new pastor.

"Hey—how are you?" Mike said stepping into David's small office with the draft in his hand.

"Good, thank you, yourself?" the young colleague replied, in a tone that was neither chilly nor warm.

"Listen, I was just wondering, is this something you're working on?" Mike said, holding up the paper.

"Where did you get that?" was the immediate challenge.

"Someone from deacons shared it with me. They seemed to think it was being considered as a faith statement for the church."

"Well, what you have there is a rough draft. I'm surprised people are passing it around—we specifically asked them not to do that until we had a chance to discuss it."

"So that is the plan, then. Somebody has you working on a faith statement for the church."

"I wouldn't put it quite that way. It just seemed to me we could have a little more discipline when it comes to what we teach, since I'm supposed to be in charge of that sort of thing. Right now we're all over the place."

Mike glanced up at the plaque on the wall from Princeton Theological Seminary and realized he was in over his head with this younger colleague. David was ready for the conversation; Mike, who was acting on impulse and passion, was not.

"I couldn't help noticing that it seems pretty strongly Calvinistic. Was that the idea? Are we thinking about bringing in Calvinism as the official doctrine of the church?"

"I would say Calvinism is the *historic* doctrine of the original New England church," David replied carefully. "All the old Puritan churches were strongly Calvinistic. This isn't anything new. It's more like going back to our roots, like Ezra and the great return."

"And what about the second article? Can you give me an idea of what that's all about?"

"Second article?" David said stone-faced.

"Yes—the one about love being an attribute of God."

"Oh! That. Well, yes, that's true. Love is an attribute of God."

"Excuse me if I'm wrong, but it seems to be saying love is not even the first attribute of God."

"Love is important. Obviously. But other things are important, too. You can't just talk about love all the time or you're giving an unbalanced picture of God."

"So that's what this is all about, then. It's an attack on people who talk too much about the love of God, in your view."

"I don't know what you mean by 'attack.' It's an attempt to provide some balance to what we say about God. That's all."

Mike looked at him for a moment. "And what about Charles? Is he on board with this?"

"He knows about it. He's seen it. I'm in charge of Christian Ed, so he's letting me do my thing, which I respect."

"But he hasn't specifically said whether he agrees with this document or not?"

"He hasn't said one way or the other. But I think he would have spoken up if he had a problem with it."

The conversation was over. Mike was there to get information, not to try to change minds. His suspicions about the second article were confirmed. It was indeed there for the purpose of censuring those who teach that God is love. He wasn't imagining things. But there was a loose end—a big one. The missing factor was Charles. Did he endorse what David was trying to do, and to what degree?

Mike went directly to his office.

"Come on in!" Charles said smiling. He seemed to be in a good mood.

"Do you know about this?" Mike said, paper in hand.

"Whatcha got there?" Charles replied, extending his arm. Mike handed it to him.

"Bill gave me this. Somewhere he got the idea that he was going to have to sign it if he wanted to lead a Bible study."

"Oh, sure. I know what this is. It's that thing David's working on with Christian Ed. He wants to try to bring a little order to our usual joyous chaos. And good luck with that."

"But do you agree with what he has here?"

"I'm not sure I know what you mean by 'agree.' I do think we could be a little bit more clear on our doctrine, what we believe. Basically what we have here is a zealous young man right out of seminary who's determined to shake us up and make us fly right. Do I agree completely with every single thing on this page? No, probably not. But I also don't want to crush his spirit before he manages to get out of the gate. It's a harmless little piece of paper. Why don't we just let him go with it and see where it takes us?"

"I don't know if I would call it 'harmless.' Not if people are going to be asked to sign it. Not if it results in someone like Bill being told he can't lead Bible studies anymore."

"It's not going to go that far, believe me. This isn't a witch-hunt. I told you, it's just an enthusiastic young guy stretching his wings a bit. Besides, it might be a good thing for us to have a churchwide conversation about what we believe and why we believe it. Call it a learning opportunity."

Charles was so jovial and so unconcerned that it took away some of Mike's own concern. He did not seem to be taking the faith statement too seriously and scoffed at the idea of it being used as a loyalty oath. He also seemed to agree about Bill, which made Mike feel better.

And yet Mike did not feel completely reassured. He could not take the personal element out of it. He taught that "God is love," but according to the faith statement love was just an attribute of God. Where did Charles stand on this question? Mike couldn't help feeling he was being coy. He "probably" did not agree with everything in the draft, but which part? What about article two? Did he agree with it? And if so, how did he feel about Mike preaching that God is love?

Mike did not come right out and ask him because he was afraid of the answer. Something told him he already knew.

HE IS RISEN INDEED

MIKE DID NOT hear anything more about the faith statement over the next few weeks, but this did not mean his life was uneventful. For one thing Frank was fired, just a week after Easter and the outflowing of services praising the risen Lord and his compassion and meekness.

It seemed he had committed an unpardonable offense. Susan had specifically asked him to remove the unsightly orange sanding barrels from the entrance area, where they were to be replaced on Easter morning by urns full of beautiful pansies that Debbie Burns had been nurturing in her sun room since February.

Frank did not forget to do it. There was a possibility of snow showers in the forecast, so he thought it would be wiser to leave the barrels in place, just in case. Unfortunately he neglected to check in with Susan and apprise her of his plan. When she arrived at church she was furious. Not only were the barrels still there, but Debbie Burns had not left her urns because, in her words, there was no good place to put them. The pretty flowers were displaced by dirty fifty-gallon drums, and it was Easter.

It was the last straw for Susan. Not only had Frank screwed up again, but he deliberately flaunted authority and refused to do what he was told to do. She exploded at the trustees meeting on the following Wednesday and managed to get enough votes on her side for termination—six to three. She hated to do it, she "liked Frank personally and had nothing against him," but it had to be done. He had been a bad hire from the beginning and just had to go.

Mike was sick when he heard the news. He could only imagine how Frank felt. How could they be so heartless, so cruel, at Easter no less, when Frank and everyone else was still recovering from an unusually harsh New Hampshire winter?

He drove over to his house. Frank greeted him warmly and invited him in for a "cup o' Joe," as he called it. They sat down in his humble kitchen and Frank had a weary smile on his face.

"I'm so sorry," Mike began in a heartfelt way. "I just can't believe this happened."

"It's okay," Frank said, sounding philosophical. "I guess maybe it's a blessing in a way, because to tell you the truth they were driving me crazy. Especially her. I don't know what her problem is. I just couldn't do anything right in her eyes. I tried. I really did. I thought I did okay, but she sure didn't see it that way."

"Well, if it's any consolation, I don't think you did anything wrong. There was snow in the forecast. I remember it. They can't blame you for the caprices of Mother Nature."

"Oh, yes they can. They did. I got reamed out but good."

"Well, maybe you're right. Maybe it is better this way. I thought you did a great job, and other people did, too. She just never could get past—"

"The alcoholism. No, I know. A lot of people have a hard time getting past that. Hell, I do myself. It's day by day, and that's about all I can tell you."

"I hope you don't let this get to you. I don't want it to keep you away from church on Sunday morning."

"Oh, I'm not going back there. No way. I'll never set foot in that place again."

"Well, another church, then. Let me introduce you to the pastor at First Congregational. He's a really good man and I think you would like him."

"No, thanks anyway, Pastor. I'm not really thinking about church right now. I've got to get me another job or find some other source of income before the creditors catch up with me. In other words, I'm going to be busy."

Mike's heart absolutely ached at these words and the defeated tone in which they were uttered. "The thing is church is important. You told me so yourself. You can't let people chase you away."

"You're telling me I need church; I don't know. I've still got AA. I go there every week and the people seem a lot more spiritual to me than some of the people I ran across at church. Or at least they're a lot more encouraging."

"Sadly, that's true. But what they don't give you at AA is God."

"Oh, we talk about God. It's not church talk, but it's pretty deep sometimes. Don't forget, these are people who've been to heck and back. They've got a lot to say on the subject."

Mike left this little visit feeling very upset. He was angry at Susan, boiling angry. There were two sides to every story—but all Susan ever saw was her own. She was incapable of seeing his side or, God forbid, Frank's. It wasn't so much that she was wrong as she was being unreasonable. She had a prejudice against Frank and would not let it go, and this caused her to look at his work too negatively and to be too eager to find fault.

Then he thought about his own role in the disaster. He was the one who in his starry-eyed idealism had encouraged Frank to apply for the sexton job and recommended him to the board. Why hadn't he minded his own business? He knew Susan continued to nurse a grudge against him. Why had he put poor Frank in that position, between himself and the wrath of Susan Cantor?

Saturday night came and he went to church and was watching for Frank as people wandered in and out, but he was not there. He went to the main service the next day, still hopeful, but again there was no sign of him. He did see Susan, however. She smirked at him as if to say "I won." He refrained from saying anything, in spite of his anger. Why give her another opportunity to tell him how wrong he had been and how much trouble he had caused?

Then there was another crisis in the church involving the Cantors. It seemed Fred was trying to get Simon Renz thrown off the board of deacons. His offense? He had been seen at a strip club, and a deacon of the church could not be seen at strip clubs; it was setting a bad example.

It turned out things were a bit more complicated than that. What actually happened was Simon had gone to a bachelor's party for the son of a good friend, dinner at a restaurant in Portsmouth, and afterwards the younger set had dragged them off to a bar for some more lively entertainment. Simon claimed not to know it was a strip club until he was already inside and it was too late, and in any case he had gotten out as soon as he could.

It didn't matter to Fred. He saw things in black and white. As far as he was concerned, the deacons had a high calling in the church and had to hold themselves to a higher standard. It was obvious to him that a deacon of the Pine Cove Community Church could not be spotted in a strip club. It was like giving church approval to that type of squalid behavior.

The deacons were in an uproar. Fred was popular—he was the chairman for the second year in a row—but Simon was also popular and had a reputation as a sincere, unassuming Christian who did a lot of good for a lot of people. Simon was too devastated by the whole mess to defend himself, but Bill spoke up for him. What about Jesus going to the houses of the "sinners" and sharing bread with them? Was this any different?

Well, they had quite an intense discussion over this question, and in the end the board voted not to expel Simon. The only one who was really dead-set on expelling him was Fred, and even he abstained from voting when all was said and done. There were three abstentions among the nine deacons, which gives an idea of how divided the board was over the issue.

And then just when it looked like it was all over Mike got dragged into it. He wasn't mentioned by name, and he wasn't there to defend himself, but Fred had to get the last word in, and what he said was that this illustrated the problem with teaching that God is love and all mush and sweetness and there is no hard edge to God, no wrath or dividing line between right and wrong. This is what comes from watering down the "true religion."

This news came from Bill. Mike was shocked.

"But what makes you think he was talking about me?"

"It was obvious. Everybody knew who he was talking about."

"Everybody? Really?"

"Yeah, I think so. You're the love guy, right? You're the one who always talks about love."

"You mean that's my actual identity—the 'love guy'?"

"Yes! That's what they call you now."

"Oh, great. So I'm responsible for someone supposedly going to a strip club because I preach about love. That's ridiculous," Mike blurted, unable to conceal his irritation.

"Well, get used to it. There's a new spirit in this church. People want to play the part of the prosecutor. And it seems like so much of it is going on behind the scenes. They come to the deacons and they already have their minds made up and things worked out."

"Who is 'they'?"

"Fred and Charles—and now David. They seem to think they need to take control of the agenda and show us heathens the right way to do things."

"And what about the faith statement? Is that being done behind the scenes too?"

"Oh, definitely! They keep saying he's doing it with Christian Ed, but the people I talk to from Christian Ed don't know anything about it. David and Fred are the ones cooking it up, and I wouldn't be surprised if Charles was in on it too."

Mike sensed Bill was right. It did seem like people were trying to pull strings and manipulate outcomes. After all, he would not even have known about the faith statement if Bill had not told him. Things were happening and nobody seemed to hear about them until they were already half-hatched. For the first time in his two years he began to feel that the atmosphere at Pine Cove was becoming political. There were some, apparently, who felt they needed to give their special guidance to the church in order to save it from itself and the ignorance of the herd.

To Mike, this was what had happened with Frank. There were only a few people opposed to him. Most of the other people he talked to thought Frank was doing a fine job, but a few naysayers had carried the day. And what reason did he have to think that there would be any other result with the faith statement? Fred was for it, apparently, which meant Susan was for it and they would be lobbying hard with their social set and leaning on Charles.

Mike could see it being approved in the end. They would make up some malarkey, say whatever they had to say, to get the church to approve it.

DISPUTABLE MATTERS

A COUPLE OF MONTHS went by and summer came and there was no more word about the faith statement. The Saturday night service continued to grow and Mike kept himself busy with that and other things he was responsible for, including the counseling which took up more and more of his time. He did not go to the deacons' meetings. No one invited him, and frankly he was starting to think ignorance was bliss.

But it wasn't; ignorance is just ignorance. It turned out the faith statement had not gone away. It was laying low for the summer while people were preoccupied with other things. Now fall was coming, the unofficial restart of the church year when all the pastors and parishioners were back from their vacations and things got serious as they ramped up to the holiday season; and sure enough, the faith statement reared its ugly head again.

There were rumblings, and this time not just from Bill. Mike was hearing things from several back channels, which led him to believe that the movement was gaining momentum. He had not seen or heard much about the faith statement since Bill had shared the first draft with him. Both David and Charles had reassured him it was just that—a first draft headed for discussion and revision, possibly extensive.

Mike used this implied promise to calm himself down over the summer. He knew the statement in its original form would be a disaster for him. It might mean having to leave the church. But more than that, it was inimical to who he was and what he believed. The purpose of the faith statement was to draw lines and cast down the gauntlet on who was and who was not a Christian, but Mike believed that "if you confess with your mouth that Jesus is Lord and believe in your heart that God raised him from the dead you will be saved."

In short, he tended to be quite tolerant of doctrinal differences within the umbrella of creedal orthodoxy. He did not agree, for example, with everything the Catholic Church taught about the sacraments, at least as far as he could understand it; but for the sake of the spirit of unity he was willing to assume that he might *not* understand it; that it was not necessarily saying what he thought it said or had been told by his Protestant professors.

Mike was a "Protestant" by birthright, but he wasn't really protesting anything. No, more than anything he wanted unity among Christians, just as the founder of the faith commanded. The old wars between the Catholics and the Protestants had made him sick when he studied them in seminary. What a terrible time for the church, what a blot on Christianity! No wonder so many in New England had turned to Unitarianism or Universalism.

But David really was a Protestant in the original sense, and he was not only protesting the Catholic Church but also those in his own church who did not seem quite up to his exacting standards. Of course he had the best intentions. In his mind he was a light-bringer. His mission was to make Pine Cove safe for the elect, and the faith statement was his sword of fire.

Mike knew it was a sword because he was on the receiving end. It burned him every time he looked at it. He didn't even have to read it and he could still feel the burn. Charles had indicated that no one would be required to sign it, but Mike wasn't sure he believed him. If it came to that, and he refused to sign, they could cut him loose. And then where would he go, at his age, a failure in his first parish? Who would have him?

The more Mike thought about it, all alone in his apartment, the more real this possibility seemed. It wasn't just David and his dark seriousness that make him uneasy; it was the opposition he had been experiencing from the Cantors and even Charles. He was already something of an outcast, with his orphan service, an outsider; but now this new faith statement made him feel like he was not wanted. And he could not help wondering if that was someone's intent.

Feeling isolated, and desperate for guidance, he decided to drop in on one of his favorite professors at the start of his August vacation. They sat out on his back porch (we will call him "Professor Johnson") and Mike quickly found his way to what was really on his mind over a glass of fresh-brewed iced tea.

"Does it seem kind of negative to you, or is that just my imagination?" Mike said after showing him the draft.

"Bracing, like the Northern clime from which it came," Johnson relied with a faux shudder. "Of course it's negative. It's the Great Negation. It negates the value of existence, which is nothing more than a 'lump of damnation.' That's how we wind up with 'pure doctrine,' much like Plato. If you negate everything as if it had no value, then what you have left over is a pure negation. Matters become 'pure' in an epistemological sense, anyway."

"But the thing is it doesn't just divide believers from non-believers, which is what such a statement is supposed to do. It also divides sincere believers from other sincere believers who might not find all that negativity quite so appealing."

"That's the other 'Puritan dilemma,' the one we don't talk about so much," Johnson agreed. "The Puritans were united as long as they used the notion of their purity to divide themselves from the Church of England, but as soon as they reached our fair shores they began to be divided amongst themselves. It seems once you start dividing yourself over purity, it's hard to know when to stop. And it wasn't only Roger Williams or Anne Hutchinson. They were just the most famous examples. Apparently Haynes and Ludlowe didn't think Massachusetts Bay was pure enough either, and they were the original leaders."

"They divided themselves for the sake of purity, but there is no such thing as a pure church," Mike suggested.

"That's the dilemma. The Puritans were unhappy with the Church of England. That's why they left. But unhappiness is a ravenous beast. It can never be satisfied because everyone is basically unhappy. As far as I can see, there is only one way out of the logical trap we have set for ourselves with our quest for purity, which is to accept the unconditional love of God. Otherwise we seem to have division upon division, as the denominations prove; forty thousand of them, all for the sake of purer doctrine."

"But that's just it. This document seems to be subtly trying to *downplay* love, with all the discussion of the various 'attributes of God.' Or am I reading too much into it?"

"That's exactly what it's trying to do, like Plato in the *Symposium*. The Puritans, because of their fondness for negation, were very much enamored of the wrath of God shown in the Old Testament and its purifying power. But you can't really be in love with wrath and also be in love with love. Now to be fair, they were responding to people who had a tendency to make *everything* into love, including the cat killing the mouse. But the attribute argument is a two-edged sword, because of *ousia*. You can say that judgment is an attribute of God—but no one says 'God is judgment.' And the same is true of righteousness, and holiness. You can't put those attributes in the place of the predicate nominative because they just don't fit."

"But you're saying you can do that with love, as in fact has been done, which suggests that it's more than just an attribute of God."

"Well, that's what people like you and me think, anyway," Johnson said with a chuckle. "Also it seems to me that the other so-called attributes are actually attributes of love, when you come right down to it. What does it mean to be righteous? It is to love the Lord our God with all of our heart and soul and minds and our neighbor as ourselves. So righteousness is actually love. It isn't anything other than love. Same thing with judgment. It's love that determines whether any given judgment is just, since 'all of the commandments are summed up in love.'"

"And what about holiness? Their little faith statement seems to indicate a belief that it is essentially different from love."

"In that case, please tell me what it is. In some circles there is a sense that holiness is 'wholly other'—a pure negation of our mixed existence, a force of transcendent resistance to human depravity, and specifically through this resistance, numinous. But this is a hollowed-out holiness. There is no content in it. Ask them for a tangible example of holiness and they will be unable to provide one. Holiness cannot come into existence because then it would be tainted by existence and become unholy, much as Plato's supreme being cannot be pure intellect and also have any contact at all with the material world. And yet Jesus was a living, breathing being, fully man as well as fully God, and without sin. That is, he was holy."

"The cross is holy, and the cross is said to be love. But am I wrong in thinking this thing (Mike held up the draft) tries to make holiness out to be the *opposite* of love, or at least very different?"

"No, you're not wrong. That's exactly what it's doing."

"But you don't agree. You seem to think they're pretty much one and the same thing."

"I do. Don't you?"

"Yes, of course I do. I completely agree with everything you've said. But when I tried to make this same argument to Charles, he wasn't impressed. Admittedly I didn't make it as well as you do."

"I don't know how well I make it either. The 'pure doctrine' has been around for six hundred years and isn't going anywhere. When I was young I used to debate with my Calvinist colleagues about this sort of thing. I don't do that anymore."

"I would like to follow your example. I certainly don't want to stir things up, if it can be avoided. But some good people are going to get hurt if this gets approved by the church."

"What about Charles? What's his take on all this?"

"Charles is playing his cards very close to the vest. When I ask him about it directly he denies that anything has been set in stone or anyone would be required to sign it."

"Sign it! They're going to make you sign this thing?"

"Well, that's not perfectly clear yet. We have a young pastor from Princeton who thinks we need more rigor in our teaching. That's what he is apparently recommending."

Professor Johnson gave Mike a searching look. "I'm surprised at Charles. I didn't think he was the kind of guy who would go for something like this, for litmus tests. But sometimes in life we are called upon to actually put this 'faith' thing of ours to the test. It sounds like this may be one of those times for you."

Mike left in a daze. It was gratifying to find some confirmation of his views in one of the Wise Ones, which was how he saw Professor Johnson, but the final comment was frankly devastating. It seemed prophetic and confirmed all of Mike's apprehensions over the past few months. If the young lion continued to push with the faith statement, with Charles stealthily supporting him, there was nothing Mike could do about it. He couldn't convince them any more than Professor Johnson could convince his friends. Besides, it was Charles's church.

Yes, it was supposed to be Christ's church, but Mike wasn't sure how many of the parishioners knew the difference. Pine Cove had been nothing, at least in the sense of numbers and impact, before Charles came along. He was the direct link to the church for most of the seven or eight hundred people who showed up on a typical Sunday to hear his incredible sermons. Mike could not imagine openly opposing him. It was like opposing Moses.

He spent the rest of his vacation wandering around the coast, staying in random bed and breakfasts and doing a lot of walking along the ocean, which he loved. But the beautiful waves breaking on the shining shore only made him more gloomy, since he could not share them with Janet; since he was out on the beach walking by himself when almost all the other men his age were with a mate. He smiled at them, he said hello, but their curious looks made him feel conspicuous and made him feel alone.

Eventually he made his way back to his lonely apartment. He was trying to decide what to do with himself on his first weekend back when he saw in the *Gospeller* that David was going to be preaching at a new Sunday night service geared to the youth. Mike decided to go and see what he had to say. He did not go to discredit David or catch him in some error. On the contrary; he went to exculpate him. He got it in his head that it was fear that was keeping them apart and hoped to allay those fears by putting himself in David's shoes, trying to see things through his eyes.

It did not work out quite that way. David's text was "Do not judge." At first this seemed promising. "Do not judge" was one of the most important watchwords of Mike's existence and of his theology of a church rooted in love. But it turned out his young colleague had his own interpretation of this admonition. According to him, the words did not really mean what people thought they meant. When Jesus said "do not judge," he did not mean that you should not judge. What he meant was you had to make yourself perfect *before* you could judge.

After all, isn't that what was meant by the exhortation to "remove the log from your own eye, and then you will see clearly to remove the spec from your brother's eye"? What Jesus was really saying, averred David in his ingratiating manner, was that the way to judge others rightly was to make yourself right with God and clear up your own vision. Jesus was not condemning judging per se. He was condemning bad judging and commending purity.

Pastor David assured his listeners that they could become godly judges. Those who were born again had the power to become a holy priesthood, capable of wielding the sword of judgment with justice and precision. They were God's Elect, after all, a special group with a special dispensation, and it was part of their great calling to be the judges of the world, to show it the error of its ways and set it right again, to be a light in the darkness and moral squalor of this benighted age, and in the end age to come.

Mike thought his head was going to explode as he sat there in the dark feeling like a spy, silently listening. The shocking thing was not just that David was dead wrong, at least in Mike's mind, but that he was so utterly convincing with his silver tongue and cherubic face. Mike almost found *himself* being convinced by the dazzling display of wit and learning, or at least argued into submission. He looked around at the youth group kids and a smattering of interested adults and saw them all smiling and nodding their collective heads. No one seemed surprised by what they were hearing.

Why should they be? They were not equipped to question someone like David, a pastor of Pine Cove Church and Princeton graduate. Besides, he was flattering them. He made it sound like they would be the righteous judges of their fellow beings when the end times came and even now. He was handing incredible power over to them—power that was reserved for God alone, in Mike's mind. "There is only one lawgiver and judge, he who is able to save and destroy. But who are you that you judge your neighbor?"

This sermon on a sleepy August evening opened Mike's eyes to his predicament. David was compelling and would become his nemesis if he had the church leadership behind him. Mike was out of his depth. He was not smooth. He would lose his temper in a fight and David would calmly cut him to pieces.

Because yes—there was going to be a fight if he chose to oppose the new direction the church was taking. He would have to stand up to them like Paul standing up to Peter, but Mike was not Paul and he knew it. He was not a genius like Paul or doctrinal expert and did not pretend to be. He could not marshal subtle arguments that put people in a box from which it is impossible for them to escape. Paul did just that—and still they persecuted him.

The sermon told him Bill was right: there was a new spirit in the church, the spirit of judgment. Or maybe it wasn't so new. Maybe the church wasn't quite as kind and loving as he had believed when he first arrived. He thought about Fred and Susan Cantor and their Bible study. He thought about some of the sermons he had heard Charles preach that made him blanch. He thought about the firing of poor Fred. Maybe David didn't bring this spirit of judgment into Pine Cove Church but was just a catalyst.

It didn't matter. Either way, Mike was left on the outside looking in. He stared at this thin, intense young man as he stood up in front of the small congregation and all of a sudden he felt like Elijah fleeing from Jezebel. He lost his nerve.

THAT THEY MAY KNOW YOU ARE MY DISCIPLES

THE SEPTEMBER DEACONS meeting was coming up fast, and Mike overheard the church secretary telling someone on the phone that they were going to discuss the faith statement. He decided to go. He was a little surprised to find the heads of all the key committees in attendance—not just Christian Ed, which was to be expected, but Missions and Trustees as well. It was a de facto church council. Apparently things were more advanced than he realized.

They went through the usual motions of the reading of the last month's minutes and old business before jumping right in. David circulated the faith statement. Mike took his copy and began to examine it. His ears started ringing as the words on the page came into focus. It was exactly the same version that he had seen previously. Exactly the same!

For several months he had been calming himself by clinging to reassurances from both David and Charles that the statement was merely a draft, with the implication that there would be major revisions. But there had been no changes over the summer. The statement was still the same hot sword that had sent him into a tailspin the first time he read it.

The words seemed even more unrelenting than he remembered, perhaps because of the gravity of the gathering. He stared at the second article:

> There are four main attributes of God: loving kindness, righteousness, holiness, and judgment. None of these is more important than the others; all must be taken into account in knowing God and worshipping his majesty.

He had taken the trouble to look at other faith statements. There was nothing on this topic and no language like this in any that he found, including the famous Geneva Confession, which was written by Calvin himself. Calvin had formulated the idea that love is an attribute of God, but apparently he did not think to include it in his own faith statement. No, David's draft was the only faith statement Mike had seen with such pointed language.

So who was it pointed at? His intuition told him it was pointed at him. He studied David as he talked. Why was he doing this? His young colleague had never expressed any reservations about what Mike was preaching—at least not to Mike himself. For that matter, he had never gone out of his way to talk to him at all. And then all of a sudden there was this. Where was it coming from? Was it a sneak attack, as it seemed to Mike, or was he imagining things?

And why all the secrecy? Mike would not have even known the faith statement existed if Bill had not shared it with him. No one talked about it during the Sunday services. There had been no mention of it in the *Gospeller*, the church e-newsletter. No one said anything about it at monthly staff meetings. True, they were more like coffee klatches than official business, but wouldn't you expect something like this to come up?

If the faith statement was as important to the church as David made it sound, then why not talk about it openly? Why not discuss it from the pulpit on Sunday mornings? Charles had not mentioned it, not once, as far as Mike knew. He who was always full of news about Big Things and Big Initiatives had not said a single word about a doctrinal statement that would touch virtually everything in the church and set the tone for years to come.

Again, why? Was there a reason for this conspicuous lack of transparency? Could it just be an oversight? Mike could not help wondering. He thought about Bill and his concern that the church was being taken over by a small but determined clique. The draft was being presented to all the senior leaders in the church without ever having seen the light of day. Only a select few were involved in the creation of it, and they seemed to be trying to ram it through as a fait accompli.

But who were "they," and why were they behind it? Who had the most to gain from implementing such a statement? Mike's mind went immediately to the Cantors and their implacable opposition to him. Fred was there, of course, as chairman of the deacons, but Susan was there as well. She was not the chairman of the trustees. She was not one of the principal leaders of the church, at least officially. And yet there she was, with a wry little smile on her face that seemed to say "this is going to be good."

Was the faith statement something David and the Cantors were cooking up to get rid of him? No—it couldn't be. Mike tried to disabuse himself of this paranoid notion. But then he looked at the article about God and his attributes and wondered again what it was doing there. Fred was one of the few people in the church who was interested in arcane points of theology. Fred called himself a Calvinist, and it was clear he didn't like Mike. Was the second article his handiwork? Was this their way of dealing with him, possibly getting rid of him? Mike wondered.

"So as many of you are aware," he heard David saying, "we've been putting some thought and energy into the concept of a faith statement for the church. All of the major Evangelical churches have statements like this. And the reason is simple. This kind of statement gives focus and cohesion to a church. It gives you an identity. People want to know where we stand. I hear this again and again—'Pastor, what do we stand for? What do we really believe?' And I think these are important questions. You can't go out and make disciples for Christ unless you know what you believe. You can't help them come to faith unless you are clear on your own faith. And there's something else, too, which I've become aware of in my role as youth pastor and in charge of Christian education. We could use some discipline around what we teach in this church. We have a lot of people and a lot of teachers, and that's great; but it's also a challenge, because we want to make sure we are aligned, we want to make sure that what we teach is what the Bible teaches and there aren't mixed or wrong messages going out. Which is what the little paper you have in your hands is all about. This is a distillation of the best faith statements from churches all around the country. I spent quite a lot of time researching it, making sure it's inclusive enough for the diversity of our wonderful congregation without violating the spirit of the Gospel or the historic doctrines of our church. And I've also talked to quite a few people in the church and included their input in the draft."

There was silence as everyone studied the document. Then Bill spoke up. "So pastor, just out of curiosity, what made you bring this up now? What were the specific concerns that needed to be addressed?"

"I wouldn't say there were any specific concerns," David replied, a little too condescendingly for Mike's taste. "There are always concerns about getting our message right, or there should be. The thing is, I have a role here. I'm supposed to look at what we teach and how we go about teaching it. And then there's the question of best practices and what other Evangelical churches are doing. All in all, it just seemed helpful to have a document like this for guidance. Not just for other people, but for myself, to keep myself honest. As I said, I looked at a lot of other churches that are similar to ours in size and spirit and it seems like almost all of them have something like this. So it must be rather important."

"I can certainly see the usefulness of a faith statement in these crazy times, but I thought we already had one in the creeds."

"Well, I guess you've noticed we don't really put a lot of stock in those old creeds. But we do have a specific heritage, a proud heritage rooted in our Pilgrim fathers, and in my mind it makes sense to have a faith statement that reflects this heritage. Not a creed, but a statement about Pine Cove and why it is such a special place, why so many people flock here to hear the Gospel."

"I agree with you," said Marsha Blackmun, one of the deacons. "This place is special. Let's get the word out there, because I think people need to know what they're missing."

"Let me just put my two cents in," Fred Cantor said at this juncture. "I am completely behind this and have been since day one. I think this is a great thing, and I think Pastor David has done yeoman's work in putting this thing together and getting consensus from top leadership in the church. I'm in business and let me tell you something about business. You don't get anywhere without a mission statement. It's a highly competitive world out there, and you need to know why you exist and what you have to offer if you want to succeed. And I see this the same way. Not that we're competing with other churches, but we're competing with the devil for human souls. Right? That's the most important work of all, and I think we need to be clear on what we believe so we can be as effective as possible."

"But I'm still not sure I understand what's wrong with the creeds we already have," Bill persisted. "I had the impression they were the basic foundation documents of the church."

"The *Catholic* Church," Fred corrected him, with a bit of a leer. "Says right in them, 'catholic.' Go check. Those creeds were okay maybe for different times and different places, but we're not part of the Catholic Church, and it makes sense to have something other than their old creeds to say what we are and what our mission is, especially in these perilous times when faith is under attack everywhere we look."

"So you're saying this faith statement separates us from the Catholic Church. It puts some distance between us and them," Simon Renz said, also skeptically.

"We're not trying to put any 'distance' between ourselves and anyone," David said. "That's not the intent here. The fact of the matter is our church and all the original churches in New England are rooted in a certain doctrine. That doctrine has been under attack by people who are opposed to Christianity and the Bible. You hear people sneering about the 'Puritans.' Well, in reality, there were a lot of good things about the Puritans. What they really wanted to do was to purify the faith and go back to its roots. Which is exactly the kind of thing we need today, when there's so much confusion about what we believe and where we stand."

Mike had had enough. "Basically what you're trying to do is bring Calvinism into the church. Isn't that what this is all about?"

David smiled thinly. "Well, yes, Calvinism is the historic doctrine of the New England churches. In fact I can show you a covenant statement from this church when it was just getting started as the Second Congregational Church way back in 1738 that is pure, unvarnished Calvinism. Quite refreshing, really."

"So we agree. This is about Calvinism. Because what I'm hearing is a lot of talk about 'defining our mission' and 'clarifying our teaching' and so forth, but what we actually have in mind is identifying ourselves as a Calvinist church."

"You say it as if it were a bad thing," David said with a laugh. "The Pilgrims and the Puritans who started the church in New England were Calvinists. This simply acknowledges the fact that, yes, we have historic roots. And those roots are important."

"John Calvin was one of the greatest men in the history of the entire Church," Fred thundered. "He's the right man for our times. We have too much of this stuff in this country of multiculturalism and everything under the sun. I for one welcome bringing back the old-time religion. It was good enough for Abraham; it's good enough for me."

"I kind of doubt that Abraham was a Calvinist," Mike replied, and then immediately regretted the sarcasm. "If you want to bring a faith statement into the church, that's fine. It's not up to me to tell the Pine Cove Church it can't have a faith statement. But I do think it's important for everyone to understand exactly what that statement is. For instance, article five is a pretty big statement with some important implications. 'By divine election, he chooses those whom he would save and give eternal life and condemns those whom He hates.' I assume everyone here knows this comes from Calvin's doctrine of predestination?"

Mike looked around the room. David, Fred and Charles were all smiling, but the smiles did not look comfortable; everyone else was looking at him blankly, confirming his suspicion that they had not really read the document carefully or considered its consequences; which was another way of saying they were not conversant with the controversies entailed.

"I don't understand this part about 'Condemns those whom He hates,'" Simon said. "I thought God loved all of his creation."

"That didn't stop him from destroying it in the Flood, or having the unfaithful Israelites swallowed up by the thousands when they sinned," Fred sneered. "That's the sovereignty of God. He does what he pleases with his creatures. If you don't accept it, then I don't know what to tell you."

"I'm not that comfortable with this either," said Joan Fletcher. "'Whom He loves and whom He hates'? That just doesn't sound right to me."

"It's exactly right. 'Jacob I have loved, but Esau I have hated.' This is one of the most important things we can teach. Is God sovereign, or not? If he is, then he has the right to do what he wants with his creatures. He has a right to make them 'vessels for destruction,' if that's what he wants to do or feels needs to be done for the sake of the elect. And if he *isn't* in charge, then it's all a matter of chance and human will—and we're in trouble."

Mike sat listening to these arguments and was troubled. He saw some resistance from the board, but the combination of David and Fred was too much for them. They were hearing arguments they had never heard before and had no real way of evaluating.

"What about you, Pastor?" Joan said to Charles. "Do you agree with this?"

Charles looked a little startled to be singled out at this juncture. "Well, you know some of these doctrines are hard to understand. I think the language might be kind of stark, but I have to say it is traditional. We do need to affirm the sovereignty of God. Whether we do it exactly in this way is something we can talk about."

Mike could not stop himself. "I agree wholeheartedly with the sovereignty of God. I'm just not sure this describes it. But let's look at some of the other points here, while we're at it. How about article two? What's that all about?"

"What do you mean?" Fred said. "It's the traditional teaching of the church."

"The Calvinist church, maybe, but not the church itself. The Bible says 'God is love,' but according to this love is just an attribute of God."

"That's exactly right. It is an attribute. The Bible's not just about love, my friend. It wasn't love that struck those people dead in the desert. You can't just go around giving the impression 'God is love' and anything goes. God is many things. 'God is light.'"

Now David jumped back in. "To me, this is one of the most important articles in the statement. Fred's right; you don't want people thinking God condones everyone and everything. They need to understand that he's also a God of holiness and judgment, or they're likely to have a little surprise coming when they stand in front of him on the last day."

"I didn't say he wasn't," Mike replied. "I was just questioning the idea that love is an 'attribute' of God. It's specifically the word 'attribute' that I'm interested in. I don't remember seeing it in the Bible. Maybe you can show me where it is?"

"Oh, this is just splitting hairs," Susan Cantor said, throwing up her hands in aggravation. "We have a brilliant young pastor from Princeton Seminary. Can't we at least give him a little benefit of the doubt? He's been working very hard on the faith statement, takes it very seriously. And after all, what we teach in this church is important. We can't just leave it to chance."

Mike didn't agree that it was hair-splitting, but he also did not bother to respond. He'd said enough. He was happy to find there were some skeptics in the room who weren't afraid to speak their mind. Besides, this was just a preliminary discussion; there was plenty of time. He decided to wait and fight another day.

But Bill caught up to him on his way to the car. He was hot.

"They cooked this up," he said, brandishing his photocopy of the faith statement. "I told you. It's this little group of people trying to take over the church. And what was Susan Cantor doing there? She's not a committee chairman."

"Unless you mean the Flower committee," Mike joked. "I assume she invited herself. They want to show a united front. But I thought Charles's reaction was interesting. I'm not so sure he's one hundred percent behind this. He could just be letting David off the leash a little."

"No, don't you get it? They're using David and his faith statement to get at you."

"What?"

"I thought you used to work in a corporation. It's the old good cop, bad cop routine. Charles is going to sit there like the Cheshire cat and pretend to be above it all, and meanwhile he walks out of here and tells David 'Go get 'em.'"

"Oh, I don't believe that. I can't see him doing that."

"I couldn't either—until this. Here's the thing. You have somebody upset with you because there are too many people going to your service right now. You were supposed to fail, or at least have the common decency to be mediocre. And now they're mad at you for failing to live down to their expectations."

"First of all, it's not 'my' service; it's the church's service. And I can't imagine them being mad at me for bringing more people to church."

"Have it your way. I'm just telling you how it looks to me."

These comments were not helpful. Mike was already too much inclined to be suspicious of David and Charles and Fred and their motives. Bill confirmed his misgivings and took them to a higher level. He knew the Cantors were still mad at him. They were very vocal in the meeting. It was pretty clear they were pushing the new statement.

Then again, they wouldn't be quite so blatant about it if they were trying to get rid of him, would they? Mike tried to take the high road. Maybe they were just honest Calvinists with a passion for the pure doctrine. Maybe they were sincere about wanting to save people from error. It was possible they were not thinking of him at all when they drafted the faith statement but just focusing on making a clear summary of what they believed.

But he could not quite put Bill's interpretation out of his mind. After all, Bill had simply articulated what he himself was feeling.

YOUR FAITH HAS HEALED YOU

THE FAITH STATEMENT continued to rankle, but Mike was too busy with the Saturday night service and counseling and church activities and the bustle of fall to obsess over it. A month went by, and more people started coming to the service, and his sermons were stronger again, reaching new levels of insight and communication, thanks to the time off in August and the rest.

Then something strange happened, something he was not anticipating. A young dark-haired woman by the name of Chloe Novella started coming to the service. She had impressed herself on his memory because she was a little frail and too stiff in her movements for someone her age—and because she had two very active young boys who seemed to overwhelm her a bit.

After a service in early October she approached him with her greetings. "I guess you're wondering why you've been seeing so much of me lately," she said with a crooked smile.

"Well, I was hoping it was because you felt welcome here," was his somewhat puzzled reply.

"Can I tell you something? I'm not really a church person. I haven't gone very much since I was a kid and my parents made me go. But I guess I'm getting kind of desperate. I need help."

Mike looked at her and saw her frailty and his heart went out to her. "Is it something you can talk about?"

"Oh—yes," she said with a little laugh. "It's not anything like that. I have rheumatoid arthritis. That's all. The doctors—they're trying different things, but nothing really seems to work for me. Even chemotherapy, which I really can't afford. It just seems to keep getting worse and worse."

"You're doing a good job of coping," Mike said admiringly.

"I don't know. I use up so much energy just getting out of bed in the morning. It's not just the pain, but I'm exhausted all the time. I don't want to be like this anymore. The worst thing is it's hurting my family. I can't be the mother I want to be."

"I'm so sorry. I have a good friend who's struggled with it all her life. You are very brave."

"Well, the thing is I have this feeling you can help me," she said, kind of shyly.

"You do?"

"Yes. That was such a beautiful sermon you preached a few weeks ago about the cripple at the pool and the healing power of God. I just can't get it out of my head. I want to be healed so much, I can't even tell you."

"You can be healed. I believe it. Your faith can heal your body."

Mike did not know quite where these words came from. They came from him, but they also did not come from him. He had prayed many times for sick parishioners. In most of those cases, he had no clear discernment about the outcome. Sometimes it was for people with cancer, and he would not know how to pray because he had no insight into what was possible. He prayed for healing but had no sense of assurance that healing might come.

There was a difference this time, however. Somehow he felt intuitively that this woman could be healed. It was the first time he'd had such a feeling and he was surprised by it. She wanted to be healed, she needed to be healed. For once he felt positively that healing was not just a distant memory of past glories but something as close to this poor woman as her own hands. Mike did not consciously put himself or his own wants or prejudices into the interaction at all. This feeling that he had, this good feeling, simply came to him of its own accord.

"I know, I believe I can be healed. I do. Can you help me?"

To this, at least, he had a precise answer. "God can heal you, if it is his will. I have no power to heal you myself. But I am very happy to pray with you, because I believe you can be healed."

"Do you? Do you really believe it?" she said.

"Yes, I can tell you in all honesty that I do. But I think the more important question is whether *you* believe it. Because I think we see in most of the healing miracles that the person not only wanted to be healed but believed they could be healed."

"No, I understand. And I completely believe it. That's why I'm here. Something told me to come to you and ask you to pray for me. This has been going on for several weeks now. This is not something I would normally do. It's something I feel like I almost have to do. I wake up in the middle of the night thinking about it. Who am I kidding? I wake up in the middle of the night anyway because of the pain."

"Do you feel comfortable praying now?"

"Yes, I want to pray now. Is that okay?"

"No—it's fine."

Mike put his hand on her shoulder and they bowed their heads. "Lord, this good woman comes to you now in complete humility, seeking your healing power and grace. You know how much she is suffering. You know how much she has endured and how difficult this terrible disease has been for her. You also know her faith and her belief that she can be healed. Please come to her now in all your power and glory and grant her healing. Please fill her with your Holy Spirit so that she might be filled with life and health and might come to know you better. Please restore her to good health so she can be the mother and wife she wants to be and can serve you. In the name of Jesus Christ our Savior, amen."

These words came from Mike but they were not exactly his. There was no strain or effort, there was no fishing around in the mind for the right words to say, they just seemed to spill out of him. Something else happened too, at that moment. He did not know what, exactly, but he felt something had happened. It was not like an inrushing or a loud wind. It was more like a tangible lightening of being.

Mike did not know quite what to do with himself. He opened his eyes and removed his hand from her shoulder. She opened her eyes and was smiling.

"Are you all right?" he asked.

She nodded. "I felt something."

"I did, too," he said, a little sheepishly.

In the week that followed, Mike fell back into his busy routine, but he did not forget this encounter with Chloe. He felt good about it; he did not have any of the misgivings he normally felt when he prayed for healing, for reasons he himself did not understand. Her desire to be healed and her belief that she could be healed was palpable to him, and this made the entire experience seem far more positive and gratifying than anything he had ever done along those lines before.

He found himself wanting to call her and see how she was doing but did not have her number. It seemed he would have to wait for the following Saturday and hope she showed up. The day of the service came and he did not see her. He was looking for her, but she was not there. Then the hall became crowded, and it was no longer possible to see her even if she did come in; not without actually standing up and turning around.

So he forced himself to settle back into his seat as the worship team appeared and began to lead the congregation in songs. After the opening prayers came the announcements. There were the usual advertisements for youth group, church bake sale, upcoming fall clean-up day, and so forth. And then there was a quiet voice from somewhere in the back.

It was a woman's voice, and Mike thought he heard the word "healing." He turned and saw that it was Chloe, and began to tingle. Greg stopped her and asked her to come down front. She was too shy to comply, so he sent the wireless mic to her through the crowd.

"I'm sorry, I just wanted to say a wonderful thing has happened to me. I've had terrible arthritis ever since I was a teenager. Sometimes I could barely get out of bed, that's how bad it was. And it made it so hard for me with my kids. Anyway, I came to Pastor Mike last week after the service, and he prayed for me—and I was healed. I don't have any pain at all or any stiffness in my joints. I'm not even taking any medicine. I just wanted to say, thank you so much. Thank you, God. We serve a mighty God. I can't even express what a difference this has made for me."

She became flustered and offered the microphone to anyone who would take it. Mike asked for it. "Chloe, I am so glad to hear that," he said. "I can't even tell you how glad I am, because I know how much you were suffering. But I do have to correct you on one point—it wasn't because I prayed for you. I am a very imperfect instrument. No, you believed you would be healed. You really believed it, and your faith has healed you, just like Jesus said. You have a very strong faith, and that is a beautiful thing. So no, I haven't given you anything; you've given everything to me. And to all of us. Thank you."

There was warm applause at the conclusion of these remarks. Mike was in a rare state. It was easily the most remarkable thing that had happened to him during his ministry or all his years in the church. He did not take any credit himself—his disavowal was perfectly sincere—it was not for his sake that he was in a state of exaltation but purely for Chloe. And for the congregation, that they had an opportunity to witness this amazing display of the healing power of God, that their faith might be built up and nourished.

He saw her after the service. She came to him in the reception line, still kind of shy. She looked different, her posture and everything about her.

"Surprise!" she said with a bright smile when she reached him.

"I'm so glad to see you. You look wonderful."

"I feel wonderful. This is the best I've felt in at least fifteen years. And usually this is a hard time of year for me, the damp and cold."

"Well, I'm just so happy for you. And happy for me. I learned something."

"Really? What did you learn?"

"I learned that healing is real. Not that I ever doubted it. But I'd never had any first-hand experience of it. Not like this, anyway. And this has been just amazing."

"Well, I can tell you it's real. Look, I can bend my fingers—no pain," she said, flexing her fingers for him to see. "I can walk with no pain. I can't tell you how much of a difference even that makes—just being able to get around. Honestly, I can't thank you enough."

"You can't thank me at all. I didn't have a thing to do with it," Mike protested. "It was the power of God, that's all. And I feel very, very privileged to have seen it, very blessed."

"IF THIS MAN WERE A PROPHET..."

MIKE REMAINED in this exalted state through the following week and an October drenching—and then the bottom fell out. Audrey Popovich came bombing into his office one chilly day around lunch time, just when the sun seemed to be making an effort to break through the clouds. He could tell right away that something was terribly wrong.

Audrey was a strong (vocal) Christian and a leader in the youth ministry of the church. Her husband Greg was the worship leader, and they made quite a dynamic duo and were easily the most recognizable couple among the laity. Mike did not know her well, but he had never seen her with anything other than a smile on her face. She was not smiling now.

"You caused this. You brought her into the church," were the first words out of her mouth.

Mike stared at her in perplexity. "Caused what?"

"Someone's spreading a rumor that Clarissa is having an affair with my husband."

"Oh, that's impossible," Mike said dismissively, although his mind went immediately to the scene he had witnessed at Easter, the scene he now wished he had not seen. "He would never do anything like that."

"Not on his own he wouldn't. But he could be tricked into it. She was after him from the start, asking to be on the worship team. I could see it right away. I knew she was up to something."

"Now let's just calm down a bit. I can see how upset you are, but first of all, I don't know a thing about this. I haven't heard any 'rumor.' And on top of that, I just don't believe it. I don't believe it could happen. I know how devoted Greg is to you and his family. He's one of the finest Christian men I've ever known. I think you need to sit down and have a good talk to him before you rush to any conclusions."

"Why bother? He's just going to deny it. This is exactly what I've been afraid of, since the first day I saw her up there. I knew she wasn't what she seemed. I knew she was trying to get her claws into him, with those short skirts and tight blouses."

"Okay, but do you have any actual evidence that something's going on? Did you see anything? Did somebody else see something?"

"No, of course not. She's not that stupid. She's not going to do it out in the open."

"Was there a letter, an e-mail, a phone message?"

"No, there was nothing like that. Okay, I'll tell you. I heard it from Darlene. She said she caught them together—more than once."

"Caught them? Doing what?"

"They were alone together! I don't know what they were doing, but they shouldn't be alone. It's not right. And you're just trying to change the subject. You were the one who brought her into the church and insisted they put her on the worship team. You ruined my family."

"I did not insist on any such thing. I merely asked—" He stopped because he realized what he was about to say might implicate Greg.

"Asked what? Yeah, I know all about it. And you knew exactly what she was like. You knew what her past was like and you went ahead and did it anyway, because it was a feather in your cap or something, because it made you look good to save this poor woman. Yeah, that was a great idea. Thanks. Now you can try explaining it to my children."

"So let me just make sure I understand. Darlene said something about 'catching' them together, but she didn't say exactly what. I mean, it could be anything. It could be completely innocent. Right? Couldn't it?"

"So what, you're trying to blame this on me now? Like I'm the mad housewife or something? You were the one who brought her into the church and put her in the band. You're going to pretend that didn't happen?"

"I'm not trying to pretend anything. I'm just trying to suggest it may not be what it seems. I certainly hope it isn't. But in any case let's give them the benefit of the doubt, since we don't really have any concrete evidence. Maybe Darlene misinterpreted something she saw. I don't know. It's possible. What if I sit down with you and Greg and Darlene and we try to talk this thing through?"

"You are the last person in the world I would want to sit down and have a talk with. It's like you don't even want to admit you did anything wrong here!"

"Sit down with one of the other pastors, then. It doesn't matter who you sit down with. If they decide I was in the wrong with something I did, so be it. The main thing is for the two of you to be talking so you can find out what's real and what's not real. That's the only way to know how to address it, or if it even needs to be addressed."

"You're just trying to protect her. You're just trying to keep her in the band so she can do her fancy violin solos and make you look good."

"Honestly, that has nothing to do with it. This is a very serious charge. We don't even know if it's true. All we have is some anecdotal evidence from someone who won't even say what she's seen. We don't know what Greg would say about it, or at least I don't, and we definitely don't know Clarissa's side of the story. And that's important. We have to be careful we're not just slandering someone."

"I'll tell you what's important—saving my marriage! I want her off the worship team, and I want her off now. I'm coming to you first to give you a chance to do the right thing, but don't think I won't go over your head if you don't do something about this. Don't think I'm going to just sit around and let her destroy my family and my marriage."

"Okay, let me talk to Clarissa first. If you still feel you need to go over my head after that, then by all means go right ahead and do so. I'm not trying to stop you."

"Like you could stop me!" she said and then stormed out.

Mike was dumbfounded. There were so many thoughts and feelings rushing through his mind that he didn't know where to begin. The first was horror at the idea that the rumor might be true, what that would mean for Greg and Audrey and their family. This thought made him sick to his stomach. Such a perfect couple, such a wonderful couple, the adorable little girls.

The second thought was a nagging one that he was trying, unsuccessfully, to keep out of consciousness—the hug he had witnessed at Easter and their apparent awkwardness when they saw him. He remembered it all too well. He remembered the suspicion he was not quite able to keep himself from having. Then again he had watched them closely over the weeks that followed and seen nothing—not even a hint of impropriety or unusual attraction.

He had buried the whole thing in his mind, forced himself to forget it, chased the horrible phantom away by telling himself he could not trust this particular memory. Thus when the first words came out of Audrey's lips he hit a wall. He came up hard against his own suspicions and hit a wall in Audrey's obvious pain and new evidence that, frankly, he did not want to confront.

But then he also thought about that new evidence. Just what had Darlene seen? This was important. Was it a quick hug? If so, it could be innocent. Was it sharing a laugh, a pat on the back, standing too close when they were doing harmonies together—what? He had to know the exact accusation in order to evaluate it. Unfortunately he could not go to Darlene without asking Audrey's permission. He could not betray her confidence.

One more thing he did not want to think about, and that was Clarissa. He really did not want to think about that. No, he could not simply throw her off the worship team. He knew it would be a crushing blow. How would he explain it? A jealous wife? Rumors? Caution? How? What kind of a message would it send to Clarissa, who was so obviously enjoying her role on the team and the new life she claimed to be living since she had started coming to church?

Could he risk destroying all that by accusing her of something that might not even be true? He did not see how he could. It made his heart ache just to think about it. Such a terrible accusation, so raw, so angry, so destructive! He was having a hard time imagining how he could even bring it up to her. But he knew he had to. He couldn't bear the thought of some other pastor approaching her who did not know her and might not understand her or care about her the way he did.

No, he would have to be the one to talk to Clarissa, and he dreaded it. He absolutely dreaded it. He could not talk to Darlene or Greg, not without Audrey's permission, but he had a duty to talk to Clarissa, if for no other reason than to warn her. And he had to do it before Saturday, before she went up there on the stage without having any idea about the possible explosion that was brewing or what was being said about her.

He agonized over it all afternoon as the world outside got wetter and gloomier and colored leaves tumbled to the ground in a smear. He tried to do other work, tried to work on his sermon, but could not. Too distracted, too upset. Finally he called her and left a message on her cell. She called him right back. Could she drop by that evening for a little chat? She said she could. She could tell something was not quite right, try as he might to conceal it in the tone of his voice.

He did not go home. He did not eat supper. He just stayed there, praying, pondering, pacing, but mostly praying. The longer he waited for her to arrive, the more worked up he became and more oppressed in spirit. He wanted her to be innocent—for her sake, not his—but he could not convince himself that she was. He wanted to spare her any pain, but there was no way to broach the subject without causing pain, and no way to let her go out on that stage on Saturday without broaching the subject.

Finally she arrived, and he had never felt worse in his life, not even when he had to call his daughters and inform them their mother had terminal cancer.

"Hi," she said. (He could feel as she said it that she was expecting bad news.)

"Hi. How are you?"

"I don't know," she said with a nervous laugh as they both sat down. "I'm not sure. You scared me. What's this all about?"

"I'm sorry, I didn't mean to scare you. That's the last thing in the world I want to do. Oh, how do I say this? Honestly, I don't want to hurt you."

"Hurt me! You won't hurt me. What is it?"

"Well, I had a little visit today—from Audrey."

"Audrey? Greg's wife?"

"Yes. Maybe you already know what I'm going to say."

"I don't have the slightest idea. I know she doesn't like me."

"She told you that?"

"No, I can sense it. She's not exactly subtle."

"No, I would have to agree with that. She's not subtle. Well—here's the thing. She came to me all upset, claiming there was something between you and Greg."

"'Something'? Could you be a little more specific?"

"Okay, so as best as I can understand it, she believes someone is spreading rumors."

"About me and Greg? Are you kidding?"

"I'm just the messenger here. I didn't say I believed it."

"Believe me, there is nothing going on between me and Greg. He's not my type."

"Is there anything that someone might interpret as something going on?"

"Well, we're on the worship team together. We see a lot of each other, with rehearsals and all. We're friends. So I suppose it's possible for someone with an evil mind to put all of those things together and come up with a wild accusation."

"And that's the way Greg sees it, too? I mean—how can I say this?—you haven't picked up any signals from him of any kind of special interest?"

"You're going to have to ask him about that. All I know there's no 'special interest' on my part, except I like him and I enjoy playing with him. That's all I can tell you."

"Okay, I guess I'm going to have to talk to Greg."

"So what happens now? I mean, where is all this going?"

"I'm not sure. I can tell you she's really upset. She's insisting that I take you off the worship team. Not that it's up to me to make that decision."

"You're kidding me, right? She wants me off the team? Based on what? Some rumor? I mean, this is ridiculous. Here I am, donating my time to do this, giving up all kinds of work to help out, and this is how I get treated? Why?"

"Don't worry, you don't have to leave the team," Mike said, showing more confidence than he really felt. "I'm going to see if she'll let me talk to Greg, and then I'm going to try to talk to the two of them together and see if we can't get this ironed out."

"No, I mean I'll gladly step down, if that's what they want. This doesn't strike me as Christian behavior, but what do I know? This is all new to me."

"Well, it could be nothing. Let me talk to them and see what I can do. In the meantime, just please—don't even think about this. I mean I know that's kind of hard to do, but just try to put it out of your head. It's probably just a big misunderstanding."

They chatted a little more, but she had not eaten dinner yet and wanted to get home. Mike walked her to the door and gave her a little reassuring pat on the shoulder as she departed. He stepped out of the office and happened to look down the hall.

There was Charles, watching them.

ONLY GOD KNOWS THE HEART

MIKE'S BLOOD RAN COLD when he saw the senior pastor. He could only imagine how it looked. He was in his office at night with an attractive young woman who happened to be wearing a mini-skirt. He patted her on the shoulder as she left. He was trying to encourage her after the devastating conversation, but there was no way for an outside observer to know this, especially if that observer happened to be of a suspicious turn of mind.

He went back into his office and closed the door and sat there in a daze. What was he going to do? He had an accusation and even a threat from Audrey Popovich. He had a heated denial from Clarissa. No, he did not tell her not to play on Saturday night. It was not fair to punish her when he didn't even know if the accusation was true. It was not fair to crush her fledgling faith under the burden of prejudices about "her kind."

He was ashamed of what had just happened, ashamed for the sake of Christ and his church, ashamed that someone who had turned wholeheartedly to the faith and given so much of herself to the church was now the object of a malicious accusation, one of the most hurtful accusations anyone could make. He was ashamed of the judgmental attitude implied in Audrey's comments about Clarissa. He was ashamed of his own cowardice in not standing up for her more stoutly, in letting Audrey browbeat him into unseemly compromise.

And yet…and yet…he did not know for sure if the accusation was false. He did not have the blessed assurance he desired, the certainty that encourages bold action. All he knew was what he heard from Audrey and now Clarissa. One was defensive and angry, perfectly natural under the circumstances, while the other was hurt and staunch in her own defense—also perfectly natural. If the accusation was true, then his heart went out to Audrey. If not, then he felt compelled to defend Clarissa. But was it true? He did not know.

He almost found himself wishing Clarissa had broken down and confessed. Not that he wanted the rumor to be true, but by standing firm she had put him in a difficult situation. A Solomonic judgment was called for, but he did not feel very wise. He did not have any firm sense of discernment or clever means of forcing a just judgment. He knew what he wanted to be true, but he was not sure he could trust his own motives, since he had been a strong supporter of Clarissa from the start.

At the same time Audrey was not going to let this go. She made a threat about Clarissa and the upcoming service, and he had to address it one way or the other. What he really needed to do, he felt, was talk to Darlene, the source of the rumor. After all, it could be that Audrey was simply overreacting. He had to know exactly what Darlene saw and why she felt the way she did, but of course he couldn't call her without betraying Audrey's confidence. So he called Audrey first.

"Is this a good time to talk?" Mike said.

"Let me just step outside," she said in a low voice. Mike heard the sound of a door opening and closing. "Okay, what is it?"

"I talked to Clarissa."

"You did! What did she say?"

"She completely denies it. She says there's nothing going on."

"Of course she said that. What do you expect her to say? She's not going to just come right out and admit it."

"I don't know, I think she might—if there were anything to it."

"You can think what you want. I know what I know. Did you tell her she can't be on the worship team?"

"No, I didn't feel it was appropriate, since she denied everything."

"Well, she better not be up there. I don't care what you think. I better not see her up there on Saturday night or you'll regret it."

"Look, I completely understand why you're upset. I would be upset too if this happened to me. But the thing is, we don't know if it's true. We just don't know. Darlene says something's going on. Clarissa says that's nonsense. I would love to find out who's right, but so far I've only been able to talk to one of them."

"That doesn't have anything to do with it. She shouldn't be up there in front of everybody, showing off. You're the one who put her up there. You make her go away."

"You know I can't do that to her. Think about it, put yourself in her shoes. What if somebody made an accusation like this against you and it was completely untrue? How would you feel if people just assumed you were guilty? It would crush her."

"I don't care! Get rid of her."

"Again, I understand why you're upset, but I can't 'get rid' of anybody until I know what the facts are. It would help if I could talk to Darlene."

"Okay, but then why are you calling me?"

"To get your permission."

"For what?"

"What you told me was confidential. I can't just call Darlene out of the blue and say, 'Audrey says such and such.' I have to make sure you're comfortable with me calling her and telling her about our conversation."

"Oh, is that what this is all about?" she said with a bitter laugh. "Fine—talk to Darlene all you want. But stay away from Greg. I don't want him dragged into this."

The thought occurred to Mike that he had already been dragged into it. The thought also occurred to him that his sense of decorum was wasted on Audrey. She laughed at him for wanting to alert her. On the other hand, if he had been so foolish as to call Darlene without telling her first there was every possibility that she would have gone ballistic. Such was the volatile and unforgiving situation in which he now found himself.

He had the green light he needed; now all he had to do was summon up the courage to make the call. It was an imposing task. Darlene was thirtyish and not married, and there was a reason for that: she was a strong cup of tea. Overweight and overbearing, she projected a psychic armed perimeter as forbidding as any barbed wire. Mike had never felt confident talking with her; less so now, when so much was on the line, including potentially her credibility.

But he called anyway. She sounded surprised and happy to hear from him. For a moment he had the crazy feeling that she thought he was calling to ask her out on a date. This made what he had to say even harder.

"So I understand you had a little conversation with Audrey," he said, attempting to sound natural and not exactly succeeding. "About Clarissa."

"Clarissa! What are you talking about?"

"So you don't know anything about it?"

"I don't know. You're the one who called. You tell me."

"Audrey seemed to think there was an—accusation of some kind—about her husband. Is that true? Did you say anything to her like that?"

"Not about Greg. The other one."

"So you don't think Greg has done anything wrong."

"I don't know what he has or hasn't done. I hope not, but I wouldn't put it past her."

"Just to make sure we're on the same page here—you're referring to Clarissa?"

"Of course! Who else? You're telling me you haven't noticed what's going on there?"

"What I'm trying to find out is what *you* think is going on. Did you see something?"

"They were—you know—together," Darlene said defensively.

"Together? Can you be more specific?"

"Together. I mean, one time I saw her lean her head on his back after a rehearsal. That seemed a little weird. Then there was the time he jump-started her car for her. They were still there after everybody left. And all the talking they do. The bantering back and forth during rehearsal. It's just not right."

"Maybe they're being friendly. You know how musicians are."

"Yeah, I know how they are. That's the problem. You heard her on Testimony Night. We don't want that kind of thing going on around here."

"I'm not sure I know what you mean by 'that kind of thing.' That's what I'm trying to find out. I need to know if you saw anything beyond what you just told me. Because it doesn't sound like much."

"It isn't that simple. You have to be there. They may seem like little things to you, but you don't see them all the time like I do."

"But you didn't catch them—say, kissing—or anything like that?"

"No, of course not."

"Okay, we're not really understanding each other. This is a very serious charge. You can't go around making charges like this just because they seem overly friendly to you. We shouldn't be judging people and making charges at all, if we can possibly avoid it."

"I knew you would be on her side. No big surprise there."

"I'm not siding with anybody. I'm just trying to get the facts straight."

"And I'm just trying to save a marriage. Maybe you should start thinking more about Audrey and the kids and less about your precious worship band and your superstar violinist."

"Why do you have such negative feelings about her? I don't understand it."

"I don't trust her. She's up to something."

"Has she done anything to you personally? Something to hurt you?"

"Well, no, I guess not, except for being such a prima donna all the time."

"Is she pleasant to you? Is she unkind in any way?"

"She knows how to put on a show. You can be pleasant all you want. This is about right and wrong. The bottom line is I don't like her. And I'm not the only one. She's very full of herself, whether you realize it or not. That doesn't go over so well with people."

Mike had mixed emotions about this conversation. He did not go in expecting a warm reception from Darlene and was not surprised at her unwillingness to part on friendly terms. But her evidence against Clarissa did not seem very compelling. She had not seen anything more incriminating than he himself had seen—minor physical contact and general friendliness.

Meanwhile it sounded like her misgivings may have been tinged with envy. After all, Clarissa was an attractive tall blond with a nice body; Darlene was, well, frumpy. Clarissa was a talented violinist who could play anything with ease; Darlene was a back-up singer who was allowed to bang the tambourine, but not too often. Was Darlene accusing Clarissa, not because she had any solid evidence of wrongdoing, but because she was jealous of the attention she was getting?

But while the conversation did not convict Clarissa, neither did it make the accusation go away in Mike's mind. Darlene had nothing but suspicions—but those suspicions might just be accurate. And she was not backing down. Mike knew Audrey would not be satisfied with the results of this conversation. Darlene had not swerved from her story. Nor could he share his misgivings about her motives with Audrey. He could not blacken Darlene's reputation in order to save Clarissa's.

No, there was only one person who could shed any more light on the situation, and that was Greg. He understood why Audrey did not want him talking to her husband. To ask Greg if there was any truth to the rumor was to incriminate him. Mike was very reluctant to take this step—he could not imagine having such a conversation with Greg—but he also was not willing to let Clarissa be a scapegoat. Audrey was the one making the accusation and the threats. If she wanted him to act she would have to allow him to talk to her husband.

He called her again. "I talked to Darlene. Sounds like she didn't see anything conclusive."

"That's not the way she made it sound when she was talking to me. She sounded pretty sure."

"Did she tell you what she actually saw?"

"No, I didn't ask."

"Well, I did ask, and again, it was not conclusive. In fact it was not even particularly surprising. Certainly not enough to be making such a serious accusation."

"And did you tell her that?"

"I did."

"What did she say?"

"Basically all she said was she didn't trust her. I'm sorry she doesn't, but you can't get someone thrown off the worship team just because you don't trust them."

"So I guess that's it, then. You're not going to do anything."

"No, I'm happy to pursue it further, if you really want me to. But the only way I can do that is to talk to Greg, which you don't want me to do."

"I told you—no way. I haven't even talked to him myself. I don't know how, I'm so upset."

"Then let me talk to him for you. I don't need to tell him where I got the information. I could just say there have been rumors and this would be a good time for him to be aware of them and address them before they get out of hand."

"Are you kidding me? He's going to know exactly where this 'rumor' came from. No, I have to talk to him first."

"So is that the plan, then? You're going to talk to him and let me know?"

"I don't know," she said, bursting into tears. "This is the worst day of my life!"

She hung up. Mike felt ill. Audrey was adamant; she wanted Clarissa thrown off the team. He felt her pain. He found himself almost wishing Clarissa had never come to the church. But that was the coward's way out. He was not going to humiliate Clarissa just to make Audrey happy. No, it was more than that. He wanted her to be wrong. He wanted Clarissa to be innocent. He wanted her new faith and enthusiasm to be preserved, and siding against her with Audrey and Darlene would surely destroy them.

And there was another problem too. He did not really have the authority to do what she wanted him to do. It wasn't his worship team. Greg was in charge, and Greg would not be happy if he asked Clarissa to step down without consulting him first. He would want to know why, and Mike wasn't going to lie to him. In short, Greg was going to get dragged into the mess one way or another. There was no way to do what Audrey wanted him to do without creating the uproar she wanted so much to avoid.

He did not know what else he could do. He had taken Audrey's charges seriously and talked to both Clarissa and Darlene. The next logical step was to talk to Greg—but the ball was in her court. If she wanted to make such a serious accusation, then it would have to be seriously vetted. Greg would probably welcome a chance to clear his name.

One thing Mike was not going to do, however, was throw Clarissa or anyone else under the bus just because someone wanted him to. That was not his idea of Christian behavior.

THE CUP THAT I MUST DRINK

MEANWHILE THERE WAS A BUZZ growing in church over Chloe's testimony. This was someone who had been visibly limited, if not quite crippled—tied up in knots and struggling just to get herself moving—and now all of a sudden she was a robust, smiling young woman who seemed completely free of pain. She was still small, she was still painfully wiry and thin, but she was able to stand up straight and walk without grimacing.

It was incredible, amazing. So many people had come up to her after the service and talked to her and congratulated her, and she just stood there and beamed because she was happy and felt like she had been liberated and her life was starting all over again. Soon the word started to get around to the rest of the Pine Cove community as well. Bill dropped by the office on Friday specifically to point out a write up in the church e-newsletter:

> Rejoice! Chloe Novella has a miraculous remission of her long-standing arthritis. "I prayed with Pastor Mike after the service two weeks ago, and the next thing I knew it was gone. I had the pain for 15 years, and it was getting worse and worse. Now I have complete mobility again." God is good! All glory to God!!!!

People were talking about it. Dramatic healings are not common, and the change in Chloe was noticeable. There may be healing from cancer or healing from an infection—there was often news in the church about such things—but those healings cannot actually be seen. What happened in Chloe's case was different and striking. It was like the paralytic who was commanded to take up his bed and walk. Everyone could see the transformation.

Mike felt uplifted; for Chloe's sake and for the glory of God. He did not presume to think he personally had anything to do with it. All he had done was pray; the healing was entirely from above. Still, it was the first time such a thing had happened to him. He could not help marveling at it. He could not help feeling a little glow at the privilege of having been involved in it and seen it with his own eyes. It not only built up the faith of others; it built up his own. It steadied his psychic ship after several months in stormy waters.

One unexpected consequence was another bump in attendance on Saturday nights. The congregation had already tripled since he had been there, but now it suddenly jumped to two hundred; still not a third of the Sunday morning crowd, but they were outgrowing the space they had been given. The atmosphere at the service was positively festive. Songs were sung with more fervor and there were even some enthusiastic "amens" during the sermon.

The vibe in the service was so remarkable that it helped take his mind off the very difficult situation with Clarissa. He saw her at the beginning, when the worship band went up and took their places, and his heart jumped into his mouth as he thought of Audrey's anger; but then they began to play, and the congregation began to sing, and his anxieties melted away. Clarissa did not stick out like a sore thumb after all, in spite of the omnipresent mini-skirt. All he saw was the worship team and the congregation, singing as one and full of praise and joy.

Until the service was over, that is. Audrey chose a moment to walk by him when he was alone and gave him one of the ugliest looks he had ever seen in his life. But why this look? He told her he could not do anything more without talking to Greg. She knew perfectly well that her husband was in charge of the worship team, not Mike. He was the one who decided who should come and who should go, and in fact guarded this authority jealously.

Mike had no way of determining whether there was any substance to the charges without talking directly to Greg, which was exactly what Audrey would not let him do. He had talked to Darlene, and her evidence of wrongdoing or even wrong intent was thin. True, he'd had certain suspicions himself from something he saw at Easter, but the fact that both he and Darlene had such suspicions was not, in itself, conclusive. He could not do what Audrey wanted him to do based on the information he had; but more than that, he did not want to do it. He hated the very thought of doing it and the hurt it would inevitably inflict.

But there was the look, and it rattled him. Audrey said she would go over his head. Sure enough, he was summoned to Charles's office first thing Monday morning.

"I had a disturbing talk with Audrey Popovich yesterday after church," Charles said. "Do you know anything about that?"

"I think I probably know why she came to you, yes."

"She was—not happy. She really thinks this girl—what's her name?"

"Clarissa."

"Oh, yes. Clarissa. She thinks she's trying to break up her marriage. And she's very upset with you for putting her on the worship team."

"Well, first of all, I didn't 'put' her on anything. That's not the way it works. I introduced her to Greg, and he put her on the worship team. Second, I don't know that what she's saying is true. I know she believes it, and I know she got the information from someone else who believes it, but I've talked to both of them and don't find the evidence particularly compelling."

"This 'someone' is Darlene, I take it."

"Correct. She claims she saw things, but the things she saw—if that was all she saw—could be completely innocent. If she never saw anything more than that, then there's no justification for making such a serious accusation. And besides, I think it may be a little more complicated than she's letting on. I'm sensing a little jealousy or other unknown animosity toward Clarissa that may be coloring her judgment."

"So you're saying she is not a reliable witness."

"I'm saying I think she has a personal dislike for Clarissa. Actually, no—she said it herself. And this dislike may be making her see things that aren't really there. I'm not claiming there's anything malicious going on with her. I just don't know if she's seeing things clearly."

"But what about you? Have you seen anything that made you suspicious?"

Mike blinked. "I don't know that I have or I haven't. I know they are affectionate towards each other, but then the whole worship team is quite affectionate. Except Darlene."

"But you can't say definitively there's nothing there."

"No, I can't. I wish I could. But on the other hand, I can't say there's anything that makes me think these suspicions are true. I can't judge Clarissa's heart, or Greg's, based on what I know. I can tell you that I want to think the best of them and trust them."

"I'm sure you do; we all do. But this is a very tricky situation you've gotten yourself into. If there is any truth to these charges—if something happens between these two—it will blow up in your face and in all of our faces. Not to mention the families destroyed."

"Well, I really don't know what to do," Mike confessed. "This girl is a new Christian. She's so enthusiastic and she gives so much of herself. She donates her time and seems so completely happy with her new life. I can't see us taking that away from her."

"Unless there are other reasons for her happiness, in which case this becomes a very different matter. But tell me about her. Isn't this someone you brought into the church?"

"I wouldn't say I 'brought' her in. She started coming and wound up staying."

"But isn't this the one who got up on Testimony Night and basically told everyone she was a whore? 'Looking for love in all the wrong places'—wasn't that the expression she used?"

The word "whore" hung out there naked in the space between them. "I think maybe that's a bit strong. She had a lifestyle that a lot of people seem to have these days. I'm not condoning it by any means, but I think this was exactly the reason she came to us and exactly the reason she's so happy. She was looking for freedom from all that and she found it here."

"But did she really? That's the question, isn't it? I'm all for turning your life around. Lord knows, I've seen it hundreds of times. I preach about the miracles I've seen in my sermons. So yes, I believe people can change. But I would say, 'Trust, but verify.' Someone may tell you they have changed, and someone may give every appearance of having changed, but we don't rush to put them on a pedestal or in a position of leadership. We don't put them in the worship band and up in front of the congregation until we really know their hearts."

"Again, I didn't 'put' her anywhere. She came to me and asked about the worship team, and I introduced her to Greg. It was entirely his decision."

"Exactly. You introduced her to Greg. That's the problem. That's why Audrey is so upset and why she came to me and basically unloaded on me."

"She asked me about it—I didn't ask her. Should I just have said 'no'? Not even given her a chance to prove herself?"

"Did you know about her past?"

"Not at that point, no. I hadn't even met her. She came up out of the blue and asked about the worship team. And I told her I would talk to Greg."

"And you didn't notice the outfits, the way she presents herself?"

"I noticed it, but what was I supposed to do? Tell Greg to watch out for this one—she likes to wear short skirts?"

"That's exactly what you should have done. You should have told him everything you knew. As it is she basically came recommended—by you. And that wasn't such a good idea, based on what's going on now. And what was she doing in your office the other night? You looked awfully friendly to me."

"I was talking to her about this very thing, trying to find out what's going on."

"Like she's going to tell you! Mark my words—you better put some distance between yourself and that girl. You better make sure you're not succumbing to her charms and favoring her more than you think you do."

Mike just looked at him. Bit by bit, Charles was hardening his position. He had begun by acting like Mike's friend, but at this point his face was red and he was clearly angry.

"I would be perfectly happy to talk to Greg about all this, but Audrey won't let me."

"I don't blame her. I don't think she trusts you right now. And for good reason."

"But if I can't talk to him, then I can't move forward. She wants me to have Clarissa removed from the team. I can't do that without talking to Greg."

"You can, and you will. All you have to do is tell Clarissa you don't think it's appropriate. Blame it on the outfits, if you have to. But if you know what's good for you, you're going to get her off that worship team right now. Believe me, I've seen situations like this before. If you wait, it could be too late."

If he knew what was good for him! Was this a threat? It sure sounded like it.

This conversation sent Mike into a tailspin. It was shocking to be threatened by Charles, shocking to be threatened by anyone, but especially by the senior pastor of Pine Cove Church. Mike almost couldn't believe it had happened. It was certainly a side of Charles he had never seen before, an angry side, almost vicious. It was a very jarring way to start the new week.

LET HIM WHO IS INNOCENT

MIKE WAS THROWN into the pit of agony. He was deeply concerned for Clarissa. He wanted to make the path easy for her until she had a chance to develop deep roots and could nourish herself. He wanted to "bear with the failings of the weak" because of his sincere love for her and his belief that she had found a better way of living; because he wanted her to be saved, in this life and the next.

But there was an immovable barrier to this desire of his, which was Audrey and her jealous rage. It was understandable; he could see how a musician's wife might be intimidated by Clarissa and her gifts, which were manifold. But he did not believe her fears were grounded in reality. He believed Clarissa when she said there was nothing between them. He tended to discount Darlene's gossip as the product of envy and spite.

The easy thing to do—the most circumspect, from a career point of view—was to give in to Charles and Audrey and dissuade Clarissa from participating in the group. It was also the safest thing, since he did not know for sure if Darlene's suspicions were unfounded. There was some danger in allowing Clarissa to continue—and who was he to make such a choice? Who was he to put a marriage at risk based on his own personal feelings?

On the other hand, they had handcuffed him, Audrey and Charles, by not letting him talk directly to Greg. They were the actual cause of the dilemma in which he now found himself. Their whole case against Clarissa was based on their reservations about Greg's state of mind and the possibility of him having feelings of some kind toward the comely violinist. Did Greg have any such feelings? Mike had no idea, but it would be useful to talk to him and try to find out.

He had been given a direct order by Charles to ask Clarissa to stand down. But Charles was not really his boss. God was his ultimate boss; but at Pine Cove it was the deacons. They were the ones who paid him. And why was Charles so eager to side with Audrey? What unknown demon had moved him to call Clarissa a "whore," of all things? Mike was shocked by this. He had never heard Charles use vulgar language before and had not imagined that such a thing was possible.

"Whore"? Really? What was behind this outburst? He couldn't mean it literally—Clarissa was not a whore. She may have had a more colorful past than Charles was comfortable with—or Mike, for that matter—but to call her a whore was—well—outrageous.

Mike was upset about the way they were treating her. She was not like them. She came from the same culture and ethos that Charles spent so much time reviling from the pulpit. She wore make-up, contrary to Peter's exhortation; but so did many women in the church—including Charles's wife. She wore her famous short skirts, but it was a well-heeled congregation, and many of the women liked to dress fashionably and show off their figures.

Whore. He couldn't get over the fact that Charles had actually used such a horrible word. At first he set it aside in his mind, tried to ignore it as if it had been an aberration, or maybe even a hallucination, but it kept coming back to him, insisting to be let in, as well as the sneering tone in which it was uttered; and every time it did it made him more agitated. Had Charles used this term with anyone else? No. Mike could not imagine he had.

But then this led to a different train of thought. Charles seemed very angry, but why? He had no reason to be *angry* when, as far as either one of them knew, nothing had actually happened. It wasn't as if Clarissa and Greg had run off together or been seen doing anything that would justify Darlene's suspicions. So far it was all just rumor and supposition. So then why was he angry?

What was the cause of the red face he had shown to Mike when he tried to dictate to him, the red face he could not conceal? Was it possible that his highly uncharacteristic anger was not really directed at Clarissa at all? In short, was Mike the actual target of his anger—and possibly the popularity of the Saturday night service? Was Charles using Clarissa as a pretext to become angry with Mike and show his anger in a threatening way?

Mike was like Jacob. He had taken the inferior flock that was not wanted and made it desirable. Nothing inspires jealousy like success. Charles had built up the Second Congregational Church from very near extinction and made it into the mighty Pine Cove Church; he was a well-known and respected author and speaker in Evangelical circles. He was the star, and now this parvenu had come along and was stealing some of his shine.

Charles was angry with him, and this was his way of letting the anger out. It was another clever bit of misdirection, like the faith statement. Wasn't that aimed at him too, while pretending to be about something else? In that case Charles did not even have the courage to take on Mike himself. He brought in the dour little Princeton Puritan and patted him on the back and encouraged him while he sat back and pretended to be above the fray.

Mike wasn't being paranoid. Or at least he didn't think so. He was not the only one who was inclined to see things this way. It was Bill who had planted the idea in his head originally, and he trusted Bill's judgment. Bill was even-tempered and rational. He was the kind of guy you would go to if you really needed to talk about something delicate—specifically because you knew he would be impartial, because you knew he was well-grounded and would give you good advice.

Bill was the one who had suggested to him that Charles was jealous. Mike had not solicited this opinion. It was offered gratis. He spoke up because he was worried about Mike and because he saw something going on that did not seem worthy of the church he loved. He had no selfish or ulterior motives for accusing Charles of using the faith statement as a way to get back at Mike for his success. Or at least none Mike could think of.

Mike did not want to believe that Charles was jealous of him, but he could not discount a friendly warning from someone like Bill. And jealousy also seemed like the most likely explanation for the strange outburst he had just witnessed. Charles had not called him into his office just to have a conversation about Clarissa. That was a pretext. What he really wanted to do was vent his anger with him, and Audrey had given him an opportunity.

Mike felt no small amount of anger himself. He did not like being dictated to by Charles. He did not feel that Charles was an honest broker. The highly inappropriate use of the word "whore" brought this home to him. A spirit of defiance rose within him. It was not Charles's responsibility to manage Mike. He had specifically asked to have his duties written up in such a way as to exclude supervision of the pastoral staff.

Now he wanted to assert the authority he did not really have, and Mike was disinclined to go along. In his view, he had not done anything wrong. He had not mishandled the situation. Charles implied he had, but to Mike's mind this was just a sign that Charles did not care about Clarissa or what happened to her. Calling her a "whore" seemed to indicate certain limits to his compassion for this particular sheep.

Mike agonized, and then he became offended, both for Clarissa's sake and for his own; and then he became indignant. This was one case where he felt he was on the side of right and Christian charity. After all, what was he going to do? Call Clarissa and tell her the senior pastor thought she was a whore?

No, he couldn't. He was happy to sit down with all of them, including Greg and Charles, and have an open discussion, no matter how painful or stressful that might be, but he was not willing to humiliate Clarissa and effectively drum her out of the church and away from God. For yes, he was convinced that if they did this to her, she would leave. Just like Frank, she would leave to save face. In fact he wondered if this was what they really wanted.

He did not call her. Nor did Charles call to see if he had called her. The week went by and Saturday came. Mike prayed and prayed before the service; all day he prayed, often on his knees, although he wasn't really sure what to pray for. God's light? His will to be done? What? He was not sure—but he prayed. He did not know what else to do.

He showed up at his usual time, trying to look unconcerned, and was greeted by many smiling faces, as he was always greeted, and shook a great many hands before taking his usual seat. He heard a buzz behind him and turned around to see what it was. Charles had come in. Charles had not come to the Saturday night service in the three whole years Mike had been there, and of course he knew what it meant; he knew why he had come.

He spotted Audrey, too. She did not look at him, but she had the same angry expression on her face as the week before. Mike closed his eyes and began to pray. The worship team took their place, but he did not look at them; he kept his eyes closed and he prayed. He looked up and there was Clarissa and he was filled with love for her, compassionate love. She was not full of herself, in spite of her talents. She was actually very self-effacing. She had a little smile on her face and he knew it was the look of love, the look of joy in this new thing she had found and this new and more productive way to spend her Saturday nights.

Right then and there he knew it was worth it—to him, anyway. He stood up and sang along from his heart. God is great, and he had come to worship him. Nothing else mattered at that moment. The readings went by, and the announcements, and everything else, and then it was time for him to give a sermon. He gave one of his best, on the story of the Good Samaritan.

He could feel the congregation with him. He knew where Charles was sitting but did not look at him; Audrey, either. He was determined not to let them deprive him of the strength he felt just then as he talked about one of his favorite parables. He hit the theme of Pharisaism hard. There were some, he felt, who needed this medicine. They would not like the bitter taste, but at that moment he did not care. He was not saying anything that wasn't in the Bible. It was all right there.

After the service so many people came up to him and thanked him and hugged him that he almost forgot about the gravity of the moment. Charles was not going to let him forget, however. He drew him aside into a dark corner at his first opportunity.

"What are you doing? I thought we talked about this."

"About what?" Mike said, a little disingenuously.

"About this special friend of yours. This Clarissa. I thought you were going to get her out of the worship band."

"I didn't say that. I know you want me to, but I can't."

"What do you mean, you 'can't'? You're the pastor."

"Exactly. And that's why. I don't want to see her get hurt. Besides, it's wrong."

"Do you have any idea what you're doing here? Do you know what you are putting this poor woman through, with her husband up there on the stage with that girl? Do you even care?"

"I care more than I can say. And no, I don't know what I'm doing. I'm just going on faith. Clarissa is new to the church and to God. I can't do anything to drive her away, not without more evidence than I have now."

"Just how much evidence do you need? Are you going to wait until there's a full-blown affair and that poor family has been ruined?"

"How about talking to Greg? He's the key figure here; how about seeing what he has to say? If his wife won't let me talk to him, then I have to assume Clarissa is telling the truth. I can't act without having more information."

"Oh yes you can, and you will," Charles said getting in close and pointing a finger. "You are going to call this woman tomorrow and tell her she needs to take a break from the band."

"And that's another thing. Who are you to tell me what to do? You aren't my boss. I'm accountable to the deacons, not you."

"You're right; you are. I talked to Fred and he completely agrees with me. He told me to tell you that himself."

"He didn't tell me."

"Well, I'm telling you. We are in complete agreement on this thing. You are going to call that woman and get this mess straightened out. Before next Saturday. Do you understand me?"

Mike did not respond. He just stared at him. He saw the anger in his eyes and did not respond.

Mike did not sleep that night. He tossed and turned in his sheets and did not sleep. There was no point in calling Fred. Charles would not have said such a thing if it were not true. Besides, he did not want to call Fred. He did not want to give him a chance to bully him and put him in his place, which, as Mike knew full well, he very much wanted to do.

MAN OF SORROWS AND ACQUAINTED WITH GRIEF

NO, HE DID NOT call Clarissa the next day, as Charles insisted. Not on the Lord's day. Instead he went to church and listened to Charles's sermon and wondered what he was listening to. Who was this warm, generous, expansive, spiritual figure up there on the stage pouring his heart out to the assembled throng? Was it the same man who had called Clarissa a whore? The same man who had stuck his finger in his chest?

It didn't matter. His feelings about Charles had nothing to do with what had to be done now, not if the chairman of the deacons was telling him to do it. He could try to resist, but that would mean having to take the matter to the whole board. He couldn't see dragging Clarissa's name through the mud in order to save her. She might not thank him for the favor.

Come to think of it, she wasn't likely to thank him either way, was she? But there was no way out of the bind. It was no longer a matter of holding out for a conversation with Greg. The only way to save both Greg and Clarissa any more embarrassment was to bite the bullet and do what he had been told to do. Otherwise there would be an open battle, with predictable consequences.

Mike felt sick. It went against everything he believed about the church and its mission to the lost sheep. More than that, it was dirty. But what choice did he have?

He forced himself to call her Monday night after a long day of misery.

"I need your help."

"My help? With what?"

"Well, it seems we have a bit of a situation on our hands. It's not your fault; it has nothing to do with you, really. It's just people and the way they are."

"So I take it this is Audrey again," she replied in a very different tone.

"I don't know what to tell you. I know it seems crazy. Believe me, I don't have any problem with you being on the worship team. I love seeing you up there. But some people seem to have gotten themselves all worked up over this stupid rumor, and unfortunately I've been designated as the person who has to try to calm the waters."

"I don't know what she's so upset about. I did absolutely nothing wrong. These people talk about loving one another, but they don't really mean it. They're not willing to give someone like me the benefit of the doubt."

"I agree with you. There's definitely a rush to judgment here. I'm not condoning it. In fact I think it's terrible. Basically I'm calling you on my knees. I know you didn't do anything. I'm just asking you to humor me for a while."

"You want me to leave the worship team."

"I'm just saying it might be better for now. If you could just lay low for, say, a couple of months, the whole thing will probably blow over."

"You don't really believe that," she said with a sardonic laugh.

"Are you upset?"

"Of course I'm upset! It's not the band. I'm being accused of something I'm completely innocent of. Wouldn't you be upset?"

"Yes, I would. I know how you feel."

"No you don't. You're not the one being asked to walk away."

"That's exactly what I'm *not* asking you to do. I definitely don't want you to go away. I love having you here. Please don't let yourself get turned off to church by some of the people in the church, including me and this very strange phone call. Please, I'm begging you."

"Well, I think I can give you half of what you want. I can leave the worship team, since apparently that's what everybody wants me to do. But I can't stay in the church. You can't do this to somebody and expect them to stay, slap them in the face like this."

"I'm trying as hard as I can *not* to slap you in the face."

"Sorry, you're not succeeding."

This was uttered not in a tone of defiance but hollow, like someone who has been crushed. Mike felt terrible. Why had he caved in and done their bidding? He believed in "submitting to one another out of reverence for Christ"—but was it submission or was it just cowardice? Paul did not submit when the church leaders said the Gentiles had to be circumcised. He stood up for what he believed was right. Had Mike?

Was it right to submit in what he himself believed or suspected to be a wrong cause? Or was he just using submission as an excuse for fecklessness? After all, he'd had his own misgivings about Clarissa and Greg. He said "people" were upset, but he was upset too—or unnerved—at the possibility of something happening between them. And he was doubly upset because Charles was right. He was the one who had welcomed her with open arms into the church and introduced her to Greg.

But how was he supposed to have any idea it would lead to this? Everything he had done with regard to Clarissa was from a spirit of warmth and generosity. It wasn't his idea to put her on the worship team. What was he supposed to do when she approached him? Say no? It didn't even occur to him at the time. But now he was being punished for his magnanimity. He was being punished for not being more like Charles.

The loving spirit of Christ required him to be open and take chances—and the result was agony. But here he was, feeling sorry for himself. What about Clarissa? Her happiness had been shattered and he was the one with the hammer. He could hear the anger in her voice, and then he could hear it mixing with tears. He thought about the unreasonable request he had made. Was he trying to double her humiliation? Not just to step down from the team but to face everybody after?

Clarissa was gone, a shooting star, but it was not over. Oh no, it was far from over. She did not show up at rehearsal on Tuesday night, and of course Greg texted her to find out why. When she told him he was furious.

"So I understand you told Clarissa to leave the worship team," he said, confronting Mike.

"I didn't want to, believe me. I was told to."

"'Told to'? By who?"

"Charles—and Fred Cantor."

"*They* know about this?" he replied, looking aghast.

"Unfortunately, yes. Charles heard about it from Audrey, and then I guess he talked to Fred."

"Audrey! What are you talking about? She didn't say anything to me."

"No, she was too upset. Please don't be angry with her. I think she was kind of goaded into it."

"By who?"

"Well, I think you better ask her about that."

"This is unbelievable. Absolutely unbelievable. All you people talking about this behind my back. Why didn't you just come to me and ask? I could have told you it was a bunch of crap."

"Well, again, Audrey didn't want me to come to you."

"You can't get off that easy. You can't go around making these kinds of accusations and then just blame it on Audrey. You should have come to me before it got out of control. And who are you to tell Clarissa she can't be on the worship team? That isn't your decision to make."

"Again—I didn't really have a choice."

"You had a choice. You could have stood up for her. This stinks. She didn't even have a chance to defend herself."

Mike was stung. Should he have stood up to Charles and Fred Cantor and refused to ask her to step down? Maybe—but it seemed like an impossible situation. If only Audrey had let him talk to Greg, everything might have been different. But he couldn't tell Greg that.

And *still* it wasn't over. The next day there was a call from Audrey herself. "I just hope you're proud of yourself if this ruins our marriage."

"Why? What's the matter now?"

"Greg's mad at me. He's acting like it's all my fault. Apparently that's what you told that woman."

"I told her you were upset. What was I supposed to do?"

"You were supposed to tell her to get out of the stupid band! Nobody said you had to go and turn Greg against me. I suppose you think you're getting your little dig in on her behalf."

Mike became hot. "You should have known he was going to contact her. But you wouldn't let me talk to him."

"Well, now you've got him feeling sorry for her. He won't even talk to me. Thanks a lot!"

With that she hung up. Mike was devastated. Yes, he felt sorry for Audrey and the pain she was going through—but it was not his fault. He had simply done what she asked him to do; no, demanded that he do. Did it not occur to her that her husband would be upset? If she suspected him, why wouldn't she talk to him? Mike couldn't understand it. What had prevented her from simply sitting him down and telling him what Darlene was saying?

Was she afraid of him? It didn't seem likely. Greg was one of the most easygoing men Mike had ever met. Was she ashamed of giving credit to a rumor? She should have been ashamed, as far as Mike was concerned, especially considering the source. In either case it was her refusal to talk to Greg that led to him being surprised and his angry reaction. Mike had nothing to do with it, and it was very unfair of her to try to make it seem like his fault.

Audrey's anger and meanness caused a change in him. Now he stopped feeling sorry for her and began to feel sorry for Clarissa and the pain he had caused through what must have seemed like betrayal. He thought about her open, honest spirit. He thought about her unfeigned cheerfulness and what a gift it was. Clarissa brought sunshine instead of rain. Her good nature and lack of pretension made people smile.

He thought about her standing up in front of the congregation on Testimony Night, just saying what was on her mind and where she was coming from, not trying to hide or cover up her rough edges, as everybody else on the stage was doing. She had done a beautiful thing, opened herself up to them, made herself vulnerable by trusting in their goodness—and they went right ahead and stabbed her anyway.

"They"? Who was he kidding? He was the one who called her. He was the one who made her feel like dirt. And now *he* felt like dirt. The right and wrong of it had seemed so clear. He had his marching orders. He was doing what the church wanted him to do, even though he did not want to do it, in part to keep the mess contained and avoid a public uproar.

But now Audrey's continuing assault made him see his clarity in a different light. He had allowed himself to be pushed into taking sides—had he taken the wrong one? After all, who was innocent in all this? Not Audrey. She was too quick to believe a rumor and too quick to judge. Not Darlene. There was a commandment about this sort of thing, and she had broken it. Not Charles. He had shown his true colors when he called Clarissa a whore.

No, the only one who was truly innocent was Clarissa, assuming her denials were true. She had not done anything wrong—and she was being punished! Darlene was not being punished. She was probably thrilled to learn that Clarissa was gone and in any case did not seem like the sort of person to see any fault in her own behavior. Audrey and Charles were not being punished. Their behavior was outrageous, in retrospect, but they were only too happy to see Clarissa gone.

It occurred to Mike that there were some instances in life where the old idea of justice simply did not hold. People who did terrible things were not always punished by a guilty conscience, not when they were convinced they had done right. The people who killed Christ were glad to see him go and felt no pangs of guilt over what they had done. And the people who drummed Clarissa out of the Pine Grove Community Church also did not see their own cruelty. In their minds they were upholding the purity and sanctity of the church. They were the righteous ones.

And what is righteousness? Conformity? Something else? Christ dined with sinners. He "did not come to call the righteous but sinners to repentance." He allowed the sinful woman to wash his feet. He saved the woman caught in adultery. He talked to the woman at the well. He called a tax collector. If he was righteous in trying to save the lost, then was it right to shun someone like Clarissa? Was it right to draw her into the church and then drum her out when she failed to conform?

Mike knew *they* did not see it that way. What they saw was Pine Cove Community Church, this idyllic place composed of people just like themselves. They were like the ones who condemned Christ for his wine-loving ways. For them, righteousness was all about appearances. It was dressing a certain way. It was doing certain things. It was saying the right words. Clarissa was an anomaly. One way or another, she had to go.

Mike was the one who felt bad about what happened to her. He was the one who had hurt her. And what made it worse was he allowed them to *make* him do it. He bent to their will, but why? They were not going to thank him for it. He didn't expect any gratitude from Charles, but now he had no illusions about Audrey either. He did what she asked him to do, against his own will, and she was angrier and nastier than ever.

No, they did not see the cruelty, but he did. It was all he could see. It was Frank all over again. The more he thought about it, the more he was horrified by what he had done. Had he really called

Clarissa and asked her to step aside? How could he be so unfeeling? He was filled with self-reproach. All he really wanted—all he ever wanted—was for her to find a home in the church and find Christ. She had come, but he had chased her away.

He called her. She did not answer, and when the voice message came on he was not ready for it. "Hi, Clarissa. It's Mike," he heard himself saying. "Sorry I missed you. Wanted to talk to you, if you don't mind. I'll try again later." He was upset with himself. The tone was wrong, stilted, strange. It was his own awkwardness coming through but it sounded like something else. That night he tried again. Same result. He called the next morning. He called again in the afternoon, and still she didn't pick up. And then the truth finally began to dawn on him. He took a deep breath while he waited for the beep.

"Hi! Me again. I'm kind of getting the feeling you don't want to talk to me. Can't say I blame you. I know I treated you badly. Anyway, I just wanted to tell you that I love you very much and think you are a very special person. You have been on my heart ever since our last conversation. I don't know what to tell you except I can't say enough how sorry I am for everything. I loved the way you responded to the word. I was very impressed by that, by all the insights you had. And I am impressed by you, by your cheerful spirit and your enthusiasm. Anyway, I hope you don't give up on church. I hope you give it another chance, because—"

The message timed out, and he was left gasping for a conclusion he didn't really have and did not feel he deserved to have, under the circumstances. He didn't dare to try calling her again to finish what he had been trying to say. He was afraid he had already said too much.

IN THE TEMPLE COURTS

A COUPLE OF WEEKS went by and Mike did not hear anything more about Clarissa. Greg did not say anything about it; Greg was hardly speaking to him at all, except when they had to talk about the service and the selections they were going to make. Charles also did not say anything, either to thank him or even to acknowledge that Clarissa was no longer on the team.

There was tension, which they were careful to conceal from the congregation. Greg was angry about what had happened and the affront to his honor. Audrey was angry with Mike and would not even look at him. Even Darlene seemed angry, in spite of the fact that she had gotten what she wanted, or at least what Mike imagined she wanted. What did she want?

But at least it was quiet now. Mike's mind began to clear a bit as he looked forward to the holidays, starting with Thanksgiving at the house of his oldest daughter, Irene, and her husband in Maine. He was looking forward to getting away, spending some time walking on the shore, watching the waves come in and letting the salt breeze take his cares away, if they could.

Then in early November he received a surprise visit from Don Baker, the visitation pastor. Don had an official look on his face, which he was trying unsuccessfully to hide. It put Mike on his guard, but even so he was not at all prepared for what happened.

(Don) "So listen, I heard about that wonderful healing you had in the Saturday night service, that dark-haired girl—what's her name?"

"You mean Chloe."

"Yes, Chloe. Always loved that name. Sort of reminds me of Shakespeare and fairies and sprites and all that. Anyway, I hear she was healed from—what, arthritis or something?"

"Yes. She had a terrible time coping. But as far as I know, she's been pain-free since then."

"'As far as you know'…there hasn't been any official follow-up?"

"No, why would there be? I mean I do see her in church every Saturday. I think if anything had changed she would have said something. But she always seems smiling and happy."

"But of course that doesn't necessarily mean she was healed. She could just be compensating—wanting it to be—you know how supple the human mind is."

"I suppose it's possible. As I said, she hasn't said anything to me."

"You know, I always wondered. Why didn't you invite her to come to our monthly prayer service? We have a wonderful time together."

"I would have been happy to. She just approached me after one of the services—I didn't expect it—" He felt himself walking into a trap.

"So she just came up to you after the service? Then what happened? She asked for healing?"

"Well, no, as I recollect she asked me to pray for her."

"Right then and there? In the reception line?"

"She waited for the line to go down. Basically it was her and me at that point, although there were still some people lingering in the room, mostly staff."

"And you prayed."

"Yes."

"Just out of interest, can you tell me what you prayed for?"

"Oh, I don't know. I think I probably said something about how much she was suffering and then asking God to come and heal her. I'm not really an expert at these things, like you. I wasn't really planning to do the prayer. It just happened."

Don had the unofficial healing ministry in the church. There was no "healing pastor" per se, but it was something he had studied, and something he was very much interested in. And he was the one who led those monthly healing services he alluded to.

"Well, it's not a matter of being an expert, I suppose. It's just about praying in the right spirit. It's kind of tricky, as you could imagine. Anyway, what happened then? Can you tell me?"

"I don't know if anything really 'happened'; anything dramatic, anyway. I remember having the feeling she would be healed. I remember that much. But nothing more."

"Did you say this to her? You thought she had been healed?"

"No, I don't remember saying anything at all. But what's this all about, if I may ask?"

"Oh, nothing, nothing." Don said retreating with a quiet laugh. "You know the foolish knots we sometimes tie ourselves up in over things like this. Well—I might as well come right out and tell you. I guess some people have been questioning whether there really was a healing. I don't know, I've never heard anything like this come up before, but I guess it was probably because there was such a big deal about it."

"There was no 'big deal' at all," Mike replied, trying not to get angry. "Chloe got up in the middle of the service the following week and told everyone she had been healed. That was it. They do things like that every single week in the Sunday service."

"I know, I know," Don said, looking quite abashed at this point. "I'm not the one saying there was such a big deal about it. But there was an article in the *Gospeller*, and a lot of people have been talking about it. So I guess that was a big deal to some."

"Who exactly are these 'people'?" Mike inquired

"Oh, I don't know. Various personages. Fred Cantor came to me to talk about it, and I guess I didn't give him what he was looking for, so he went to Charles. And then the next thing I know I have Charles calling me to his office and we're having a little conversation about the miraculous healing. Charles never calls me to his office, by the way, so that was a little surprising."

"And their concern is?"

Don looked very uncomfortable. "I don't know. I guess they want to make sure it's verified. You know how some people are, they're always worried about the image of the church, or something like that. They're afraid if we run around saying we've had this great healing and then it turns out it wasn't exactly the case—"

"Then we'll have egg on our face."

"Yes, I guess so."

"Funny, I never remember them being concerned about this before. But what reason do they have for doubting? Did they say?"

"Well, I guess some people are saying they don't really see any difference."

"And by 'some people,' you mean Fred Cantor."

"Yes, he was the one who said that to me," Don confessed. "But apparently someone else actually said it to him first. Audrey Popovich, of all people."

Mike sighed. "And now they've sent you out to investigate."

"Well, I don't think it's anything like that. Like I said, I think they're just trying to gather the facts. It's not a big deal. They just want to make sure we're not saying anything that isn't true."

Don didn't stay too long. Mike sat there staring at his place after he was gone. He probably sat in that pose for fifteen minutes as if half-expecting Don to walk back in and tell him it was all a joke.

He didn't blame Don. He really didn't. He knew they had put him up to it. Don was a very sweet guy, a retired pastor who was brought in to do the visiting Charles didn't want to do. He also just happened to have this deep and long-standing interest in healing and, pretty much on his own initiative, had started the monthly healing service.

But Mike was outraged nonetheless. So this was the new angle they were going to use to come at him. They were trying to make him sound like some kind of glory-hound, going around promoting a healing he had performed and putting his name in the newsletter and causing a lot of superfluous chatter—about himself.

First of all, he had not performed any healing, not even in his own mind. He was not in the habit of confusing himself with the true Physician. He had simply prayed with Chloe, at her request, as any pastor in the church would have done. It was God's power that healed her, if she had been healed. And he believed she had. She herself said so.

Nor was he trying to promote himself. He gave all the glory to God in every conversation he'd had about Chloe. He wasn't even the one instigating these conversations. People were curious. What was he supposed to do—refuse to tell them what happened? As for the newsletter, he didn't even know the article was in there until Bill pointed it out to him.

So was this Fred's new tactic for disparaging him? Claiming he faked a healing in order to glorify himself? It certainly seemed like it. The only conclusion he could draw from the visit from the hapless Don was that they had sent him to investigate. Don was their Inquisitor. Had a miracle really taken place? What was the evidence? And how had it taken place? Had all the proper protocols been followed?

This thought made Mike laugh. Did Christ follow protocols? No, he followed his heart. He never would have healed the man with the withered arm on the Sabbath if he had been following protocols. It got him into a lot of trouble. But Mike knew he couldn't point any of this out. They would just accuse him of making himself equal to Christ.

And what about Audrey? Was she really the instigator in all this? Mike could not believe the change in her. He had always thought of her in the most generous terms, a sweet young mother with a kind Christian spirit; he had put her up on a pedestal, but she was turning into a bit of a harridan. Was it really necessary to accuse him of fraud? If she had doubts about the healing, wasn't there some less spiteful way of addressing them?

This was serious, more serious in his mind than the faith statement kerfuffle. In that case they were simply trying to marginalize him; here they were actively involved in an effort to denigrate him and damage his reputation. Charles could have deflected the whole thing by protecting Mike from scurrilous accusations; for that matter by saying something as simple as "we don't know" at an opportune moment. Instead he seemed to be facilitating the inquisition.

And why? Because Chloe had been healed? Because the Saturday night service was popular? Because Clarissa had come into the church under his tutelage? Why?

He fought these bitter thoughts. There had to be more to the story, more than he was aware of. It couldn't be as raw and ugly as it seemed. He tried to put himself into a state of suspended animation in order to protect himself from his own internal monsters, which at that point were threatening to consume him. Don't overreact, he told himself again and again. Maybe it's not what it seems. Maybe it's all perfectly innocent.

These hopeful thoughts came to an end on Thursday at the staff social, however, the monthly venue for the pastors to get together and chat and nurture a sense of camaraderie and connectedness. It was not generally a venue for business. They were more likely to talk books or sports or even the weather than to dive into anything having to do with the church.

Which is exactly how things started off on this sunny November afternoon—until Don started filling everyone in on poor Millie Parsons and the battle she was waging with a UTI that had gone septic.

"Maybe we should send Mike over to see her," quipped David with an expression that could be interpreted in several ways.

"Don't send me," Mike replied. "I hardly know her. Don's the one she has the relationship with."

"Maybe you can bring her some of those special healing powers of yours."

"Unfortunately I can't claim to have any special healing powers."

"Now he tells us," Charles chimed in, maintaining at least the appearance of pleasantry. "But to get serious for a moment, we should all be very careful about any claims we make when it comes to healing. It's too easy for people to debunk them and make us look like charlatans, or worse. If anyone thinks he has seen a healing or been part of one in any way, let's agree to bring it up here first, with the whole group, before going public. Okay? That way we'll have a chance to talk about it and come to a meeting of the minds on what we really think happened."

Mike couldn't help himself. "I think that's a great idea, but of course it doesn't have anything to do with what happened. I never 'went public' with anything. Chloe got up in the middle of a worship service and gave her testimony. There was nothing I could do about it."

"No, and I'm sure you didn't encourage her," David said, his smile veering slightly.

Mike looked at him for a moment, stunned. "I did absolutely nothing of the sort. I don't tell people what to do. I didn't even know she had been healed until she stood up and announced it. It was as much of a surprise to me as anyone else, believe me."

"But the problem is we don't know if she was healed. Calvin made it pretty clear that healing miracles did not pertain to the modern church and obscure the glory of the gospel. And why did he say that? Because people were faking miracles."

"'Faking?' So you're saying she lied? Why? What reason could she possibly have to lie?"

"I don't know—because you told her to?"

Mike burned.

"Now, now; let's not get into speculation," Charles piped up. "There's no evidence yet that there was anything fraudulent going on here. It's just that some people are upset by the whole situation because they feel they were taken by surprise. I think we need to stick together as a church, and especially as a group, so we can avoid things like this in the future. That's all."

Mike did not reply to this, did not react to the "yet." He forced his feelings down, like forcing down reflux, a little vomit in the mouth. At least now he had a clearer picture of what was going on. He did not sense any antagonism from Don or the other two pastors; it all seemed to be coming from David, and, perhaps to a lesser extent, or at least less openly, from Charles.

David's motives seemed clearer now. Somehow Mike had found himself on the other side of the Calvinist divide from his intense young colleague. Now that David mentioned it, he did remember hearing something about Calvin's disavowal of healing miracles in seminary. They had a big name for it, which he forgot. But the fact was that Mike did not have a dog in this race. He did not come into this thing either for or against Calvin's position on post-apostolic healing miracles. Chloe asked him to pray for her, and he did. Should he have refused?

More mysterious was Charles' reaction. He had shown no sign of being opposed to healing miracles in the past. He supported Don and his ad hoc ministry. True, he didn't make a big deal about it, but Mike had never heard him express the kind of doctrinal reservations that David was raising now. No, it didn't seem to be doctrine that had him and David joined at the hip in the present instance. It was the animus they had toward Mike.

Once again Charles could have stepped in and stopped the whole thing at the beginning. He was the senior pastor. He knew that the Bible says "as much as it is in your power, make every effort to live in peace with everyone"; Mike had heard him preach on this verse. And he just sat there and allowed David to humiliate him in front of the other pastors with his outrageous insinuations and sneering attitude.

Which raised a troubling idea—were they in active collusion against him? Had they been talking about him behind his back, strategizing against him? At this point Mike could not put it past them. His anger and his hurt made him suspicious. They certainly seemed to be on the same wavelength. How was it possible if they had not been in communication with each other?

Once again Charles had managed to make himself seem like the moderate one, the reasonable one, the father figure. But this was not really what he was, not in Mike's view. Not with the little "yet" he had slipped into his comment. After all, Charles was the one who had sicced poor Don on him. For that alone he deserved a good whipping, making Don do his dirty work and pretending it was for the good of the church.

Whether actively colluding or not, he and David had the same goal, which was to put Mike in his place. It had never been clearer to him than it was now.

AS FOR ME AND MY HOUSE

THE NEXT BIG THING that sneaked up on him was the final push for the faith statement. Mike had not heard any more about it since September. It was his impression from the deacons meeting that support was lukewarm, so he was hoping against hope it had somehow gone away, that the perpetrators had come to their senses and realized how much damage they were likely to do to the church with their hair-splitting.

But this was one miracle that had definitely not occurred. There was an email inviting him to a church council meeting where a vote would be taken on whether to present the statement to the congregation. It was full of a lot of airy persiflage about "careful thought and prayerful study" and the "historic mission of the church," etc. All this pretty rhetoric made Mike ill. The faith statement was an act of aggression, as far as he was concerned. It was aimed directly at him.

Well, no, this could not really be the case, could it? He was not so vain as to think that the whole world was preoccupied with him. More likely he was an indirect object of the assault. It felt personal to him because it left him out in the cold. If this was where Pine Cove Church was going, then he was no longer part of the church or its mission. He was a satellite anyway with his little Saturday night service, but even there they would not leave him in peace.

The meeting was a week away, and Mike spent much of the interim worrying and fretting. He tried to take comfort in the fact that there were prominent people like Bill who did not agree with the statement, but were they equipped to deal with someone like David, a trained theologian who spent a good deal of time thinking about these things? Besides, David was grimly determined to carry the day, while they were merely hurt and confused.

What about the rest of the staff? Mike wasn't sure where they stood. They had remained silent during the discussion in September, but this was not surprising. It is hard to take a position when you have a mortgage to pay. Charles was making a show of not taking sides, and it was easy for them to follow his lead. Whether this was part of his strategy Mike did not know.

The appointed day came, and Mike's nervous system went on high alert as he walked into the meeting room and found an inconspicuous seat. He fidgeted as David covered pretty much the same territory as before. At first the discussion was tentative. A couple of people thanked him for his hard work. Then Helen Lent opined that "it would be a good thing to have a faith statement if people didn't know what they were teaching or teaching the wrong thing."

Mike silently groaned. Did Pine Cove Church really have a problem with people "teaching the wrong thing"? This was the justification that was being used for the faith statement, but no one had ever produced any concrete examples. The only dubious teaching Mike had encountered in three years was Fred's claim that the Beast of Revelation was the Catholic Church—and Fred was one of the biggest proponents of the faith statement. Which seemed kind of ironic.

Some more praise was offered, and then there were a few questions, which were deftly handled by David, with support from Fred. Julie Brown expressed a tentative reservation about the "lump of damnation" and was promptly beaten down by the chorus. Same thing with Will Barnstead and predestination.

Mike longed to lend some support but felt abashed. For one thing, it seemed like the momentum in the room was strongly behind David. For another, he suddenly felt a little like a stranger. They all seemed so close, so much of one mind, and he was just the pastor of the Saturday night service that only a couple of them ever attended and the rest did not take seriously. If they—the church—really wanted to go in this direction, who was he to object?

But then Simon Renz started speaking. Mike had a soft spot for him. There were never any agendas when it came to Simon, never any games. His heart was in the right place, even if he did have a tendency to wear it on his sleeve.

"I have to go along with Pastor Mike on this second thing," he heard Simon saying—and immediately felt himself stiffening. "I know we talked about it last time, but could you just explain it to me again? I'm a little slow."

"Sure, I'll be happy to talk to that," David said in his unctuous way. "Let me just say, first of all, that we're not saying God isn't love. I know some people are trying to make it sound that way, but that's not the case at all. Clearly the Bible says 'God is love,' and we agree wholeheartedly. But you have to look at the whole picture, not just one verse. And the Bible has a lot to say about God. God can be angry. God can be vengeful. God can be jealous. He's even described as being full of wrath. Now think about that for a moment. If God is full of wrath, then he can't be full of something else. He's full. But then how can we also say 'God is love'? Well, it turns out the answer is quite simple. These are different attributes of God. Yes, one of those attributes is his loving-kindness. But there are other attributes too, and they are just as important and need to be taken seriously. God is 'holy,' for example. There's an absolute dividing line between God and man, and you just can't call that dividing line love. It's something else or it can't be holy."

"Okay. I guess that makes sense. But bear with me. I'm still struggling with this a little. I mean, to me, God is love. He's kind, he's 'slow to anger,' he's forgiving."

"Good discussion. I completely agree with you. God is incredibly kind and forgiving. But in order to receive that forgiveness we need to understand that we are 'sinners in the hands of an angry God.' Maybe you've heard that expression before. It's from a famous sermon that was preached not too far south of here back in the Great Awakening. We have to know exactly where we stand with God in order to come to him in the right way and be in a right relationship with him. It's not good to fool ourselves into thinking we can cozy up to him and be his friend."

"That's interesting. I seem to remember an old hymn that goes 'What a friend we have in Jesus.' Maybe that's why we don't sing it in church anymore."

"The point David's trying so patiently to make is we have to be serious about what we're doing," Fred jumped in. "God expects a lot from us. 'Be perfect as your father in heaven is perfect.' When you come to the faith, some things have to change. You can't just go on sinning and expect God to keep forgiving you. That's 'cheap grace.' You can't just go to a strip bar and think everything's going to be all right. That's the whole idea here. Take the holiness of God seriously so we can be a light to the world."

The people at the meeting who were deacons understood the "strip bar" reference and were either looking down or at each other with wide eyes. Mike lost his cool.

"I believe the 'idea' is we cannot be perfect. Can't you even read your own statement? In one breath you tell us we're 'totally depraved,' and then you tell us we have to be holy or we're out. Which is it? We can't be both."

Mike was shaking when he finished. Fred responded calmly. "Well, we already know where you stand, Pastor. You've made it perfectly clear. You think you know more than John Calvin and Jonathan Edwards and Martin Luther and all the other great heroes of the church, but I'm not so sure about that. I think they may have known more than you think they did. I don't know from some of the things I've seen going on in your own service that you know better."

"What 'things' are you talking about?"

"Well, like this person you put on your worship team," Susan chimed in. "I understand, yes, the Gospel is for everyone. Jesus ate with the sinners and tax collectors and all that—I get it. But we have to have certain standards in the church. Now you bring in this person who fully admits her lifestyle leaves something to be desired, even brags about it, and you turn around and put her on the worship team. Why? What's the big hurry? Can't she sit in the congregation like the rest of us for a while before we put her up in front like that?"

"So this is a personal attack, then?"

"'Personal'?" Fred said. "No, it's not personal. All we're saying is holiness is important. You can't just throw the baby out with the bath water for the sake of love."

"And what is holiness?" Mike rejoined, his voice rising against Fred's condescending sneer. "Looking a certain way? Acting like good upper middle class American Christians? According to the Bible, holiness is to love as Christ loved."

"Okay, okay—I think we may be getting a little off the track," Charles said in a conciliatory tone. "The idea isn't that we have to agree perfectly on every single little thing in this statement. What this really is, is a way of helping us to define ourselves somewhat, putting our identity out there, as it were. And I have to tell you, historically, this thing is right on. We have Thanksgiving coming up, and we're going to celebrate the incredible accomplishments and incredible faith of our Pilgrim forefathers, and let me tell you something—this statement is right down the line, as far as what they believed. If we could go back to the Mayflower in a time machine and show it to them they would have no problem with it whatsoever. It would be just their cup of tea."

This was uttered in such soothing tones, and with such stirring rhetoric, first in praise of Thanksgiving, and then of the Pilgrims, of whom no self-respecting Evangelical could have anything negative to say, that it simultaneously silenced the room and also calmed much of the emotion that had been stirred up by the exchange. But it was, ultimately, a statement on behalf of David's document. Its intent was to steer them in the direction of approval.

Bill noticed. "Okay, I think we've heard enough times now that this statement is historically sound. I'm a history buff myself, and I certainly wouldn't want to go against the Pilgrims. But Pastor," he said, addressing Mike, "obviously you feel strongly about this second point. Do you feel you can support a statement like this, if we go ahead and ratify it?"

Mike looked at him and loved him. He knew what he was trying to do. In Bill's mind, Mike's answer to this question would carry the full weight of pastoral authority. The problem was Mike knew this was not the case at all. His opinion did not carry the same weight with most of the others in the room that it did with Bill or people who attended the Saturday service. Most of them hardly knew him. Still, he felt he owed him an honest answer.

"No, I can't go along with this. And it's not just the second point. There are other things that I don't completely agree with."

"Well, you know, sometimes that's the way it is in a church," Fred said, slapping his hands on the table. "Sometimes we have to make decisions knowing they won't be popular but they are right for the church. And as far as I'm concerned, this is right. This is the direction we should be going in and need to be going if we want to be on the right track for the future. Make no mistake. There will be some folks who will want this to fail. But I feel very strongly that this is the time when we need to band together and make a stand for what's right and for God."

Mike did not even bother responding to this blast of vacuity. He saw it for what it was; if others couldn't see it, he did not think he could enlighten them.

There was some more talk, much less pointed and contentious, and then there was a vote. The faith statement passed, seventeen to seven. Mike was in shock. The rest of the meeting seemed to drag on forever. Several people cast funny glances in his direction as he sidled toward the door. He could not be sure what these looks meant. Curiosity? Sympathy? Pity? Confusion?

WE PLAYED THE FLUTE FOR YOU

IT TOOK A LONG TIME for Mike to recover from this meeting—or maybe he never really did recover. First of all, what they had done to Simon was disgusting. It was nothing more than an ad hominem attack, but ad hominem attacks of that particular nature happened to be effective in a conservative church setting. The shock of any hint of immorality rendered all other arguments moot. Simon could not muster a reply, and Mike had been extremely daring to take up his cause.

Mike thought about his own little outburst and was not satisfied with himself. The sneak attack on Simon caused him to lose his temper and take the low rhetorical road of ridicule and vituperation. He jabbed when he should have parried and only succeeded in making himself look bad. Most of the people sitting around the table had no way of knowing that his anger was on Simon's behalf. All they saw was a sour reaction to some arcane point of doctrine.

His own intemperance did not excuse the counterattack, however. It was inappropriate in the extreme to bring up Clarissa as an example of the supposed shortcomings of his theology. Most of the board did not know Clarissa, which took the whole episode out of the realm of reality and turned it into a simple morality tale. Mike was on the losing end of this narrative. He had shown bad judgment, allowing a woman of questionable character to join the worship team. Of course things were much more complicated than that—but how could he explain it in such a setting?

What troubled him the most, however, was David and his response to Simon. As far as Mike was concerned, the argument about God being "full of wrath" and therefore having no room in his heart for love was pure sophistry, especially since the cause of God's wrath was specifically the lack of love seen in his people, their lack of charity and kindness and justice. But as he sat there listening to his young colleague he also realized he had no answer for him. David was smooth-tongued and Mike was not. He could not reason dispassionately with him over something that touched him so dearly.

When he did try to speak up what came out was an outburst. This made him made him look unprofessional compared with David. He was personally invested in the argument; David was not. He was arguing for a heartfelt attachment to the love of God; David was merely articulating an intellectual position that he had learned from textbooks. Mike could not contend with him because he felt too much while David felt too little.

Suddenly Mike saw himself as Christ before Pilate. There was nothing he could say that would not be misinterpreted and twisted against him; so he became determined, from that point forward, to say nothing. A sense of doom and helplessness descended on him. Charles, David, Fred, Susan, Audrey, and now even Greg—all these were arrayed against him. What could he do, the pastor of the orphan service that nobody really knew, except pray? It was not possible for him to prevent the faith statement from being adopted or avoid the negative consequences to himself.

The churchwide vote was on the first Sunday in December, an unseasonably bitter day. David, Fred, Charles all got up and spoke fulsomely in favor of the faith statement; no one said anything opposed, perhaps unwilling to be subjected to the kind of scrutiny that had been on display in the council, or else wanting to go home to a warm fire and football. The motion passed easily, with probably eighty percent of those assembled giving up a hearty "aye" and the rest dozing off.

Oh, and then there was a surprise motion—from Susan Cantor. She gestured for the microphone and proceeded to thank David and the deacons for coming up with such an excellent history-affirming document for Pine Cove, which to her was very inspiring. Then she made a modest proposal. How about having all the leaders in the church sign it to show their support?

This idea was presented in such a reasonable-sounding way and with such heartfelt appreciation for the hard work of "Pastor David and Christian Ed" that how could they refuse? There was another motion, and another vote, and this one was not perhaps as enthusiastic as the first, but it still passed with a clear majority.

Mike was devastated. Essentially what these two votes meant was he no longer had a place to lay his head. He was now officially at odds with Pine Cove Church and its doctrine. Funny, he had not set out to be at odds—but he could not bring himself to sign the faith statement. And he knew such a refusal would lead to trouble. He knew there were dark days ahead, could feel it in his bones, just like he could feel the December chill creeping through the thinly glazed north windows.

A couple of weeks went by with no more news about the faith statement and Mike began to wonder if he had dodged a bullet. Maybe someone had realized that asking people to sign it was a little provocative. But it turned out they were just waiting for the holiday season to pass. January came in hard, with temperatures in the minus 20 range, too cold even for snow, and he began to hear rumors about a decorative version of the faith statement that was being created for framing. At the end of the month he saw something on a table in the alcove near Charles's office. He knew what it was without even looking at it.

An email went out encouraging everyone to sign it but especially the church leaders and any teachers. Charles sent out an email of his own saying he had been proud to apply his John Hancock in a prominent spot and hoped that others would do the same, since David had done such a fine job of crafting it. Mike walked by the table every day on his way to his office and could see the fake parchment filling up with signatures. He kept on walking.

They gave them three weeks to sign it. When the grace period was up, Fred called Mike.

"Pastor, I didn't see your signature on the faith testimony," he purred in the blandest tones.

"No, and you're not going to see it, either."

"Well, I think you may want to reconsider. It's pretty much mandatory for leaders."

"'Mandatory'? When did that happen?"

"That's what the church said. That's what they voted on."

"That's not what they said, but in any case I won't be signing it."

"Have it your way."

The next day Mike noticed that the fake parchment was gone. They had taken it to be framed. There was a notice in the *Gospeller* reminding everyone to come to the 9:30 service on Sunday and partake in the "dedication ceremony." Mike went; morbid curiosity got the best of him.

They certainly made a big deal of it. It was handsomely framed in faux gold and mounted prominently in the entrance hall, close to the main doors. There were speeches and more fervent invocations of the "Pilgrim fathers" and their love of God and the pure doctrine. Mike stood in the back, off to the side, taking in the spectacle and especially watching the faces of the principal players. They were smiling and he was smiling, too; but the smile did not reflect the inward man.

Mike began to wait with dread for the inevitable, like a famished deer in the predatory winter woods. Susan was on the board of deacons now, and Mike knew he had no more hope of mercy from her than from her husband, who had moved on to the trustees. Indeed, she seemed to be the more relentless of the two. She had the hardness of old money and a memory that burned like the eternal light. He had been disrespectful of her husband, and she was not going to let it go until he had paid the full price.

For a while nothing happened. The long month of January dragged by, its pale sun cleaving to the horizon, and then Lent came, and then Holy Week and daffodils, and there was no more news about the faith statement. Then Mike had a visit from Bill. The issue of the signatures had come up—specifically the fact that Mike's was not among them. Was it intentional or an oversight? Susan told the board about Fred's conversation with Mike. Apparently it was intentional.

There was quite a bit of discussion about this. Susan insisted something had to be done if, as it seemed, Mike did not support the mission of the church. In her view signing the faith statement was mandatory for church leaders, including pastors. Simon and Bill tried to rebut this notion but did not get very far. Finally Bill asked the board to let him talk to Mike. They agreed—with the stipulation that some definite action would have to be taken if he "continued to be stubborn."

"I'm afraid I've got some bad news for you," Bill told Mike. "They've sort of issued an ultimatum about signing that stupid faith statement."

"I wondered when they would get around to that," Mike said from behind a weary smile.

"I don't know where they got the idea it was mandatory—that was not the case at all. It was just supposed to be a sign of support."

"But that was always their end game. There was talk about it from the very beginning, even though Charles promised me it would never happen."

"Well, he seems to have forgotten about that. Some people have noticed you didn't sign it, and they're trying to make a big deal about it."

"By 'some people' I assume you mean Susan Cantor."

"What is her problem, anyway? They don't even go to your service."

"Oh, she thinks I did something terrible to Fred way back when I first started. I didn't agree with something he said about the Catholic Church and made the mistake of saying so."

"That's it? That's the bad blood between you and the Cantors?"

"That's where it started. There were other things too, but I don't think they would have been as bad if we hadn't gotten off on the wrong foot."

"You could always disappoint them and sign it."

"I'm just too darned stubborn to sign it," Mike said with a smile.

"But you're playing right into their hands. That's what they want you to do."

"I know that. I just don't care. Not anymore. Not after some of the things that have happened around here. Anyway, it's too late. It's already been framed and hung up."

"It's never too late. I'll take it down myself and bring it to you."

"No, don't bother. It really won't matter in the end. There are certain people who want to get rid of me—if it isn't this, it will be something else. And to tell you the truth it would be a mercy-killing at this point. They've sucked all the joy out of it for me."

Bill brought the bad news back to the board. This time Susan laid down the law. If Mike would not sign, then he "should have the common decency to move on." This caused a little uproar at first, but then it became apparent that the groundwork had already been laid. Susan had been sowing her seeds and was dealing from a position of strength.

Again Charles did not intervene. Bill looked at him but he would not return the look. He sat there, quiet and grave, observing the proceedings but saying nothing and keeping his feelings to himself. The rest of the board took this as a sign that he was not opposed to Susan's initiative.

Her own words were that it was painful, very painful, but it had to be done if they were going to be true to their word. No, they would not do anything right away, for the sake of the congregation. They agreed to spend another month thinking about it and praying about it. But Susan did not let up on her campaign. She continued to lobby for dismissal. It wasn't just the deacons; it was everyone within her considerable sphere of influence.

Mike's purported shortcomings were brought forward again and again. He was teaching about the love of God but not about the holiness of God. He had encouraged the trustees to hire a sexton who was an alcoholic, leading to disastrous consequences. He brought someone into the church who was known to have a loose lifestyle and put this person on the worship team, where she had caused a good deal of (unspecified) damage. He seemed to think it was okay for a deacon to go to a strip club.

Once the bad-mouthing began, it became an avalanche. There were dark hints about his shortcomings as a theologian. He did not seem to know very much about the Bible, not as much as a trained pastor would be expected to know. He openly admitted, when confronted with a passage from Revelation, that he had not studied the book carefully and was not familiar with the commentaries on it. He even contradicted Matthew Henry, one of the most highly respected theologians of the Protestant church. And of course he questioned the teachings of the new faith statement, which were the teachings of the New England fathers.

Mike would not have known anything about all this maneuvering if not for Bill. No one else said a word to him—not Charles, not Fred or Susan, none of the other staff. Mike saw Charles regularly, but there was no mention of a discussion on the deacons. He didn't hear about it from his parishioners because for the most part they were a separate group from the rest of the church. Most of them had no idea that he was even under attack or in danger of losing his position. They were vaguely aware of the new faith statement through the church newsletter but were not aware of any controversy. Mike did not talk about it during the services, which were their main point of contact with the church.

Yes, Bill was the only one who showed him the courtesy of keeping him in the loop. And Mike knew what this meant. The end was near when people stopped talking to you but not about you. This was not going to be an open and transparent process, as one might expect in a Christian church. No, it was more like dealing with HR. Not that he was surprised. He had always known there was a possibility that the church leaders would be required to sign the statement. He'd also suspected there would be consequences if he refused. He did not know exactly what those consequences were but assumed all along that dismissal was in the mix.

Still, it was devastating. It is never pleasant to be on the chopping block, never pleasant to have one's value called into question; but it was perhaps more difficult to be a pastor in such a position, a spiritual leader. It amounted to being told that he was not fit for the role, not fit for the anointing he had received. It amounted to being deemed unspiritual and an enemy of the church and the faith. How would he tell his congregation? It broke his heart to think about it.

He did not recognize the picture of him that was being painted by Susan and her allies. Perhaps the most astonishing rumor to reach his ears was that he had a "pornography problem," as it was delicately phrased. Apparently he had admitted to someone that the only way he could overcome an attraction to online pornography was by refusing to have Internet in his apartment. Bill came to Mike with this one as soon as he heard it. Mike was grieved to have to tell him that he had indeed said something to "someone."

He didn't reveal who. He did say he'd said it to help him. Just as St. Paul called himself the worst of sinners in order to show his empathy with others and help them in their struggle to work out their salvation with fear and trembling, so it seemed to Mike that the best way to help Arnie was to be honest and not pretend to be "holier than thou" or above the struggles he was having with modern culture. Then the remedy might have more of a chance to be efficacious.

This was the *et tu brute* stab, as far as Mike was concerned. He realized at the time that Arnie was not happy with him and the counsel he received. Mike's willingness to make himself vulnerable did not impress him. He was looking for hard and fast answers, not empathy. He was the kind of guy who did not show vulnerabilities to others, probably not even to his wife, nor was he interested in having his pastor show them.

Mike noticed that Arnie appeared in the story as "someone." Apparently he was hiding behind a cloak of anonymity while shooting his poisoned arrows. Mike looked back on the whole foolish episode and shook his head. He never should have opened up. It was like casting pearls before…well, it was a very foolish error, in any case; a green error for a pastor who was too idealistic and trusting and not yet acquainted with the realities of the job.

Mike burned over this for days. Finally he decided to call him.

"So I understand you told someone about that conversation we had last fall about the little problem you were having."

"What! Who told you that?" Arnie replied defensively.

"It doesn't matter who told me. I had the story repeated to me by someone else. But here's what I don't understand. You were coming to my service. You're still coming to my service. Why are you trying to get rid of me?"

"Get rid of you? What the heck are you talking about?"

Mike realized right then and there that Susan's crusade had not gone beyond the board of deacons. Arnie didn't know how his tale was being wagged.

"Why are you telling people this story? I don't get it. What are you trying to accomplish?"

"I'm not trying to accomplish anything. I just told one person. It was over a beer after a round of golf. Are you saying they're trying to use this against you somehow?"

"That's exactly what they're doing. And they're succeeding."

"I swear, I had no idea. I'm so sorry."

So much Mike wanted to say to him here. He wanted to ask him if he didn't understand that he had been trying to help him, making himself vulnerable that way, but the answer was obvious. No, of course he didn't. Clearly he had not understood at the time, and there did not seem to be any way to make him understand now. He was a successful businessman, bright enough about that sort of thing, but not necessarily bright about spiritual things. Or maybe he just didn't want to be bright; maybe he didn't want to let down his guard.

In any case, Mike did not pursue it any further. He'd gotten the information he wanted. It was not a consciously malicious act on Arnie's part; or at least he was not part of the posse that was pursuing him. He also had his suspicions about who the unnamed interlocutor was. He'd heard Fred was a big golfer. There were a lot of golfers in the church, but he knew that Fred and Arnie golfed together on occasion. All the facts seemed to fit.

So Fred and Susan were out to bring him down, and nothing was off the table. Mike did not make any further attempt to combat them or their calumnies. He withdrew into himself.

KIM

MIKE WAS AT A LOW EBB. He did not know if he could go on any lower and still function, still put one foot in front of the other, still bother to eat and breathe. Then he met Kim.

There was a meeting of the town Commission on the Elderly, and he had been invited by one of the Saturday nighters, Millie, to hear what they had to say about the possibility of housing, about which he was quite passionate, and had said so from the pulpit.

Anyway, he was sitting there waiting for the meeting to begin, distracted and even nauseated by all the dark energy surrounding his existence, when an attractive middle-aged woman came in and sat across the table from him. He looked up and saw her and she looked up—and, well, they noticed each other.

She had sandy hair and pleasant, open features. He wasn't thinking about women at that troubled moment in his life, for that matter had not been thinking about women much at all since Janet died, but he definitely noticed Kim. There was something about her that he liked right away, most of all her good-natured smile and open countenance. They lifted his spirits.

He stole several glances at her and caught her looking inquisitively at him. Directly at him. He couldn't help himself—he glanced down at her left hand. No wedding ring.

She spoke several times during the meeting, and he was impressed. First, she seemed very intelligent. Not just book learning but the other kind too. She was as astute about the dynamics around the table as she was well-informed on the topic at hand. Some people are part of the dynamics, and some people are able to absorb them and make themselves a catalyst in a positive sense. That was Kim.

Mike noticed that he liked looking at her while she spoke. Yes, he literally noticed this, as if he were observing himself. It was not a sexual thing; it was something else. He felt like she was a kindred spirit and found himself taking pleasure in this discovery. All right; the experience might not have been quite so pleasant if she were not so attractive. He was aware of her good looks. But there was more to it than that. He felt like he already knew her.

Afterwards he was standing in the hallway, waiting for Millie (one of the all-time great talkers) and trying to amuse himself with the memorabilia on display, which of course meant nothing to him, when he noticed Kim approaching in his peripheral vision. He did not look away from the exhibit, but his entire being went out to her. He longed—longed—to turn and say something—but what? His strong feelings neutralized him.

She walked behind him and he could feel her walking by as he stood there staring straight ahead and not seeing what he was staring at—and then she stopped.

"Hi," she said, extending her hand in a friendly manner. "You're one of the pastors at the Pine Cove Church, aren't you?"

"Guilty," he replied with a foolish smile. "And you're Kim."

"Yes. What did you think of the meeting?"

"I thought it went pretty well. I'm optimistic that something can get done. The town certainly needs it."

"Oh, I hope so. Millie told me you were a big advocate. Much appreciated. Every little bit helps."

"I'm afraid I didn't help too much in there. Just trying to get up to speed. You know what they say about fools and keeping your mouth shut," Mike babbled, and then there was a bit of an awkward silence.

"Say—I hope you don't take this the wrong way, but would you like to go out for coffee some time to talk about it?"

"I think I'd like that very much."

They set a date for Friday, at a coffee shop they both knew. Through the dullness and pain of the last six months Mike began to look forward to this meeting. He had not had any opportunities for love or female companionship since Janet died. For a long time he was not looking for any. He was crushed by her rapid and horrible demise and simply lost all interest. Then he found himself in an environment that was not conducive to finding someone new. Almost all of the women he met at Pine Cove who were his own age or close to it were married.

True, there were a couple of women who had, well, attached themselves to him in his new position. He had been warned about this sort of thing at seminary. It was the position, not the person, that made pastors seem attractive to certain women; and besides, he was not really looking for a relationship. Things might have been different if he had been attracted to either of them, but he was not. Besides, he was still in deep mourning.

The years went by and he was *still* in mourning. Man's tender flame—his perpetual enthusiasm for woman, flesh of his flesh—was dampened in him by the sadness that continued to linger from seeing his beloved wife shrivel away to nothing and also from his position, which enforced a sense of rectitude in matters matrimonial, and, finally, on account of the kids; because he could not quite imagine telling them that someone was standing in for the mother they loved, because he loved them so much and was afraid of doing anything to damage or alienate them.

So no, there had been no one since Janet, at first no desire at all, and then repressed desire. He had not felt the spark of love for many years. He felt something with Kim, however. He was not quite sure what it was. To be truthful, it could have been something as mundane as the fact that she approached him. At that time in his life, when he was feeling so alone and isolated in his vocation, it was flattering to have an attractive woman invite him out for coffee. It made him feel valuable again, wanted.

And she was attractive. In an intelligent way. There was something in her face and the faint laughing lines around her eyes that kindled not just desire but interest of a more elevated kind. Mike was very much in need of a friend just then, a kindred spirit, someone to talk to. He wondered if he was seeing one in Kim.

For the first time he did not think of Janet. It was not the smell of death that came to him now as he looked at her but the smell of spring. Whether this was because of the terrible situation at the church, or his deep need for safe haven, or other causes, he did not know. He noticed her and was intrigued by her, and then she approached him. She came to him almost like a dream and spoke to him and he stood there looking at her and not quite believing what was happening.

He tried to check the warm flow of these feelings. There was no reason to think she was interested in him. She saw the need for senior housing in town and he did too. He had spoken up in the meeting and made his feelings plain; and when he was done he noticed her looking at him, without actually looking at her, and he noticed a smile on her face.

Oh, that smile! There are ironic smiles, stupid smiles, Mona Lisa smiles of indeterminate significance, smiles of sheer delight, forced smiles like flint; but her smile combined good humor with intelligence and a certain tranquility of spirit and idealism and right-mindedness. Or at least he thought he could see all these things in her smile. (He was falling in love without knowing it.)

Can you really read so much into a smile? He laughed at himself. These were moldy old ideas, the dreams of philosophers about outward appearances and what they convey, which in fact could be nothing. "Stop judging by appearances!" The truth is he knew nothing about Kim. The things he thought he saw in that smile—did he really see them? Were they really there—or was he just getting desperate at his rapidly advancing age, desperate in his loneliness, which was never greater than at that moment?

Besides, he knew absolutely nothing about her, except for what he had observed in the meeting. What did she do? What were her likes and dislikes? For that matter, was she attached? How could someone like her not be attached? And if she wasn't—was there a backstory? Which was worse—the likelihood of her being attached, which made her unapproachable—or not being attached, which suggested—just what?—to his overactive imagination.

Was she attracted to him? People have funny ways of looking at pastors. They don't see them as human beings. A warm smile from someone like Kim could very simply mean "you're a pastor and I want to like you for reasons I myself don't quite understand, and for another set of different but related reasons—which I also do not understand—I want you to like me." He had seen it hundreds of times. People want to like and be liked by pastors. If only they knew what pastors are really thinking and feeling!

The other possibility was she meant what she said and simply wanted to see him for business. They were both interested in the same thing—housing for the elderly. There was some opposition on the board. They were natural allies and it was perfectly natural for her to have an interest in him. She wanted to form an alliance against the Philistines in town.

And yet, and yet—no, he didn't think he was deceiving himself. Not really. She had looked at him in the meeting. Their eyes had met in a business-like way at first and then in a way of surprise and recognition. She smiled and he thought—felt—he could read her mind. He thought she was attracted to him. He definitely knew he was attracted to her.

All these thoughts kept running through his head, the kindling of love and the self-preserving urge to dampen it, over and over again. Indeed, he could think of little else. It was certainly more pleasant than thinking about what was going on at church.

Finally the much-anticipated day came. He went to the coffee shop early, so anxious was he for this little appointment, had built it up so much in his mind, imagining things he could not even allow himself to imagine but also was not quite successful in suppressing, so he went there fifteen minutes early—and she was already there! They sort of laughed when they saw each other. It was as if they had caught each other's secret.

Still, Mike kept it all at arm's length—himself from his own feelings, that is, not from Kim per se—from the warm beast that was making its presence known—the beast of love that comes in like the sweet columbines of spring and then, too often, like a wrecking ball—he pushed those feelings down as he sat with her and tried not to look at her—or at least not to stare—he pushed those feelings down and all the more they arose—kept telling himself he was there as a pastor—this was business—something important was at stake—

But they did not stay down because it seemed obvious from the start, from their first quiet words together, from the fact they were both early for the appointment, and finally from their embarrassed laughter, that elderly housing was not the only thing on Kim's mind. They could not help themselves. There was something between them that neither one of them had started and over which they had no control. They both knew it and were too old and maybe too lonely to fight it or even to have doubts about it.

Refractory. That was the word that kept popping into his head. Funny how the mind works, how such a word pops up in the most unlikely situations; but he was thinking of this desire inside him for tenderness and intimacy, not so much for the other thing—he was old enough not to be purely physical—he did not pretend to be spiritual either but at least he knew he had a spirit—and his spirit sighed at the sight of Kim and took delight in her presence, not quite knowing whether she was real or an illusion.

At first it was all about the housing, perfectly proper. Kim had a sweet flame for the cause of the elderly and a heart for their travails and the strange situation in which they found themselves, where modern medicine had lengthened their lives without making them any richer or more independent, in fact had attacked their independence by filling them with the innumerable ailments and general physical deterioration of old age.

She had an elderly mother herself who happened to be in nice housing somewhere down by the Cape. She knew what a blessing it was, giving them independence and various levels of care at the same time. She was passionate about it, in a quiet way. She expressed her unhappiness with the intransigence and coldness of certain factions who didn't want "those kind of people" attracted to the town by the honey of affordable housing.

They both agreed, they fed on each other's passion. But that was not all they talked about. Something was pulling them in another direction and neither one could quite resist it.

"So I hear you lost your wife," she said at some point with an awkward smile that he recognized as being awkward because he already knew her real smile by heart. "Millie told me."

"Oh—yes. Seven years now. Funny, in some ways it seems like yesterday, and in other ways—so long ago."

"That's natural, I think, no?"

"I think it's natural. To tell you the truth I don't know anymore." He blushed at this unplanned and somewhat—refractory—outburst.

"You're still wearing your ring. You must have loved her very much."

"She was my life. To tell you the truth, I didn't realize it until she was gone."

"I know exactly what you mean. I took mine off, but I waited a long time. And then I felt funny about it for a long time. Guess I still do."

"So you're—" He didn't know quite what to say.

"Same as you. My husband died of a massive heart attack about ten years ago. Forty-four years old, in great shape, avid jogger. Such a shame. Happened while we were at parent's night. We came home—my son Jason and I—and there he was, just lying on the living room floor. I can't even tell you what ran through my mind at that moment. It was horrible. But he was already gone. The ambulance got there in no time flat, but there was nothing they could do about it."

"I'm so sorry. There's nothing wrong with not wearing the ring. It was a long time ago."

"Can I be perfectly honest with you? I finally took it off because it was driving people away. I can't believe I said that!" she said blushing.

"What?"

"Well, you're probably going to think I'm desperate, but when a woman gets to a certain age it gets harder and harder to find—well, someone worth finding. Sorry—as a pastor you know what I mean. Or maybe not. Anyway, a wedding ring doesn't exactly help. I wore the rings for a long time, but then one day I took them off to do the dishes and somehow just never got around to putting them back on again. In fact they are still on the windowsill above the kitchen sink. So that makes me a terrible person, right?"

"Not at all. In fact what I think is wearing the ring after the—person—is gone is like holding on to the past and something that isn't there. No, let me rephrase that—obviously it's something that isn't there. Every now and then I look down and notice the ring and I don't even know what to think anymore. Is it for Janet's sake? Or is it self-pity at this point—or something worse? In any case I have an excuse. My knuckles are so swollen that I'm not even sure I can get it off."

She laughed. "Well, anyway, you outed me. Am I being too forward? Inviting you out to coffee and all?"

He looked at her and a thousand responses ran through his mind. But he was fifty-six years old and he didn't have any illusions or anything to gain or lose; so he simply replied, "No, I'm glad you did. I—was interested in you, to be perfectly honest."

She smiled and looked down. "Well—thank you for that. Has there been anyone since—?"

"No. No one. That was when I decided to go to seminary. So I guess I've been otherwise engaged, to make a pun I didn't intend to make."

"And of course there was the grieving process."

"There was. It's been quite the process. How about you? Has there been anyone for you?"

"Not really. Nothing serious. I just haven't been interested. Well, that's not quite right. I haven't found the right guy to be interested in. I may be desperate, but I'm also kind of picky. And it's so hard to meet people. I mean, how do you do it, at our age? I'm not going to go to some bar. I never was a bar person anyway. Where do you go?"

"I don't know. I guess you just try to stay involved, try to be in situations where there are other people and don't succumb to the temptation to shut out the world."

"You mean like the Commission on Aging," she said with a smile that was—well, tender.

Mike realized he was in danger of being overcome with deep emotion at that moment. He had been under terrible stress for over six months now, feeling so isolated and unwanted on so many levels—and this attractive, intelligent woman, who called herself picky, who from all appearances had every right to be picky, was intimating that he might be someone who was worthy of her interest. So many emotions! He hardly knew what to do with them.

This little meeting was at noon. It was a beautiful spring day, so they decided to go for a walk at a park that Kim knew. They walked and they talked and all of Mike's burdens seemed to melt away, all of his aloneness and sense of the whole world being against him. They walked and they walked some more, strolling really, and the sun shone and Mike breathed in the fresh country air and felt himself beginning to heal. It was connection. It was acceptance, friendship, for someone who felt very lonely at that juncture in his life.

Strange, isn't it, how you can be the pastor of two hundred souls and still feel alone, actually terribly alone? But Mike did. He did not feel he could afford to get too close to anyone, to let himself become anyone's fast friend. It did not seem fair to the rest of the flock. So he kept a discreet distance. There were some couples that he really would have liked to get to know better, become close to, but he kept his distance for the sake of the flock.

And then there was all the pressure he had been under and the sense of rejection coming from Charles and others. He really could have used a friend, someone to talk to, someone who would listen to him sympathetically and give good counsel, stand by him in good times and in bad. He was certainly friendly with Bill, he liked Bill very much; but it was not the same. He was a pastor and Bill was a parishioner, and there was a wall between them.

He basked in the warm glow of friendship with Kim, walking together in the sun. It was easy to talk to her and for her to talk to him. They talked so openly that it seemed like they had always known each other. They had so much in common. They wound up spending the entire afternoon together. It was Mike's day off; he was in no hurry to return to his lonely apartment. They visited a couple of shops and got ice cream and it was all very nice, on that beautiful spring day in April, the sunshine Mike needed.

They went out to dinner several times after that first date, and to a movie, and even to a concert in Boston. Kim shared his love for the faith, although she preferred a quieter worship experience than Pine Grove. Mike told her about some of the good things that were going on, about the growth of his service. He also told her some of the bad things, like David's faith statement and the attempt to use it against him. Kim was outraged. How could people be so cruel?

One warm spring evening after they went out to dinner Mike showed her his apartment. Oh gosh, it was the first time he had been alone with a woman like this in over seven years. But you know what? That's not really what was on his mind. He'd just had the visit from Bill about the Arnie rumor and was feeling particularly battered. He did not have any selfish designs on Kim, unless it is selfish to cling to someone like a life raft when you are drowning.

They spent a perfectly lovely evening together listening to favorite songs on the stereo, he in his easy chair and she on the couch he had kept from the family room of the old house. He tried not to think about Janet sitting on that same couch or what she would say about the present arrangement. At one point he got up to get Kim a glass of wine, and she followed him, and when he turned around they came together, by accident as it were, and they just looked at each other.

Mike took her in his arms and there was a lot of emotion in that embrace. It was tenderness. There was a kiss, but it was not exactly the passionate kiss of youth. It was a different kind of groping altogether—two people trying to reach other—a kiss with a lot of thinking in it and a lot of water under the bridge. It was a kiss of not quite knowing about the kiss or if it was comely for people their age to kiss but also wanting the merging of two souls that the old poets loved to talk about in their lips, so much wanting it, so much wanting not to be lonely or alone anymore.

They went back to the couch and sat down together, and then somehow after a certain amount of time they were lying down; the couch was deep and easily accommodated them. They kissed again, but it still wasn't really that kind of kiss, the one you might expect. It was more like a friendly affectionate kiss.

Mike could not help it. His eyes filled with tears.

"What is it?" she said.

"Oh—I don't know. I'm just so happy right now. Having a hard time believing it's real."

"You don't think I'm real?" she teased.

"Oh, you're real all right. I'm just not sure I can believe how lucky I am."

"What a romantic thing to say. Don't you think I feel lucky too?"

"I don't know," he said honestly. "I'm thinking maybe I'm in a little over my head here."

"Well, you keep thinking that way. I like it."

"So you agree with me, then?"

"No, but I like to keep you on your toes. I may be desperate but I have my pride."

He laughed. "You are too good. And I'm glad you were 'desperate.' You know I would never have had the courage to make the first move."

"Well, I had a four-year head start on you. You'd be amazed at what four years can do."

They lay there talking this way for hours, silly nonsense, enjoying it very much like a man who has been deprived of meat and drink for a very long time, and then they fell asleep. That was all—they fell asleep. After all, he was a pastor and they were not married. Fully dressed, except for their shoes, they lay there on the couch and fell asleep, in each other's arms. Did anything else run through poor Mike's mind as he lay there with this funny, warm, attractive woman in his arms? Well, maybe. But he took being a pastor seriously. It stood between him and the ancient passions or obsessions of his sex.

In the morning he made her a nice breakfast, fresh-brewed coffee and bacon and eggs and toast, although he was not exactly the world's greatest chef—he did his best. She ate what was put in front of her with a smile, never letting on if there was anything she might have thought to criticize, and then she left.

She kissed him. He did not want to let her go.

BUT DO YOU LOVE ME?

IN THE WEEKS that followed Mike began to open up to Kim, or "Kimbers," as he took to calling her. He wondered if they were falling in love—if people their age can still fall in love—if it is possible to *fall* and also *wonder* at the same time. He told her everything—yes, even the bad or embarrassing things—the campaign against him by a small but well-heeled minority—the disaster with Frank—his misstep with Arnie—Clarissa and all the strange and almost fateful circumstances surrounding that unseemly episode.

Kim latched onto the Clarissa thing. Was he interested in her (with a smile)? Mike denied it. Her attractiveness was an important part of the story, but the only thing he felt for her was an incredible sense of sadness at how she had been driven away. "But she wasn't really *driven* away, was she? She left of her own accord (still smiling)." Yes, she did leave of her own accord, Mike admitted. Kim was satisfied. She didn't want him thinking too much about the "very attractive" Clarissa.

As you may have noticed, Kim tended to be quite forthright. This was not because she was "desperate," as she laughingly described herself. It was because she was unafraid. She said what was on her mind—with love. This openness was good for Mike, once he learned to embrace it, a real gift. He was able to say things to her that he could not imagine saying to anyone else; and in his present situation, this was very healing.

Why? Because he trusted her. Her nature and—he flattered himself—her feelings toward him gave him the freedom to trust. This thought dawned on him one day, and then he fell deeply in love with her. Whatever he had been holding back melted away. He was not afraid of being happy anymore, not holding on to the world-weariness of older men, not wondering whether she really was what she seemed (he believed in her completely), not worrying about whether he deserved her (he knew he didn't).

A couple of weeks went by and Mike was so happy being with Kim that he sort of forgot about the uproar at church—until Bill came to him looking kind of pale.

"I guess you probably heard about the meeting the other night."

"Not really. No one said anything to me."

"What! You've got to be kidding. Charles hasn't talked to you?"

"I haven't had a real conversation with Charles in probably two months."

"This is unbelievable. They're not even going to give you a chance to defend yourself."

"Do I need to defend myself?"

"Well, you might. I guess I can tell you, since apparently no else is. Susan is on the warpath. You didn't sign the faith statement and she just won't let it go. She's talking about a church vote."

Mike gulped. "On whether I go or stay?"

"Yes. And it could come soon. Which is why I can't believe no one has said anything to you."

"Is it just her or is the whole board going along with this?"

"It's definitely not the whole board. A couple of us have been opposed from the beginning. For that matter I don't think there are many people who are actually for it. But that's the thing. She's framed it quite cleverly. This isn't a vote on the brutal proposition of throwing someone out of his job. No, she makes it sound like it's just a vote on church doctrine."

"So it's not about me. It's about the church's 'mission' and all that hifalutin stuff."

"Right. And that's where she's got the people in the middle. They don't want to say no to her because they don't want to hurt the church—or they're afraid of being accused of false doctrine. They're basically kicking the can down the road by agreeing to take it to a congregational vote. And then Charles refuses to say anything. He just sits there listening to it all with a straight face, which gives the impression that he's on board."

"Clever. He's got her doing his dirty work for him."

"That's the way it looks to me. I don't know, I hate to be so cynical. But the idea that they could actually engineer a vote to get rid of someone like you is just mind-boggling to me. What about all the people in the Saturday night service? It's going to be a disaster. They'll all leave."

"Not really. I don't think so. You're underestimating Charles. He will find a way to smooth it over and make everything come out right."

"Well, you're probably right about that," Bill said with a chuckle.

There was an awkward silence as they stood there looking at each other, neither one knowing quite what to say, since they both knew what was coming.

"So there's going to be a congregational vote," Mike affirmed.

"Right. And watch out for Susan. She has all these other issues she keeps bringing up."

"Let me guess. Fred. Clarissa."

"And that pornography thing, too."

"What! She's still talking about that?"

"She's brought it up a couple of times. Everybody just sits there and looks awkward. By the way, what exactly happened with that?"

"Oh, I was just trying to show him I understood his predicament and wasn't pretending to look down from some pedestal of righteousness."

"Sounds like you were trying to help him."

"Correct. But I learned a valuable lesson. Never underestimate the value of a façade."

"Have you tried explaining this to people?"

"What's the point? Someone like her would never understand."

"Well, you're probably right. She doesn't really want to understand. I just hope she has the good sense not to bring it up in front of the whole congregation."

"Let her do her worst. I'm ready for it."

That's what Mike said, and very calmly too, or rather with the appearance of calm, but inside he was having a meltdown. So there was actually going to be a congregational vote on whether or not he would be allowed to stay. This wasn't just some shadowy far-off possibility anymore; it really was happening. And Bill was right. Susan was not going to let up. She was now personally invested in the outcome and would do whatever she had to do to finish the job. He could expect neither mercy nor understanding from her in a public confrontation.

The fairy charm of Kim and springtime was broken. Was this really happening? Were they trying to get rid of him? He did not think it would turn out well. The Saturday night crowd would support him, he hoped, but they represented a small fraction of the church. The rest did not know him and had no way to evaluate the charges that were being thrown around.

It was an all-out campaign on Susan's part, and the Cantors were one of the first couples in the church, both in leadership participation and in giving. Besides, the whole church had adopted the faith statement, which he refused to sign. Bill was right about that, too. It was a simple matter for them to say he was opposed to the mission of the church and therefore should leave. He did not see how he or any of his supporters could overcome this argument.

Two weeks went by after the chilling visit from Bill. There was another deacons meeting, and then a call came from the church secretary to stop by Charles's office for a chat. Charles was acting more and more like the bureaucratic mandarins Mike had known from the corporation, with all of their little intimidation tactics.

It was a sunny but chilly May morning when Mike went in there, all nerves and gloom but trying very hard not to show it. Charles informed him, in a calm and even voice, that the deacons realized he had not signed the faith statement and on the basis of this had voted to bring a motion before the congregation for his dismissal. It was all very cut and dried. Charles put on his usual chirpiness, but the wall between them was evident.

"Why are you doing this to me?" Mike said with a tight smile, looking him cold in the eyes.

"I'm not doing anything. This is the board of deacons."

"But you're not doing anything to stop it. You're letting it happen. Why?"

"This is a church decision, not a Charles decision. It breaks my heart. But the church has decided to go in a certain direction, and it seems you are not willing to go along with them. You refused to sign the new statement. It's as simple as that."

"This isn't about the church. This is about me. You don't like the fact that the Saturday service is doing so well."

"On the contrary, I'm thrilled about the growth of the Saturday night service," Charles purred. "I think Greg and the worship team are doing a fabulous job reaching out to a younger constituency."

"But I'm the 'love guy,' and that's where the problem comes in."

"As I've said on numerous occasions, 'God is love.' Gosh, I don't say it; the Bible says it. This isn't about you or what you are teaching. This is about the church and calling her back to a historical understanding of her roots and her doctrine. It's about healing the times. It's about consistency in our message and how we share the Gospel."

"And would you still have this noble sense of mission if the Cantors weren't involved?"

"Not sure what you mean. The Cantors care deeply about Pine Grove. If they're behind something, then that's a good thing, in my opinion."

"Not just because they have a lot of money, as you've said on previous occasions."

"That has nothing to do with it. They've worked hard for their money—it wasn't just handed to them. The most important thing is they love this church and want to do what is best for it. Anyone who loves this church is entitled to have a voice."

"How about Frank Crane? He loved this church, and Susan Cantor had him run out of here over nothing."

"You can't compare Frank Crane to the Cantors."

"No, you can't. And that's the problem."

Mike's face was bright red as he rose and walked out very deliberately. He couldn't believe what had just happened. No kindness, no meekness, no warmth or spirit of generosity, no commiseration; instead Charles had simply sat there and lied to him, over and over again. Was this what they had in mind when they talked about Christian behavior? The "holiness of God"?

He was amazed at the sheer disingenuousness of it all. "I'm not doing anything." Of course he wasn't doing anything—he was having his surrogates do it. "I'm thrilled about the growth of the Saturday night service." Charles liked the growth, maybe, but not Mike's role in it. Very clever, the way he tried to make it sound like it was because of the worship team, which was his creation; to pretend to be tipping his hat to them when in fact he was tipping it to himself. But the worship team had been in place long before Mike arrived and there had been no growth.

Why couldn't Charles acknowledge this? What was so hard about giving someone his due? Mike was not trying to outdo him. He was not boastful or prideful about the growth of the service. In his mind it wasn't about him or his success; it was about the harvest and reaching the lost sheep. Mike wasn't drawing people away from Sunday morning. All of the growth on Saturday night was from new members. Wasn't that a good thing?

He was genuinely surprised and humbled by his success. He certainly never attempted to take credit for it. He saw himself as an instrument and nothing more. But for Charles to pretend he wasn't jealous of him—it was too much. The senior pastor's cool behavior told the tale. Consciously or not, Charles saw him as a rival and was determined to cut him down to size. And as far as Mike was concerned, the whole thing with Susan and the faith statement simply proved it.

Speaking of Susan…"The Cantors love this church and care deeply about it." Now that was quite a statement. Mike hardly even knew where to begin. For instance, what did Charles mean by "the church"? Pine Cove Community Church? Oh sure, the Cantors gave every indication of loving it. They were generous donors. They served on committees and were active leaders. But they were also the ones who declared that the Roman church was the antichrist.

This was not "the church" as Mike understood it. "The church" was not a specific place like Pine Cove but the body of Christ. To love the "the church" was to love Christ and his teachings and the way he comported himself, not some local organization with buildings and grounds and a sizable investment fund. To love "the church" was to love the last and only commandment Christ ever gave, on the night before he was crucified.

But was this what was seen in the Cantors, the self-sacrificing love of the cross? Mike could not bring himself to see it that way. It did not show a Christ-like love to vilify Catholics. It did not show a Christ-like love to attack and belittle a man because he had been an alcoholic. It did not show a Christ-like love to scorn Clarissa for being different and not dressing the way they thought she should.

"Whore"—wasn't that the word Charles had used? Did it come from a Christ-like love?

Was he really supposed to believe that Charles was not influenced by the fact that the Cantors had a lot of money? He did not want to believe it. He deliberately withheld judgment as an act of the will—"do not judge." But he could not be blind to it. Charles had taken sides. After this conversation there could no longer be any question. His days at the church were numbered.

DEN OF THIEVES

FROM THAT POINT ON, from the meeting in Charles's office on a chilly sunny morning, Mike began to be consumed with anger. The resentment he had been pushing down for months found its way to the surface and insisted on being served. All he could think about was the conversation with Charles; not so much the revelation that his position was in jeopardy, but the glib dishonesty and the way the facts were twisted to put him in the worst possible light.

He could not spin, not even for himself—he was not one of the spinners. It was one of the main reasons for wanting to leave the corporation, which was mostly spin. He was a doer, a very different breed from the spinners. Doers don't spin because they produce, and perhaps for this reason they never develop the most characteristic of all human skills: the ability to dissemble. Men are made to twist the facts, born enemies to the truth, Mike told himself in his bitterness.

Such insights only made things worse, however. He lost control of the anger, like a guy who gets a little too cavalier with the steering wheel. He found it harder and harder to smile and be pleasant, not just in his interactions with staff and church leadership but with his own parishioners. He found it harder to preach. The mounting anger burned out something sweet in him and left a great emptiness where his spirit should have been.

He would get up in front of the congregation and begin to talk—only now he heard himself talking. The sound of his own voice came back to him and sat awkwardly in his ear. Some self-conscious thing crept in between himself and his listeners. He who had always been highly attuned to others was now attuned mostly to himself. No longer was he following the wind where it blows. In place of that sweet wind was a grim instinct for self-preservation.

A couple of weeks went by but the anger did not abate; no, it was still waxing. Then the hardness began to grow into him and annihilate him. He was the outcast, he was the one they were all talking about. It was behind his back but he knew they were talking. People came to him and told him what was being said, and his anger and frustration grew. He could not defend himself. He did not have the will to do battle with someone like Susan. The lies and misinterpretations continued to pile up.

In the end he found it necessary to put on a bulletproof vest in order to keep himself sane—this was the image he kept in his mind—but since this vest was made of pure vulnerability it did not really stop the pain. It was made up of giving up, not of mettle or moxie, and was bulletproof only in the sense that no calumny could hurt him because he considered himself already dead. "Once dead, there's no more dying then"; but there's no more living either.

But this death of his was not a real death. He made a conscious effort to put his anger to death, but it did not die. It was still there but veiled, both to others and to himself, as he found out one day when a young guy in a Land Rover cut him off in traffic and Mike put the pedal on the floor and chased him like an idiot. He was ashamed of this after it was over, but he couldn't stop himself. He was losing control and he knew it.

Why didn't he pray? He did pray. He prayed all the time, whenever he thought of it. It was hard. Most of the time the best he could muster was a half-hearted "thy will be done." He prayed but did not receive the blessing, the peace of mind he coveted. The praying kept him grounded but it did not make him clean, because he was holding onto his anger.

It was not only on the road that this anger betrayed him. He came out of the Saturday night service on a beautiful June evening and found the entrance hall cluttered up with tables and people milling about. The tables weren't there when he came in; they must have been set up during the service. This seemed like the last straw. They had been in the church worshiping, and meanwhile these people, whoever they were, were in the hallway setting up their wares. Worse, it was Pentecost, one of the most important days in the church calendar, in fact the birthday of the church.

Mike approached one of the tables in a deteriorating frame of mind. "What's all this?" he said to a dark-haired woman he didn't know, gesturing to the baked goods and plants.

"It's for the new gas stove," she said. "Would you like to buy something?"

This was said very sweetly, and maybe the sweetness was the very thing that caused Mike to snap. "It's Pentecost. Is this really necessary?" he barked.

"We asked the trustees. They said it was all right."

"Well, it's not. This is supposed to be a house of prayer. Or did we forget about that?" Mike glared at her for a moment then recollected himself and walked away.

It was just the sort of thing that was starting to drive him crazy at Pine Cove—an obsession, to his mind, with upgrading the physical plant, with spending money that did not need to be spent and energy that could have been better applied elsewhere, as if there were salvation in it. They already had a perfectly good, if old, commercial gas stove, as far as he was concerned, a good make and model; but David had begun a new thing called "Soup Wednesdays" where any interested small group members could come to the church for a home-made supper and fellowship and invite their friends who might be future prospects.

All of a sudden the stove they had was just not good enough. Over a hundred people were coming, and the stove was old and had to be lit with matches and they needed something better. Every time Mike heard about the new stove he shook his head. He was a Yankee, and it wasn't the Yankee way to fix something that wasn't broke. The new stove they were looking at was almost $4,000 with a significant discount, and then they were going to have to put a new head and fan in and a new counter to accommodate it for a minimum $10,000 when all the construction costs were figured in.

Fourteen thousand dollars for a stove they didn't really need and were using to make soup once a week! He controlled his temper and stomped away. But that was not the end of it. The poor woman on whom he had unloaded began to cry, and was soon surrounded by some of her sister peddlers, who took her aside to comfort her. All of this happened in full view of the Saturday night crowd, who looked on in wonder.

The incident was reported to the deacons. Mike received a call from Charles, who was not his usual smooth self.

"What were you thinking? The trustees approved it. It didn't have anything to do with you."

"I know. I'm sorry. I didn't mean to snap at her, but nobody told me they were going to be setting up for a bake sale. Besides, it was Pentecost, one of the biggest feast days of the year."

"In case you didn't notice, we don't really do 'feast days' in this church. Those people weren't thinking about it being Pentecost. They were thinking about trying to help out."

"You mean buying a stove the church doesn't need."

"So now you're in charge of the stoves, too? That's nice. Be sure to let me know what else you think you're in charge of. That way maybe we can avoid these little mix-ups in the future."

"Again, I'm sorry. I didn't mean to make the woman cry. I didn't even know she was crying. I've been under a lot of pressure lately, and I guess I just snapped."

"Pastors don't snap. That's rule number one. Rule number two—pastors don't insult parishioners. Especially when they're trying to help the church."

Frank and Clarissa came to mind, but Mike didn't bother responding. Actually he agreed with Charles. He was ashamed of his behavior, ashamed of having lost his temper with the poor woman when all she was doing was volunteering and giving up her Saturday night on behalf of Soup Wednesdays. All she knew was that Pastor David had approved the bake sale and even contributed a few things of his own. She didn't know Mike. It wasn't personal. She had not come to show him up or disrupt his service. It wasn't "his" service anyway. He called her and apologized.

Still, was it really necessary? Did they have to set up for a bake sale while he was trying to conduct a worship service? She was not being consciously provocative, but what about David, whose brainchild it apparently was? And why hadn't they told him? He might not have been any happier about it—but at least he would have been prepared. He would not have overreacted. He would not have lost his temper. He regretted losing his temper, but what did they expect? Was it so hard to show a little respect?

Mike didn't have much time to think about it, however, because he had a call from Bill informing him that the congregational vote had been announced formally in the *Gospeller*. The church was in an uproar over the whole mess. Susan and Audrey and friends were working overtime to convince as many as they could of Mike's deficiencies. Meanwhile the people in the Sunday congregation did not know what to think. Many of them did not know Mike. Were the rumors true? They looked to Charles for guidance, but he remained stone-faced in the storm.

As for the Saturday flock—they were shocked and distraught. They couldn't understand it. Everything had seemed perfectly normal. What was going on? There were lots of anguished calls and they were full of anguished questions. This was the hardest thing of all for Mike, the declension in their eyes. The only charge he could bring himself to disclose was not signing the faith statement, but he knew other things would probably come up. A fight was coming and Bill was right. Susan would not fail to make the most of her arsenal.

The congregational meeting was scheduled for the last Friday in June. Mike was overshadowed with dread as the day approached, a stranger in his own skin. He appealed to God but all he heard was the sound of his voice. He who had a tender sensibility was now going to be subjected to public humiliation. And he knew he would have to endure it in silence. It was a referendum on him and it was in God's hands. No good would come from taking up his sword and trying to fight the temple guards; only more pain and sorrow.

Also he had to tell Kim! It hurt him to do it, crushed his pride, but she deserved to know. To his relief she was supportive. She continued to have confidence in him even when he lost it in himself. Besides, it was all very black and white to her. Charles felt threatened by Mike and had cooked the whole thing up to get rid of him. This was a bit of a simplification, but he did not argue with her. He drank in her sweet and soothing words and her loyalty.

Mike found himself going to the church less and less and spending more time with her as the judgment day approached, often driving down to the ocean for long walks on the beach in Rye or the Marginal Way in Ogunquit. It wasn't that he was slacking off; no, he was holding on for dear life. She was the only physical, tangible thing he had to cling to, his island in the storm. She informed him she was coming with him to the meeting. Mike was aghast at the thought of her sitting there listening to his fate being debated and hearing some potentially rough accusations thrown his way, but he could not talk her out of it.

The fatal date was a rainy night, a late June thunderstorm night, and Mike and Kim arrived at the church, not early and not late but exactly on time, and he led her to a seat in the back of the hall in the muted light. There was a moderate crowd; lots of empty seats. He didn't see many Saturday nighters. A couple of people greeted him and encouraged him as they came in. He kept his sad smile. In one sense he was calm. He already knew the outcome.

Things started out decorously enough. Bart Stevenson, chairman of the deacons, declined to get up on the stage and spoke in a low voice, which came across as an attempt to send a signal that there was to be no theatrics on this somber occasion. He stated the facts, as he understood them: the church had approved a faith statement and agreed to have it signed by its leaders. Mike had not signed it—Bart used the word "declined"—and indicated having reservations about the doctrine. Since the church had decided to go in a certain direction, and Mike could not in good conscience concur, it seemed to the deacons that they had no choice but to recommend severing his official relationship with the church, "without prejudice."

Mike listened to all this in growing awe and wonder. Bart seemed to be wavering even as he spoke. This was something he had to do as chairman of the board, representing its will, but Mike sensed that he probably had not realized how ambivalent he was about the whole thing until it came to actually doing it. His manner was very subdued. He looked nervous and uncomfortable. He was not simply pretending to take no pleasure in what he was doing.

Then some voices began popping up in the crowd. It seemed the support for the faith statement was not as strong in the congregation as it was on the board of deacons. Several people admitted they had reservations about the statement and did not think it should be used against a pastor as grounds for dismissal. Others said the church had approved it and could not have pastors on staff who were actively opposed to the church's official mission.

Apparently there was a lot of pent-up passion in the church over this issue that now broke out. People spoke up and voices were raised and there was a surge of emotion. There was murmuring in the crowd and rippling waves of reaction as different people spoke and were rebutted in turn. Mike looked at Kim in amazement. He had come with the gloomy assumption that it was a foregone conclusion. The church was against him; he would have to go. But now he began to wonder. Was he the unwitting leader of an insurgency?

This went on for over an hour. The situation was deteriorating when Susan got up.

"I guess people can have different opinions about the faith statement—although personally I think it's a wonderful thing, and we did vote to adopt it as a church. But that wasn't the only issue we had to look at, unfortunately. There has been a pattern of behavior here that has come to our attention, and frankly is a little troubling. I won't go into all the gory details, but to mention just one, there was a woman who started coming on Saturday night who had, let's say, a colorful background. That's not just my opinion—that's what she said about herself in front of the whole church on Testimony Night. A lot of you heard it. Well, now the next thing we knew she was on the worship team. It seems Pastor Mike wanted a violinist. Now, I'm all for violinists, but I think we need to take leadership seriously, especially worship leadership. And this was a case where a lot of people thought a bad decision had been made and bad judgment had been shown. And it caused a lot of problems in the church that the deacons had to step in and clean up."

Now Charles stood up, and Mike's heart sank. "Let me just chime in here. This sort of thing may seem a little mysterious to a lot of people sitting in the pews, so to speak, but it's actually very important. Paul tells us that our leadership must be beyond reproach, especially when it comes to morality, but in every way. I know it's hard to talk about this sort of thing. Lord knows, we're all sinners, and nobody wants to be judgmental. But we need to take what the Bible says very seriously. And in this case even Pastor Shapely expressed some concerns to me about the behavior of the person in question."

Mike couldn't help himself. He rose to his feet. "On the contrary," he called out from the back of the room. "I never said anything of the sort about the behavior of the person in question."

"He speaks!" Charles replied with a smile. "Welcome, Pastor. Didn't see you back there. But I must remind you, I specifically asked you whether you had seen anything in her behavior that was concerning, and you could not deny that you had. Now, I don't really blame you. I applaud you for supporting the young woman and can understand perfectly well why you would not want to have negative thoughts about such an attractive young lady. But again, this is a leadership question, and leaders must be beyond reproach."

Mike just stared at him in disbelief. Was he hinting at something between him and Clarissa? The other part was a downright lie. He remembered the conversation very well. He remembered Charles asking if he had any doubts about her behavior, and he remembered saying he could not positively deny it. He was simply trying to be honest and open—but this honesty was now being bent against him in what seemed to be a particularly coldhearted way.

Then Darlene stood up. "This is hard for me. I didn't mean to say anything tonight, but I'm sorry, I just have to speak. I also saw things that were—not right. I also don't want to go into all the details, but let's just say this isn't quite so pure and rosy as Pastor Mike is trying to make it seem. It was a very bad time for us on the worship team, and there were things going on that were very upsetting to me personally. I'm sorry, but I have to tell the truth. I don't want people thinking this is just something someone dreamed up or an overactive imagination."

A cold sword went through Mike's heart. He knew she was referring to Clarissa and Greg, but the way she put it almost made it sound like she was talking about Clarissa and himself, especially when put together with Charles's ambiguous comments. There was nothing he could do, however. He couldn't stand up and clarify that the unnamed person hinted at in her insinuations was Greg Popovich, the worship leader. He could not defend himself from the misdirected slander without slandering Greg. So he just sat there and swallowed his breath.

Susan stood up again. She said this was not the only "difficult situation" that had occurred with Mike. She talked about Frank and how he was hired. She talked about reservations she and her husband had about Mike's training and background after an unspecified discussion they had with him at their house. She even brought up Chloe's healing and the questions surrounding it, hinting that some of the deacons felt that Mike seemed a little too eager to take credit for something that had not even been verified.

"Excuse me! Excuse me!" There was a timid voice from the left front corner of the hall. Mike looked over and saw Chloe, looking a bit overwhelmed. "I believe I'm the person you're referring to. I have a name. It's Chloe. I had RA for fifteen years, so bad I could hardly get out of bed in the morning. And now I'm completely healed. You can see it—I'm healed. And I just want to say—thank you, Pastor Mike. I don't know why they're doing this to you or what the whole point of it is—I just found out about it today—but you are a very sweet man and you have done a lot of good for a lot of people. And it would be a tragedy to let you go.'"

Mike smiled as a tear rolled down his cheek. There was a rumble and movement in the hall as a large portion of those gathered were moved by this statement, in one way or another.

Charles stood up. "Thank you, Chloe. It's great to see you, and I'm glad you're feeling better. Not to detract in any way from your witness or the wonderful thing you feel happened to you, but I think the real issue here is how it was handled. And that's what Susan's really talking about in the larger sense, the question of judgment, the question of fitting in, being part of the team, seeking agreement and consent in the things we do so we are all on the same page and working together toward the same goal. That's the bottom line here tonight. Look, this is a terrible thing, a painful thing, and I know nobody here is happy about it. I'm certainly not. But I do think we've wandered a little bit from where we started and would like to bring Bart back to see where we stand and where we go next."

So that was his clever way of bracketing any further discussion! Mike smiled to himself when he heard it. Charles was certainly smooth and would fit in quite well in the boardroom.

Now Bill stood up. "I wasn't going to say anything, but honestly, this is ridiculous. There's been a lot of smooth talk here and a lot of not-so-smooth talk, and it's hard to decide which is more ridiculous. This is the most trumped-up thing I have ever seen in my life. This dear, sweet man came here with nothing but good intentions and love for his God and for the church. He has worked hard and been a tremendous asset. The Saturday night service has quadrupled in attendance, and why? Because of his excellent sermons. No, let me take that back. His extraordinary sermons and his Christian spirit and humility. And this is how we reward him? This is what we do to him? I've heard a lot of stories here, and I've heard a lot of spin on these stories, but let me just assure you—you are only hearing one side. You are only hearing what certain people want you to hear. And the deacons were far from unanimous on this. A lot of us think this is a travesty, frankly, and a shameful moment for us all."

Well! That was letting it all out in one blast. The crowd seemed to turn. There was actual applause after these remarks and quite a few "Amens" and "Thank you Pastor Mikes."

Now Susan took the microphone again. "Well, I'm sorry—but I just have to speak up. Some things are important and just shouldn't be let go. So somebody thinks we're telling stories. Well, you can see that Pastor Shapely is here with a friend tonight. That's not a 'story'; it's real. Now don't get me wrong. I don't have any problem with that per se. I don't think anyone would have a problem with him having a special friend after all the years since his wife died. But it has come to our attention that some of the behavior here was not exactly what we would expect from a pastor. I prefer to keep this on the deacons, but it's important for you to know the facts. There have been overnight visits with this new friend. And I can tell you that some people are upset about it and don't feel it's a good example to set for the church."

There was commotion again in the large hall—audible gasps—and suddenly Mike knew it was over. He and Kim just looked at each other in dismay. They knew the truth, but Mike did not see any reason to try to explain it. Would anyone believe him? He might even make things worse.

Bart stood up and managed to get the crowd under control. He knew it was late and didn't want to hold people up and keep them from enjoying their weekend. He asked if anyone had anything else they wanted to say. The room was silent; Susan's gambit, cleverly saved for last, had unseated Mike's supporters, who did not know how to react. They had heard from "both sides," as Bart put it, and had a good discussion—although Mike thought he looked a little embarrassed as these words left his lips. Anyway, now it was time to put the question to a vote.

At least it was close. They voted for dismissal, 138-112. A lot of people did not vote. Kim gripped his arm when the results were announced. He looked over. Her face was white. Mike stood up and helped her to her feet, and they quietly found their way to the door while people were still talking down in front. They walked straight out of the building and into the misty summer night. Mike turned around to give it one last look. He was not going to miss it.

BEAR ONE ANOTHER'S BURDENS

MIKE DID NOT GO to the service the following evening. He had a sermon ready, hedging against the outcome of the meeting, but he had been dismissed. And to tell the truth he was relieved. He had reached a point where it was almost painful for him to get up there and speak and lead the service when he knew Susan and her merry gang were out to get him, when he knew many on the leadership team did not want him there and did not think he should be speaking, including Charles. He was not one to force himself where he was not wanted.

He was relieved, most of all, that it was finally over. True, he was out of a job; true, he had no idea where he would go, since it was difficult for pastors to find new positions when they had been dismissed from the prior post. But all the months of pain and suffering were over. There was nothing hanging over his head anymore. The worst that could happen had already happened.

The hardest thing was breaking the news to the people he loved, to his parents and the two girls. He had not told them anything about the difficulties he was having, so he had to break it to them cold. He felt like a failure, a disappointment. He didn't even have the energy to defend himself or to blame it on the evil machinations of others.

They were shocked but very loving and understanding in their response. They supported him completely and were upset with the church over what had happened. His oldest daughter, who had fallen away from the church, was not surprised. It was a perfect example of why she didn't want to have anything to do with it, the meanness and hypocrisy. In a way, this hurt Mike more than anything. He did not know what to say to her.

This was so hard, telling them. So hard. The worst is over, he said to himself when he was done with his calls. But he was wrong. The thing that had just happened didn't really hit him for a couple of days. And then it hit hard. He spent much of Saturday and Sunday with Kim, but she went back to work on Monday and he was home alone in his apartment with nowhere to go and nothing to do, and that was when it started to hit him.

First came the disbelief and the outrage. He went over the meeting again and again in his mind, becoming more agitated each time. He pictured Susan with her smug expression and the spite in her voice. He went over the things she said and was amazed all over again. He felt hatred for her, not the grace of Christ on the cross. He wanted to say "Father, forgive them, for they know not what they do" but could not. He did not have the strength.

He fantasized about going to her house and confronting her and her arrogant know-nothing husband. He had all kinds of fantasies that he did not seem to be able to suppress. These were the putative paragons of Christian faith in the Pine Cove Community Church. These were the people who were held up as models of behavior and stewardship. The more he thought about their mendacity and meanness the more he hated them. He couldn't help himself.

He thought about Charles and hated him too. All of this time, these three years, he had been holding it off, ever since he had started to realize that he was not Charles's cup of tea. He had held off the hurt and the resentment and his misgivings about Charles and where his head and heart were at, but now he let it all come forward. He pictured him in his mind and he punched him in his smiling face. He curled his hands into fists and punched him in his mind, but Charles's smile did not go away!

Nor did this fanciful violence do anything to relieve his agony. It embarrassed him. He was full of hatred and rage but these things merely made him feel worse about himself. They did not give him the satisfaction he was seeking. Instead of relieving his nothingness, they made it all the more acute. Unlike St. Paul, he was not able to bear all things in good spirit—and he had not suffered nearly as much as St. Paul. He was a little man. His impotent rage simply made his littleness more apparent.

Were Susan and Fred and Charles harmed in any way by this rage of his? Not at all. They were—wherever they were—smugly enjoying their great triumph. His hatred did not hurt them. It hurt him by revealing his littleness and powerlessness. They had succeeded in ruining his reputation, but it was impossible to restore it through rage. He did not want the reputation of being an angry and vengeful man. He wanted more than ever to be meek. Even if it meant letting his enemies triumph over him.

Still, the rage did not go away. Or rather, he would chase it away with his better angel only to have it return later with equal or greater force. It came in waves, washing over him and suffocating him, following him wherever he went and marring everything in its path. He could not get to sleep at night, and when he woke up in the morning the very first thing he saw in his mind's eye was Charles's steely face. This impotent rage.

And then sometimes, to be honest, he just wanted to break down and cry—yes because of the hurt—but more because of the impasse between rage and rationalization, because of being nowhere in the middle and torn by both extremes, because of frustration. He could not cry, however. Not because he was too proud, but because he was too angry. The tears ran into iron. He became clumsy. He broke things and only half-realized it.

Bill dropped by to see him on his way home from work. Mike was glad to see him—there was no one who had been more supportive than Bill. There were condolences, and Mike tried to take them in but couldn't somehow. Something in him held those condolences off at arm's length, even while he smiled. He thanked Bill for his kind remarks. They both expressed amazement over Susan's final gambit. Mike assured him that things were not what they seemed.

Then came something else.

"So what happened to you on Saturday night?"

"What do you mean? I was here."

"Well, I think they were kind of expecting you at church, to lead the service."

"I thought they didn't want me there."

"You're still on the payroll. So basically there was no one to lead the service. I wasn't there, but I guess it was kind of awkward."

"Well, you know what? Let me just say thank you very much for the clear communications. I was not aware they expected me to come down and preach after they fired me. No one told me they were expecting it. How am I supposed to know? I'm not a mind-reader."

"Did you ask?"

"No—why would I ask?" Mike said in frustration.

"I think it might have been a good idea. I mean, don't forget they still haven't even had a conversation about what kind of package they're going to give you."

"I don't care if they give me anything. I'm sick of the whole thing and I'm sick of them. And by the way, let me tell you something. You don't lie about somebody and stab him in the back in front of his congregation and then expect him to come in with his tail between his legs and do your bidding. That's just not realistic."

Bill seemed a little surprised at this outburst. "Well, somehow we got our wires crossed. I want to make sure they do right by you, treat you fairly. But you have to be reasonable, too."

"You know, Bill, why don't you just leave?" Mike said, losing his temper. "I'm not really in the mood for this. No, seriously—just leave."

Bill tried to get him to talk, but he was adamant. After Bill left he felt physically ill. No, that is not exactly correct. For a brief moment he felt triumphant and righteous, because Bill had offended him and this time Mike had not just sat there and taken it, he had acted; he had finally fought back against their nonsense.

This sense of Achilles-like prowess soon deserted him, however, since the very person on whom he had unloaded was his best friend and strongest supporter in the church. The truth was he had wondered if they were expecting him to preach and he remembered deciding not to call and find out because of pride, because he felt ashamed and defiant. Sure, it was unreasonable of them to have expectations of someone whom they had treated badly, but he was also on the payroll, as Bill pointed out, and had been paid for June, and he had not done his due diligence on the last Saturday of the month.

So there was something to it. Bill was not wrong and they were not entirely wrong either. In fact the more he thought about it the more he talked himself into thinking he was the one who was wrong. They could have solved the whole thing by simply telling him what was expected of him. He would have gone and done his duty. It would have been the hardest thing he had ever done, getting up in front of the congregation in his state of utter shame and humiliation, pretending to smile and be in God's grace and Christ's love when in fact he was exploding inside, when he was a thousand cuts and pieces.

It would have been terribly hard, but he would have done it, if he had known they wanted him to do it. He was a responsible person. He did not let people down. Bill's reprimand had hurt him, coming on him unexpected, but he was wrong to react the way he did. He was wrong to lash out at the person who supported him most and was simply trying to help him in the awkward negotiations to come. He called Bill to apologize. He was sorry—he had acted like an ass—he didn't know what was wrong with him. Bill said it was perfectly understandable, but Mike sensed a little coldness in his voice. It cut him.

Bill was not the only one who contacted him. Many people called or sent emails expressing various levels of heartbreak or outrage or confoundment. Actually one of the sweetest conversations he had that week was with Don Baker, the visitations pastor. Don was the one who had tangled reluctantly with Mike over Chloe and the issue of her healing.

Don felt terrible about what happened. He wasn't just feigning; Mike could see the paleness and the shaking as he stood there and offered him the box of saltwater taffy he had picked up in Hampton. "If I have contributed in any way—" Mike assured him he hadn't. Don told him he could not believe the insinuations they had made about Chloe. "They sure didn't get that from me."

"No, I know; they had their narrative and everything had to be made to fit it in order for them to feel good about what they were doing."

Don sat down and they had a glass of port together and a nice conversation. It turned out Don was a secret supporter of Mike's. He'd never said this, never told him, and he regretted it. He had been quietly watching Mike and was impressed with him and what he was doing, especially considering it was his first church. Mike told him he had made a lot of rookie mistakes.

Mike went into it a little bit, relaxed by the port, exhausted and letting down his guard—things that happened with Frank and Clarissa. Don was highly sympathetic. Christ himself could not have avoided getting into trouble with the "religious leaders" in those situations, he insisted. Sometimes things get messy in churches and there is nothing anyone can do about it. They got messy with the apostles. That was why it was so important to heed the call to be "lowly and humble of heart." They talked about some of the dynamics at the church. Don did not hold back from sharing his reservations about Charles, which were similar to Mike's.

It turned out he even agreed with Mike about David's faith statement. Actually what he said was he "completely agreed." He came close to saying some sharp things about the "young man from Princeton" but managed to keep on the side of kindness. He was sorry he had not spoken out against it, however. Very sorry now. He wished he had Mike's courage, but for some reason it just seemed better at the time to go along and not cause controversy. Now that he saw the consequences, he had changed his mind.

This conversation was very soothing to Mike, very healing. He lapped it up like milk. And for a moment he did not feel quite so alone or isolated. Don had not talked to him before, not in any intimate or personal way. Oh, they had talked in the way men usually do, about the weather and sports and books and fishing and so forth, but not beyond the surface. Mike found himself liking Don very much and regretting lost opportunities. He could have had a good friend if he had seen it at the time and perhaps not been so absorbed with the Saturday night service and making a good impression in his first church.

The most remarkable conversation he had, however, was with Clarissa. She called him at the end of the week.

"I heard about what happened."

"Yes, it seems I'm not wanted there anymore."

"That makes two of us. But how are you doing? Are you all right?"

"I think so. My body parts seem to be intact. It's been a long week, but I'll get through it. I guess. Not that I have any choice."

"Well, you know, I've been thinking about you and praying for you constantly."

"Really?"

"Really! Praying! Can you believe it? I guess I'm some kind of religious nut now."

Mike laughed. "How did you hear?"

"I saw it on Facebook, where else? Greg posted something about 'Very sad news. The church voted to dismiss Mike Shapely today. We love Mike very much and will miss him.' I don't know if those were the exact words."

"Greg posted that? That's very nice."

"Yes, and very brave, considering the witch he lives with. By the way, there was never anything between us, you know. Darlene just imagined that."

"I believe you. I never said there was. To tell you the truth, I was heartbroken over the whole thing. I never said anything to you, but it was one of the worst things that ever happened to me in my entire life. I'm still recovering from it and what I did to you."

"You didn't do anything to me! You were a saint. These people just can't practice what they preach. They talk about love and forgiveness, but they don't really mean it. Anyway, I want you to know I don't blame you. I never blamed you. I think you're great, and I can't believe what they did to you. What they did to me doesn't even begin to compare."

"You were always in my heart. I was afraid we would drive you away from the church with all our nonsense."

"Not at all. You made a real impact in my life. Just wanted you to know that. And a lot of people feel that way about you."

Mike felt reconciled to Clarissa after this conversation. He felt great joy. Yes, actual joy, in spite of everything. It was a different kind of joy—a joy-in-bitterness—but it was real, and it was majestic, and he wore it like a kingly robe for a while. In the midst of all his calamity he put on this soft garment and for the moment he felt some peace.

It did not last long, however. Great consolation had come to him but he could not be consoled. He sat alone in his apartment thinking about Clarissa's phone call and smiling and basking in the warmth of some wonderful things that were said—and then he sat there too long, because the warm feelings fled. He was alone and the phone was not ringing and they came back to him, Charles and Fred and Susan and David, to haunt him.

It was an afternoon in July, dreadfully hot, and his hot anger came back to him and paralyzed him. He could not seek relief. He could not move. He sat there sweating and in agony. After all, why had Clarissa called? Because he had been humiliated. At that moment Mike discovered that sometimes even the sweetest pity and kindness can bring pain.

ONE FLESH

AND WHAT ABOUT KIM? Needless to say she was in a state of shock after the meeting. She wasn't prepared to have her love life discussed in front of a large crowd of strangers. But then she began to see the whole thing as a joke. Susan's over-the-top delivery was like an SNL parody of religionism. And of course it was even funnier to someone who knew that her pretensions of moral outrage were based on nothing.

In one sense, though, Kim was grateful for Susan's outburst. Up to that point she had been feeling a little shaken by some of the things she heard. The part about Clarissa was particularly discomfiting, the insinuation left hanging in the air by that strange frumpy woman. Susan's bizarre diatribe put everything back into perspective, however. She saw how the facts were being twisted with regard to something of which she had personal knowledge, and this helped her to frame the other accusations she was hearing.

The brutality of the meeting and Susan's viciousness only made her love Mike more, aroused her tender and nurturing side, having seen the beating he had just taken. She wound up staying the entire weekend. Not that Mike objected very strenuously. He needed her. They did a lot of driving and a lot of getting away; and when she wasn't with him, when Monday came and she had to go back to work, she was calling him and texting him. Mostly they were just sweet little messages. There was the occasional "Are you OK?"

Something changed in their relationship because of this trauma. Kim had stayed over one night before, when they did nothing but hold each other and Mike was content to just hold her. When they got back to his apartment after the meeting they did the same thing. She held him, and sometimes he was shaking, and she held him until the shaking went away. She stayed over Saturday night too. All of these stay-overs were fully clothed. They were old enough to be able to control themselves, and they did. Mike did not believe in sex outside of marriage, and Kim was glad he didn't after some of her other experiences with men.

But then Mike heard about a fiery combined deacon and trustee meeting, which had been convened to discuss his severance. Some were in favor of being generous and giving him at least two months' pay or even more, which was about what he would have received from the private sector. Some were angry at him for not preaching the last Saturday in June or bothering to show up at the office. He had walked away; why pay him at all?

Among the more militant economizers was Fred Cantor, who was now a trustee. "Besides, he's taken up with this woman," Fred said. "He's with her all the time, so I guess he's pretty much against the church now and its principles."

"What woman?" Simon said in dismay.

"The one who was with him at the meeting. Apparently they've shacked up together. And I can't see giving two months of the church's good money to someone who's living in sin."

News of this new attack came to Mike from multiple channels, not just Simon, who called because he refused to believe it was true, but even Harry Carmichael, one of his fellow pastors, who felt sorry for Mike and wanted to warn him.

Mike could not believe it. At first he was so angry at Fred he thought he was going to explode. Kim came over that night after work with some supper and Mike just let it blurt out of him, expecting her to share his outrage. Instead she laughed. He was a little startled by this reaction at first, but then he started to laugh too. It was a crazy helium-burst type laugh for the two of them. Then they fell into each other's arms and started to kiss. Not in the way they had ever kissed before. They were so much in love.

"Let's give them something to talk about," she whispered in a husky voice.

She was so tender and so humorous that Mike didn't even bother to reply. They went into the bedroom and made love for the first time. There was a great deal of tenderness in it, too much even to describe. They wanted so much to be one.

Kim went to work the next day, and then Mike was aghast at what had just happened. He was a called and ordained pastor of the church who believed strongly in the institution of marriage and did not believe in sex just for the sake of recreation. He had been outraged beyond words to find out that Fred was accusing him of something he had been studiously avoiding—not without suffering, we might add—and now he had gone and vindicated him. He had given up his high moral ground to the repulsive toad and could not feel good about this.

He scolded himself again and again for being weak, for letting them get to him, for allowing Fred to take one last measure of revenge when he thought he was done with Fred, when one of the main attractions of being dismissed was never having to encounter Fred Cantor again.

It was a sunny day and he drove down to Odiorne Point and biked up and down the coast pretty much all day, rode and rode, not fast, just leisurely, thinking about Kim and his weakness, his abominable weakness. Or was it really abominable? He loved Kim. He wanted to marry Kim, if she would have him. He could not imagine life without her. It wasn't what it seemed. It wasn't "shacking up," as Fred had put it. They were in a committed relationship. It was different.

Or were they? Mike was definitely committed. He would have married Kim in a moment, if the moment presented itself. But to tell the truth he did not feel worthy of Kim, not now. He had just experienced a crushing repudiation by the famous Pine Cove Community Church. She had seen him despised and rejected with her own eyes. Could she still respect him? Could she possibly love him and look up to him after seeing him publicly humiliated and unable to fight back?

And then there was the unemployment thing. He would have loved to ask Kim to marry him, but it struck him as being presumptuous. No, unfair. He could not expect her to marry someone who had no job and no prospects. He did not feel at all confident about finding a position in another church, not after what had happened. He could not see himself going back to the corporation. It was almost seven years now since he had left. He had no contacts, had not bothered to maintain any after the momentous decision to go into the ministry. He was in his mid-fifties, which made things almost impossible. Most of all, he did not want to go back.

He arrived at his apartment late in the long summer afternoon and was pleasantly surprised to find Kim there, making dinner for him. She looked adorable in her apron with her hair pulled back behind her ears. She served him some impossibly delectable broiled scallops and fresh green beans and brown rice. They enjoyed a nice bottle of red wine together, which she had brought, since Mike was not in the habit of keeping any alcohol in the house, except for the bottle of port he stowed for guests.

After dinner she insisted on doing the dishes. She pushed him out of the way and handed him a cup of fresh-brewed decaf and told him to go someplace and relax. He went out on the deck and gazed dreamily at the dark woods behind the house while he listened to the sounds of her cleaning up. Then there was silence. He glanced around and didn't see her and returned to his absorption in the mystic woods. Then he heard her coming up behind him. She surprised him by getting down on one knee.

"Will you marry me?" she said, smiling giddily and holding up a small black velvet box.

Mike looked down at her in amazement. "What's this?" He took the box and opened it and saw two white gold wedding rings. "Are you kidding?"

"Do I look like I'm kidding?" she replied, still smiling.

"I don't know what to say. I can't give you anything."

"How about yourself? That's all I want right now."

"But I can't support you. I can't even support myself."

"I don't need to be supported. Or at least not in that sense. Being with you is what's important. The rest will work itself out."

"But are you sure? A guy with no job, no prospects, a loser—?"

"You are *not* a loser. You did not do anything wrong. Charlie couldn't take the competition; it's as simple as that. Besides, I love you."

"You do?"

"I do. Very much. Now it's your turn to say something."

"I love you too, very much. I think you know that."

"I do. So it's settled, then!"

Mike chuckled at this play on the traditional wedding vows. He made a counter-proposal. She would have to let him pay for the rings or he could not go through with it. No self-respecting man could let his bride pay for the rings. She reluctantly agreed, and he dipped into the savings he had left over from the sale of the house.

They did not wait long. They were married in August. Neither one was interested in a big wedding; they just wanted to be together and make a public commitment. Bob Diamond did the ceremony at the church where Mike had interned. It was a small crowd, mostly family. No gifts, they insisted, although some magically appeared anyway. They went back to Kim's house afterwards and had a nice cookout. Everybody pitched in and it was fun.

Mike's parents loved Kim right away and were very glad he was marrying her. They were worried about him after what happened at Pine Cove, and she seemed like just the right "gal" to put a little stability and optimism back into his life. Mike's two girls were not so sure at first. They were hurt for their mother's sake; they could not help it. But Kim worked so hard on winning them over—just by being herself—that they were glad for their dad in the end. They agreed it was best for him. He was far too young to spend the rest of his life alone and in mourning.

Now married, Mike became determined to find a job. Nothing was developing on the church front—and besides, it took too much time to obtain a position with the laborious call process. He made a couple of inquiries at his old company, but there were no openings and no apparent interest. Not that he really wanted to go back into the corporation and his cube, but he had to have a job, any job. Otherwise he felt like he was taking advantage of Kim.

Then one of his old parishioners came to him with an offer he "probably wasn't going to be interested in"—working in the lighting department at a certain building superstore. Mike leaped at it. He was in no position to be proud. It was a better job at a higher pay than he was beginning to think he would have to settle for. It was strange at first—hard, to be honest—to see people from Pine Cove in the store, their curious looks when they saw him in his orange apron, but it could not be helped. He had a job. It was nothing to be ashamed of. He told himself he was not ashamed.

WHO DO THEY SAY THAT I AM?

WELL, MAYBE HE was kidding himself a little there. He would bump around the store and was very eager to do a good job—perhaps grimly determined to excel would be more descriptive—but he never really blended in. He stuck out like a sore thumb—in his own mind. Customers came by and he was Trapped. He wanted to turn away, instinctively felt like hiding, but company policy wouldn't let him. He had to put on his best smile and greet them, each and every one.

Then after a while he began to realize this was good for him. It was therapeutic. The large, impersonal superstore was forcing him to come out of his shock-induced shell and act in a way that was in accordance with his own ethos. He began to take some pleasure in forcing himself to meet the customers' eyes and go beyond his comfort zone. And then it stopped being painful. He did not dread it. He discovered that when a smile is returned the heart is warmed.

One day he glanced up from the screws he was sorting, all prepared to generate a smile and say hello, and saw Chloe looking down at him with astonishment and probably embarrassment.

"Pastor? What are you doing here?"

"I—work here," Mike said with a brave front. "Why—you didn't think I could do it?"

She laughed. "No, it's just—I'm surprised, that's all."

"Not hard to explain, really. I didn't have a job, and this one offered itself. So here I am! But how are you? How's the arthritis?"

"Gone! Not a trace of it. Oh—I guess I have some now and then. But nothing like before. It really was a miracle."

"I'm so glad for you. And so glad to see you!"

"I'm glad to see you, too. We miss you so much at church."

"How are things going down there?"

"Oh, they're all right. Charles took over the service."

"Charles! I'm surprised. But that's good for you," he said, catching himself. "He's a wonderful preacher."

"Not like you. I mean, don't get me wrong—I love his sermons. Very moving. But you're special. You talked to us where we were."

"Thank you so much for saying that."

"It's not just me. Everybody says it."

There wasn't much more to this serendipitous conversation, but there was plenty to ruminate over later on. First, there was the reassurance from someone he liked and trusted that he was not a complete loser and might have actually done some good in the church. He had been so devastated by what happened that he lost all sense of self-worth. He couldn't think of anything good to say about himself, and these sincere words from Chloe helped him to feel a little less self-critical.

Then there was the interesting news about Charles taking over the service. His first reaction was to see it as a cynical move on Charles's part, especially since he had never evinced any interest in the service before, had never even visited it in the three years Mike was there. Charles would not allow the growth of the Saturday night service to be squandered, no matter what its provenance. Or maybe he was just grandstanding and showing what a great guy he was.

Which raised a very painful thought. Mike wondered if it really was true that the congregation missed him. He wanted them to miss him—he could not put this vanity behind him, even though he knew it was foolish—but they were only human. It was flattering to be catered to by the senior pastor. And one thing about Charles that could not be gainsaid was his extraordinary skill as a preacher. Mike would be forgotten under the spell of that melodious baritone, he was sure.

Yes, forgotten. Suddenly he saw himself as an old man, well past retirement age, perhaps sitting somewhere in a wheelchair in a nursing home, and he saw the empty place of himself in the world. He came from the corporate environment where the worthies of the moment all move on in five or ten years and then are quite literally forgotten by the new cast that takes their place, even their names erased from corporate memory.

Mike now saw himself old and forgotten as well. It was the first time in his life he had seen himself quite this way. His children would remember him and his grandchildren, if he lived long enough to know them, but two or three generations would wash him and all of his troubles away. It would be as if he had never existed and never felt such suffering or shame. These thoughts did not purify him or make his predicament any easier, however. No, they caused him more pain.

Was his career in the ministry already over? Was all the time spent in seminary wasted? He knew it wasn't getting knocked down that mattered in the end but getting back up and into the fray. He had been knocked down many times before and always bounced back. But that was at the corporation, where he knew he was up to the job. He did not have this confidence in himself now. He honestly did not know if he had what it took to be a pastor.

He did not know if he wanted to be. The pain of the debacle was not fading away. On the contrary, it seemed he had not yet absorbed the full impact. Suppressed memories kept forcing their way into consciousness and exploding in his poor brain when he was least expecting it. He had suffered terribly during Janet's demise but this was different. This pain was about him. This was his identity being destroyed relentlessly in his own mind, over and over again.

He had high ideals when it came to church life, but the Pine Cove Church did not seem to share those ideals. They did not make it a priority to "love each other with a sincere love." They did not "stop biting and devouring" each other over disputable matters. They did not "make every effort to live in peace with everyone." They did not refrain from showing favoritism to the rich or conveniently tuning out those from lower social and economic strata than themselves.

It wasn't just that they didn't do these things. People are human. But they did not idealize them. They did not think of them as a top priority in church life.

This made him feel like a misfit, like someone trying to play with the orchestra in another key. He had his key to life, his understanding of the Gospel, his heart for the new age of grace, brought into being by a sacrifice of love, but these same things seemed to put him at odds with the leadership of the Pine Cove Church, which had other things on its mind. He could not follow their lead, and he was not the type to try to force anyone to follow him. So did that mean he had to get out of the way?

Mike thought about the fatal arc of his stint at Pine Cove. He thought about the missteps that weren't really missteps at all but impolitic. Should he have kept his mouth shut when Fred was sending all the Catholics to hell? Should he have shunned Clarissa when one of his favorite stories was the woman at the well? Should he have refrained from defending Frank against the predators who were unable to distinguish between a Christian church and their country club?

He thought about Christ and how he suffered at the hands of the religious leaders. "Blessed are you when men revile you and persecute you and utter all kinds of evil against you falsely for my account. Rejoice and be glad, for your reward is great in heaven, for so men persecuted the prophets who were before you." Beautiful words, but the problem was that Mike did not feel blessed. He understood them all too well but could not experience the blessing.

He thought about St. Paul's letters. Today Paul is honored as an apostle and enshrined in stained-glass windows, but that was not the case in his own time. His struggles were epic. There were the Jews who opposed him and his mission to the Gentiles. There were the super-apostles, the ones who have now been forgotten but who were stars in their own time. They reviled Paul and made all kinds of trumped-up and false accusations against him. Mike did not know if he had the strength to endure that kind of pain.

Then there were these words from the cross: "Father forgive them, for they know not what they do." Were modern believers any different from the Jewish religious leaders who handed Christ over to be crucified? Were they still persecuting him because they did not "know what they do"? Mike thought about the surfacy understanding of the Bible that is often encountered in church. In his mind there was a tendency to be unconscious of the depth of its words and the unbounded love in which they were rooted. The words came to the surface and were severed from their roots.

The life-meaning of the Bible is that God is love and mortal man is far from exhibiting the perfect love of God; therefore he would do well to humble himself. Christ allowed his enemies to hang him naked on a cross as a spectacular example of the value of humbling ourselves, but was the church willing to exhibit this shameful nakedness? Did the church have an acute sense of its shame in the way that Christ was naked on the cross? It didn't seem that way to Mike. At Pine Cove all the super-Christians seemed rather proud of themselves.

The church was not about the naked Christ on the cross as much as it was about a pretty picture of the cross, and him naked on it. This made all the difference in the world. The pretty picture takes away the pain. There is no shame in it for the very reason that it is a picture. It displays the cross but it does not take up the cross; by causing it to come to the surface, it moves the cross into the realm of art and narrative, the very opposite of nakedness.

The people who pushed him out of Pine Cove "did not know what they do." They were thinking about outward appearances, saving the honor of the church, as they saw it, and did not understand his passion for the lost sheep, did not even see the value of such a passion. But Mike was not comforted by finding himself in the same predicament as Christ, with whom he did not presume to be compared. In his mind he was nothing more than an anomaly, an "enemy of the people." He did not fit in at Pine Cove. Could he fit in anywhere?

Then he started thinking about what makes a successful pastor and the difference in temperament between himself and Charles. Unkind things were said about Charles all the time but they never seemed to bother him. Or at least they didn't have any visible effect. Charles was always brimming with confidence just as he was always perfectly coiffed. Mike simply did not know what to make of this. Was he faking it, or was he actually not suffering as Mike suffered?

If it was the latter—and Mike suspected it was—then did this mean that people like Charles were better suited to ministry than he was? Was he too sensitive and too idealistic to survive in the church? Charles did not share his idealism, his vision of the church as a haven of love, which may have been why the things that pained Mike did not seem so painful to him. It did not upset him to see how Frank was treated by Susan. He himself referred to Clarissa as a "whore."

Charles was successful specifically because he was happy to marshal the forces of surface Christianity, but Mike was beginning to suspect that he was opposed to those same forces. Hence he would never be a "success." He would never meet the expectations of someone like Fred Cantor and the religious leaders of his own time. If he stayed in the ministry he was doomed to suffer in ways that Charles could never dream of suffering. He did not know if he was up to it. He did not think he could survive another experience like his three years at Pine Cove.

These dark thoughts sent him down, down into the pit of despair. "Out of the depths have I cried unto thee; Lord, hear my voice." He would get up in the morning and smile at his beloved Kim and kiss her tenderly never letting her see how he felt and he would go and do his day job with all the energy he could muster but not with all his heart or soul because his soul was elsewhere, because his soul was in hell burning with an anger and shame that he could neither redress nor assuage.

Months went by like this and he never told Kim, never said a word, because he loved her so much, because he did not want to do anything to hurt her or jeopardize her love, maybe because he was afraid; months and months went by in this smoldering rage and then fall turned into winter and the sun disappeared from his life and he found himself going to work in the dark and coming home in the dark again at night, an apt metaphor for his existence.

The holidays came and went and then winter put a hoarfrost on his anger and turned it into full-blown depression. Mike stumbled through the coldest months like someone who was numb to himself, numb to the tip of his nose like when the thermometer dips to ten below. And still he didn't say anything to Kim. He did not want her to know he was depressed. In his mind it made him seem weak.

Then came March, the in-between month, neither frozen winter with its pure white snow nor lovely spring, just gray, and one morning when Mike left for work he could not even force himself to smile at Kim or kiss her with soft lips. That was the sign for her. She knew something was wrong, had known for a long time, had been trying to hide the painful knowledge from herself, but she could not hide from those hard lips.

That night at dinner she gave him a glass of red wine and then another. Since Mike rarely drank, and hadn't eaten since breakfast, this double dose soon had the desired effect.

"I'm sorry. I know haven't been very talkative lately," he said, standing with her in the kitchen while she cooked them some fried chicken. "I've just really been struggling with the whole thing—with what happened."

"Because it was terrible."

"Well, yes. It really was terrible. I guess I shouldn't be such a wuss, but there you have it. I've been—well, I guess you would say 'down.' In fact I've been so far down I was starting to wonder if I would ever come up again."

"I know. You have every right to be. You've suffered a shock. They did a terrible thing to you. Anybody who went through what you went through would be depressed—anybody. It's certainly nothing to be ashamed of."

"It's just that I'm so—angry. All the time. I know that sounds terrible. I don't want to be angry. There just doesn't seem to be anything I can do about it. I'm sitting here with you on the couch watching TV and holding your hand and I seem like I'm paying attention and acting normal but actually I'm just obsessing over things that happened, things people said to me or about me, all the crazy things that happened. And then I'm obsessing over how pathetic I am, sitting here completely powerless to do anything about it; how they all got the last laugh on me while I'm working at a department store. Poor me."

"Yes, poor you. Don't be so hard on yourself. What they did to you was unfair."

"Oh, I don't know. Maybe it was and maybe it wasn't. Maybe I'm just not cut out to be a pastor. I'm not like Charles and David. I'm not tough enough."

"Do you have to be tough to be a pastor? I thought you had to be tender."

"That's what I thought too. That's what got me into trouble."

"Not every church is Pine Cove, you know."

"No, but every church is Pine Cove in its own way."

"I don't agree with that. I don't think it's the people in the church. There were many lovely people at Pine Cove, I'm sure. I think it's the leadership. It's the message and what they're told. If you had your own church it wouldn't be like that. They would hear your message. They would be more like the Saturday night service."

"I wish I could believe that. I'm not sure I can believe anything right now, especially myself."

"But tell me about this depression. How bad is it?"

He shrugged. "Bad enough to make the occasional tree look inviting on my way home from work."

"What! Don't even say that."

"Don't worry. Somehow I always manage to keep myself on the road. But it scares me."

"Well, we're going to have to do something about that. In the meantime promise me you'll stay away from trees."

Kim made a call the very next morning, the moment Mike left the house.

SEVENTY TIMES SEVEN

A COUPLE OF DAYS went by, and it was dark and rainy and icy and miserable and cold as only March can be in a bad mood, not even any peepers yet to assuage the longing for spring. Mike felt better after the conversation with Kim, less isolated, more loved. But then he was inclined to feel worse. He did not deserve to be loved by this wonderful woman. He did not have much of a job and no career prospects and now he was burdening her with his depression on top of it. He did not deserve her and this depressed him even more.

Then it was Saturday morning, and the weather had finally broken and there was sun and even a simulacrum of warmth—the thermometer eked its way almost all the way up to sixty! Kim was out shopping and Mike was sitting at the kitchen table with a cup of coffee feeling quite numb when there was a quiet knock on the door. It was Don Baker.

Mike roused himself enough to greet Don warmly. He wanted to convey warmth to Don. A change had occurred in his attitude and feelings since their last conversation. He wanted him to know that he liked him and regretted not having shown it before. (Why didn't he just come out and say it? Men don't do that sort of thing.)

In any case it turned out this was not just a random visit. Don had something on his mind. They sat down with a cup of coffee and some Kim-made cinnamon buns that happened to be on hand.

"So—how are you doing?" Don said, and Mike knew this was not just the usual pro-forma inquiry. The tone told him it was not and there was no use to pretend. And anyway, he did not want to pretend. He was too worn out even to try.

"Okay, I guess. Well, not really."

"Perfectly understandable. I mean, you've been through a lot. It's amazing that you can still sit upright and take nourishment."

Mike laughed politely. "I just didn't think it would hit me quite like this. I wasn't prepared for it. I felt pretty good for a while. Or I thought I did. Maybe I was just fooling myself."

"You were in shock. That was a terrible blow. And believe me, I'm not the only one who's worried about you. You have a lot of friends at the church, whether you realize it or not."

"Haven't seen much of them."

"No, that's natural. Remember, they're embarrassed too. They're embarrassed for the church, because this whole thing is a huge embarrassment for the church and will continue to bear bitter fruit. But they're also embarrassed for you."

This was frank talk. Mike's ears perked up. "It's probably just as well. I wouldn't want them to see me this way."

"And what way is that?"

"You know—beaten down. Kind of pathetic."

"You mean that job you have?"

"No, not that. Well—maybe that too. But just myself. All the air gone out of my balloon."

"Don't you think it's time to start putting some back in again?"

"I'd love to. Got any suggestions?"

"Well, one thing is you need to get back into the ministry. As soon as possible. I have nothing against the kind of work you're doing now. 'The rest of the laborer is sweet.' But you were called to be a pastor and that's what you're supposed to be."

"I don't know. That's what I've been wondering about. The Pine Cove Church seems to think I *wasn't* called to be a pastor."

"That is absolutely not true. The Pine Cove Church doesn't 'think' anything. There was a trumped-up railroad job by a small faction with an agenda. To my eternal shame, I didn't stand up and do anything about it."

"What could you do? It was a steamroller. A couple of high-powered people were determined to get me out of there, and I don't see how anyone could have stopped it."

"I wonder. The other pastors did not agree with this, not one bit. If we had spoken up things might have been different. It's just that Charles can be formidable when he wants to be."

"And don't forget David."

"I wish I could forget David," Don said with a chuckle. "But he's reaping his own whirlwind. He went too far, and now even Charles is beginning to have his doubts about him. And one thing I've noticed about Charles. Once he turns on you, he stays turned."

"But what about you? You really think I could be an effective pastor?"

"Are you kidding? You need to listen better. Look, you were a fantastically effective pastor at Pine Cove for the Saturday night crowd. They love you and will never recover from what happened, no matter how hard Charles tries to win them over. You just had the misfortune to run afoul of some people who may or may not have had the church's best interests in mind. And one more thing. Not only do you have excellent pastoral instincts, but you are one of the most naturally gifted preachers I've ever heard. And that's no small thing. That's a very rare thing."

"Well, thank you. I really don't know if I deserve such praise."

"This isn't praise. This is a corrective for those crazy, mixed-up ideas you have in that head of yours. Do not let the legalism crowd at Pine Cove make you doubt yourself or devalue yourself. I've heard enough of your sermons to know your theology is spot-on. And as for the other things that happened—well, we all have our own opinions about it."

"Again, thank you. I accept the corrective in the spirit in which it was given. But getting back into the ministry? I just don't know if I can do it. I don't seem to have the energy to do it."

"Because you're depressed."

"I guess so. How did you know that?"

"Kim called me."

"That stinker!"

"Yes, she's quite the stinker. She is terribly worried about you. You scared her."

"Oh, I know. I said—well, never mind what I said. I wasn't trying to scare her. I was just trying to be honest."

"I'm glad you did. Otherwise how would she know? You can't do this on your own. You shouldn't expect yourself to."

"To tell you the truth, I'm a little scared too. I don't know where all this is going."

"I can tell you. You have two paths laid out before you. You can let this bitterness consume you and destroy your entire life. Or you can take the hard medicine now and change the future."

"And what is the 'hard medicine'?"

Don looked at him for a moment. "Pastor, you have to forgive."

"What!" Mike said with a fake laugh. "I've forgiven."

"No, you haven't. You can't even bring yourself to say 'them.' The truth is you haven't even begun to forgive them. You're still angry. That's why you're depressed."

"Don't I have a right to be angry?"

"I didn't say you didn't. All I said was you have to get rid of your anger in order to move on, in order to stop scaring Kim, and the rest of us who care about you. And the only way to do that is to forgive. Total, unconditional forgiveness. And believe me, I know how hard it can be. I'm going to tell you something I don't share with too many people, but I think this is the right time to share it with you. I had a daughter once, a beautiful, talented girl. She was everything to me. One day a boy came and took her for a ride on a motorcycle, one of her high-school friends. We never saw her again—not alive, anyway."

"I am so sorry," Mike said looking at him in wonder and thinking about how little we know about the people in our lives.

"Don't be sorry. She's in heaven. If anything I say means anything, then I have to be happy for her. But the boy lived. And believe me, it was hard for me to forgive. My dear wife, not so much; she has a beautiful, forgiving spirit. But for me it was hard. And there was something else, too—and I want you to listen very carefully to what I'm saying. I had to forgive myself as well. I let her go with him. I saw him with the helmet on and I saw her without one as they sat there in the driveway. I let them go. I had to forgive myself in the end or I would be totally lost right now. Or rather, I had to accept God's forgiveness, which washes everything clean. And so do you, or you're just going to stay stuck right where you are."

Mike sat there stunned, looking at his friend. "I don't know if I can forgive."

"Nonsense. Anyone can forgive. You just have to make up your mind to do it, and you just have to pray. If you don't, this anger of yours could literally destroy you. I've seen whole lives flushed down the toilet by bitterness over things a lot less terrible than what happened to you."

"Wow, you are a hard man."

"I have been given a word to deliver to you. I'm not kidding. It might as well have been Gabriel calling and not Kim. It came to me as plain as day. And the word is 'forgive.' Let it go. Save your life—

and Kim's too. Give yourselves a chance to be happy and free from the past."

"Okay, so I forgive. I still don't see how I can get back in the ministry. It's too easy for Charles and Pine Cove to block me."

"Again, nonsense. First of all, Charles got what he wanted. He can afford to be generous now because you are no longer there. I'm just being honest here. We all know what that was about. Second, I'll tell you exactly how you're going to get back in. There are lots of lost little churches in our part of the world. Three hundred years ago they were the center of town life; now they're lucky if five old ladies show up on a Sunday. You're going to find a church like that—or should I say a church like that is going to find you because somebody there is praying—and be very lucky to find you, by the way—and then you're going to start over. And it's going to be different. It'll be hard work, but it's going to be good. Because you have a gift."

Don did not stay long, having unburdened himself of his "word." Nor did Mike try to detain him. He was tingling. He needed to be alone. He needed to spend some time by himself to try to sort it all out, try to discover his real feelings, which were not obvious at the moment.

He knew deep down that Don was right. There was no question about it. He had a stark choice to make between self-pity and moral courage, and there was only one right answer. He could follow Don's advice and forgive and give himself a chance to get his life back on track, or he could keep holding on to his anger, this fiery monster, suckling it, feeding it every day with resentment and dark thoughts, until it destroyed him.

Right then and there he got down on his knees in the feeble March sunlight and began to pray like he never had in his life, and among all the words he used in his babbling and all the scattered thoughts and feelings and confusion and bitterness and sorrow there was one line that kept coming back to him: *Father, forgive them, for they know not what they do.*

It kept coming back to him because for the first time in his life he truly understood these words. They were not just part of a story, terrible and tragic as it might be—they were part of his own story. He was not just reading these words as someone else had said them; he was speaking them in character. Indeed, they were the only words he could think of that made any sense. They were the only words that were not nothing.

Come with us, if you dare, and see Mike kneeling in sorrow in the pale March light on his middle-aged knees. Come hear him saying these words with such fervor that there is sweat dripping from his forehead; saying these familiar old words that are suddenly new again; fumbling and unsure at first but gradually with more conviction. See him with a figurative sword in his hand, which he now proceeds to plunge into his breast to slay the dark beast that is consuming him. He wants it dead so he can live, and these words are the sword.

For over an hour he prayed. Then, exhausted, he got up and threw himself down on the couch and just lay there staring at the ceiling in a daze. A few minutes went by or an hour—he did not know—and then he heard Kim's car in the driveway. Kimmie. Kimbers. He heard the gravel crunching under the tires—very distinctly—and the sound seemed so good to him, like music. For the first time he really heard that sound. It made his soul glad.

Something had changed. He jumped up and ran to the door to greet his wonderful wife with a warm embrace.

"What's that for?" she said, smiling with surprise.

"Saving my life."

"What? I didn't do anything."

"Of course you did. You called Don."

"You talked to him?"

"He came to see me. We had a great talk. He scolded me, and now I feel much better."

"Nice to see you making jokes again. It's been a long time."

"He told me I had to forgive. I knew that but I was having too much fun holding onto my grudge."

"So that's your idea of fun! I wouldn't say it was too much fun."

"What, feeling sorry for myself? What could be more fun than that?"

"And do you think you can forgive?"

"Yes. I know I can. And I can be a better husband. Believe it or not. Anyway, I'm determined to try."

"You're a wonderful husband! It's just been hard, seeing you in such pain."

"I don't know how 'wonderful' I am. All the time I wasted when I could have been working on this, doing something about it, thinking more about you and not about poor me."

"Maybe you needed that time to get to where you are now. It wasn't easy, what you went through. Anybody would find it hard to recover from something like that."

"Well, thank God for you—and Don. I love you so much."

There was another long embrace and there were tears.

DO NOT WORRY

FORGIVING WAS absolutely necessary. He knew it. After all, forgiveness was what the faith was all about. Wasn't it? But it was also hard: letting go of the beloved infection that had been feeding and starving him all these months. Mike kept praying and gradually forgiveness came to him. He realized it one day because it was spring and he felt light. The birds were singing and the tulips were in bloom and he felt…almost giddy.

For the first time he began to feel hopeful about the ministry and the possibility of starting over. There were several openings in northern New England, but he kept thinking about Don's advice. Why waste time looking for a position in a prosperous church and trying to explain away his history? Why not look for a church that really needed him and was not likely to be so picky? It wasn't just the lower level of scrutiny that appealed to him. He liked the idea of going where he was really needed and taking on a challenge.

As it turned out, it was difficult to identify such a church from the profiles. They are no more eager to present themselves in a negative light than are the pastoral candidates. Several months went by without Mike finding an opening for which he felt moved to put in his name—until he got a call from Bob Diamond. Bob knew about an old church not too far west from Concord that had seen a steep decline in membership in recent years but had great potential, in his view. "You may not want to take on something like that." It was exactly what Mike wanted.

Mike and Kim drove over there and fell in love with it, the way you would with a rescue dog. The building was in need of tender loving care and the neighborhood seemed a little random, but there was also some charm. They could tell just from looking at it that it would be a challenge. Kim insisted she was up for one. She gave him her complete support.

It turned out the church was in such dire straits that it could barely even convene a call committee. Not too many people applied for the low-paying position—about twenty, a small fraction of what Mike was accustomed to seeing. And at least fifteen of those were not what you would call serious candidates for a small country church with decidedly country values.

The call committee seemed to take to Mike. They liked the fact that he was humble and down to earth. They knew about him being dismissed from Pine Cove but also heard about the good he had done there. They heard about the remarkable growth of the Saturday night service—not from Mike but from Don, whom he had listed as a reference. Don made it as clear as he could, without telling tales, that what had happened to Mike was terribly unfair.

Of course they talked to Charles as well, but Don was right about him. He was generous and even went so far as to call Mike a "fabulous preacher" and church-starter. This was impressive to a call committee from a small country church that had a couple of Charles's books in its library. Some of them worried about Mike. Why was he interested in a small congregation like them? Would he stay? But he addressed these questions with such sincerity and warmth that they were convinced.

Mike was installed in January. His first official service was on a bitterly cold day after a large Nor'easter. They barely managed to get the parking lot plowed and walkways shoveled in time for church, with both Mike and Kim helping out. After all that only ten people showed up. Mike tried not to be depressed.

"Do you think we're going to be able to pull this off?" he said to Kim as they made the long drive home sliding over white roads. "I almost had the feeling today, looking out at them, that they might be better off just closing their doors."

"They do seem like a rather uninspired lot," she said with a merry laugh. "But don't forget, we're not the ones who are pulling anything off. We're just the instruments. If this is where God wants us to be, then everything will be fine."

Mike was encouraged by this response. It took away the pressure he was feeling—putting on himself, really. It didn't take long for him to begin to find his way. He learned, from the almost pulse-dead response he received the first few Sundays, to scale his message down to a smaller crowd than he was accustomed to, make it much more intimate, simpler; and then he learned how to encourage such a crowd and inspire them and make them feel there was a good reason to come to church on Sunday for worship and fellowship and not just stay home and watch Joel Osteen.

He was connecting with them. His old intuition seemed to be coming back. As winter hurried by and spring came on they began to respond to him openly. The church seemed to come to life. There was a cheerful buzz on Sunday mornings instead of morbid silence and a sense of hopelessness. Crusty New Englanders would linger with him in the reception line and tell him things about themselves, their families. They started inviting him and Kim to their homes, humble as many of them were.

By Easter they were definitely starting to attract a larger crowd. Mike began talking cautiously about sprucing up the place. The leadership was receptive, even glad. And he pitched right in. He was there to scrape or paint or do anything other people were doing. They loved him for it. They began seriously talking about "the future," a topic that probably had not been broached in the church for some time, or at least not in a positive way.

One Sunday Mike got up from his usual starting place in the front pew—he did not like the ceremonial throne chair behind the pulpit—and turned around to do announcements. He felt a thrill go through him as he spotted his old friend Bill sitting in the congregation smiling at him. Mike had not heard from Bill since their last unfortunate encounter. Many times he had wanted to call him and apologize again for overreacting, but somehow he never got around to it. Then he went into his depression and lost the courage.

After church and the reception line they found their way to each other. It was April and spring had come to New England, and Mike led Bill out to the parking lot and the daffodils and the tulips so they could talk without having the usual interruptions.

"So glad to see you, such a nice surprise," Mike said with genuine warmth.

"Well, I figured it was about time I got over here," Bill said with a sheepish smile. "I've been thinking about it all winter, but the weather's been so bad."

"Hasn't it, though. Listen, I've been wanting to talk to you for a long time too. I feel so bad about what happened the last time I saw you, kicking you out. It was terrible."

"I deserved it," Bill said laughing. "It was not the right time or place, and unfortunately the words didn't come out the way I intended. You had every right to be upset. And to tell you the truth, I wasn't offended at all. I was more mad at myself for bungling it so badly."

"Still, I'm supposed to be a pastor. I'm supposed to be above that sort of thing."

"What, pastors don't get angry from time to time? Anyway, I just wanted to try to explain myself. I know I came off like I was upset with you for not preaching at that last service. Like I was on their side, agreeing with them. Let me just tell you, that was not the case. In fact just the opposite. What I was upset about was the way they were using it against you. I don't know—this isn't coming out any better than the first time," he said, laughing again.

"No, I get it. You were upset with them, and I took it as you being upset with me."

"That's exactly it. But you took it that way because I made it sound that way. I just want you to know that, as far as I'm concerned, you had every right to stay home that Saturday night, after what they did to you. I probably would have done exactly the same thing. And it wasn't like they were communicating with you or anything. If I remember correctly, Charles didn't even bother to tell you there was a congregational meeting."

"Yes, you were the one who told me. Maybe you told me one too many things, which is when I snapped. I'm not trying to excuse it. I'm just trying to explain my state of mind at the time."

"Understood. It was one too many bad things from me. And I could sense that at the time, which I think made me screw it up even more. I didn't want to tell you, believe me. I just thought you should know what was going on behind your back."

"You had the proverbial fate of the bringer of bad news. But I'm glad you did tell me. I had to know. And there's no one I would rather hear it from than you."

"Well, you're kind. All I know is I had to come see you and apologize."

"No apology needed, my friend. I assume everything is back to normal at Pine Cove Community Church?"

"If that's what you want to call it. I guess you probably know there was quite a backlash over what happened. The people from your service were completely blindsided by it—and they weren't happy. They lost a lot of good people, even with Charles stepping in. And a lot of other people were unhappy too, people who knew you and knew that the whole thing was totally bogus. There's been a lot of churning going on over there and it's still going on."

"I take no pleasure in that. I wish them all the best in the world and hope they settle down. They're doing important work."

"Oh, by the way—David's no longer the anointed one. He dragged Charles into a couple of scrapes, completely unnecessary, and that's one thing Charles won't tolerate."

"I know. The staff is there to keep Charles *out* of any scrapes. I learned that the hard way."

"My father always used to say 'Pride goeth before a fall.' That young man is a little too full of himself for my taste, and it's finally starting to catch up with him."

"He's very bright. I'm sure he'll turn himself around," was all Mike could trust himself to say.

Bill looked at him. "So you're really not mad at me?"

"Far from it. I'm just glad you're not mad at *me*. And I'm so glad to see you."

"I'm relieved. I figured you would never want to talk to me again."

"Bill, I always felt that you were one of the finest people and finest Christians I knew at Pine Cove, or have ever known. And I'm sure I felt much worse about what happened between us than you did. I'm the one who lost his temper and acted like a jerk."

"Well, I guess there's no point in fighting over who was the biggest jerk," Bill said with a Yankee smile. "I just wanted to see you again. I heard things were going well here, and I'm so glad for you and for your friend."

They parted on good terms. Bill came back the next Sunday, this time with his wife and youngest daughter in tow, the one who was still in high school. And they kept coming. It was only twenty minutes for them, about the same as Pine Cove. In June, on Pentecost, they joined the church. Mike burst into tears when he saw them sitting there. A lot of pain and other feelings were in those tears, feelings he would have been hard-put to explain.

As it turned out, Mike and Kim did not leave the little church that had welcomed them so eagerly, not after two years or even five or ten, as many in the congregation feared. And the church grew. Slowly at first but more steadily as the summer months came on and Mike was able to put together a worship team and make music an important part of the service. Some of the old-timers grumbled about this, but he was careful about how he did it, very respectful of everyone, always mixing in the old with the new. In the end they managed to come to a meeting of the minds, especially since the members were appreciative of the positive changes taking place.

It was a new beginning, and Mike was grateful to have it, after all he had been through.

THE END

ABOUT THE AUTHOR

Jay Trott is an author of essays and fiction who lives in the fierce New Hampshire woods with his wife Beth. They have four children, six grandchildren, and love long walks on the beach.

www.ingramcontent.com/pod-product-compliance
Lightning Source LLC
LaVergne TN
LVHW041806060526
838201LV00046B/1149